The Not-A-Date

Published by Implode Publishing Ltd

Chapter 1

"Tom Powell wants to see you, Mo." Angie, my team leader shouted from across the office.

"What for?"

"I don't know. He didn't say."

"What did you do, Mo?" Ryan said.

Ryan sat at the desk directly opposite mine and was a pessimist by nature. He was a glass half-empty kind of guy where as I, generally, had a glass half-full outlook on life.

It was probably about a pay rise. I'd been at Headrow Tech for almost three years, and I had yet to receive one, so it was long overdue. If the increase they offered didn't meet my expectations, I was prepared to play hardball, and suggest it might be time for me to look elsewhere.

The HR department was on the floor above mine. I took the stairs, not because I was on some kind of health kick, but because the lift had been out of order for the last two days. Mindy, Tom Powell's PA, and I occasionally had a coffee together. I was just about to suggest we meet up at lunchtime, but she picked up the phone and started talking. As I approached her desk, she could only manage a half-hearted smile, and a gesture for me to go straight in.

I sat forward in the chair. "When you say *I'm fired*, what exactly do you mean by that?"

"I mean, Ms Jackson, that you are no longer employed by this company."

"Hang on, Tom, I—"

"It's Mr Powell."

"Okay, Mr Powell, but aren't you supposed to give me a

written warning before you can fire me?"

He reached into his drawer and took out a blue folder from which he produced two sheets of paper. "That would be these." He then proceeded to make a show of counting them. "One, two."

Technically, of course, he was right. I had received those warnings, but I hadn't really taken them seriously. I'd assumed they were something everyone received from time to time. And besides, the work I did was top notch, everyone said so.

"I thought those were just meant to keep me on my toes."

"These were formal warnings. You'll notice that the second one is headed *Final* Warning." He held it up to prove his point.

So far, this wasn't going the way I'd anticipated. Okay, so maybe I wouldn't be getting my well-deserved pay rise today, but I was still confident that I could retrieve the situation.

"Tom. Sorry, I mean Mr Powell. Surely there must be a better way of handling this. How about you put me on probation for a month or even two? During that time, I promise I won't—"

"Won't what? Spend half the day working on your own app instead of doing the work you were employed to do?"

"That's very unfair. I only ever worked on it when I'd completed all the work allocated to me and—hang on, you just said *were* employed."

"Correct. Because as of now, you are no longer an employee of Headrow Tech."

I wanted to lean across the desk and pull off his ill-fitting toupee, though I couldn't help but feel that might have been counterproductive. I had to focus on damage limitation.

"Okay, but what happens now? How long is it before I have to leave? It would be really handy if you could see your way clear to allowing me to stay on until the end of the summer because I've got a couple of holidays already booked."

"You have to leave right now."

"*Now* as in?"

Instead of answering my question, he picked up the phone and said, "You can come in now."

Before I could ask who he was talking to, the door behind me opened and in walked Eddie, one of the security guys. I'd always liked Eddie because he wasn't full of himself, unlike his two colleagues.

"Hey, Eddie."

"Hi, Mo." He looked embarrassed to be standing there, cardboard box in hand.

"Please accompany Ms Jackson to her desk," Powell said. "Wait with her until she has collected her personal belongings, and then see her out of the building."

"There's no need to go to all that trouble. I can see myself out." I reached for the cardboard box, but Eddie took a step back.

"Sorry, Mo. I have to go with you."

"Okay." I stood up. "But this is your last chance to change your mind, Tom. Once I've left this building, I won't be coming back. Not even if you get down on your knees and beg me."

"Goodbye, Ms Jackson. And good luck."

Mindy still had the phone glued to her ear, but I wasn't convinced she was actually on a call. It was much more likely that she didn't want to meet my gaze. I suspected she'd known what was going to happen but hadn't seen fit to give me a heads-up. I should have known she wasn't to be trusted after what happened with our coffee shop excursions. On our first visit there together, she'd suggested it might be easier if one of us bought both drinks one day, and the other one bought them the next time. I agreed, and it wasn't until we'd placed our first order that I realised my mistake. My taste in coffee is about as simple as it comes in the shape of a black Americano. Mindy ordered some weird concoction with syrup, cream and marshmallows, which cost nearly twice as much as mine. I suppose I should have said something, but I didn't want to cause a scene. I was beginning to regret that decision now.

"I'll miss you, Mo," Eddie said as we made our way back to my office.

"Thanks, Eddie. Likewise."

As I made the walk of shame to my soon-to-be ex-desk, most of those I passed by pretended not to notice me. Except for Kathy Moore who was grinning like the Cheshire cat. She and I had always had a love/hate relationship. I hated her and she just loved to hate me right back. I was sorely tempted to pour her strawberry crème Frappuccino over her head. After all, what could they do? They couldn't fire me twice. Eddie must have read my mind because he took my arm gently. "Come on, Mo, let's get this over with."

"I told you, didn't I, Mo?" Ryan said. "I said I had bad vibes."

"It's okay. This is probably a blessing in disguise." I wasn't sure who I was trying to convince, him or me.

Eddie put the box onto my desk and stood back while I emptied the contents of my drawers into it; it wasn't a pretty sight.

"Yuk!" I wondered what had happened to that peach yoghurt.

Fifteen minutes later, Eddie held the door open for me as I stepped out onto the street.

"See you, Mo."

"Bye, Eddie.

And that was that. Three inglorious years spent in the employment of Headrow Tech had come to an even more inglorious end. Before I could set off down the street, my phone rang.

Of course. This had all been an elaborate practical joke. The guys in the office were always pulling this kind of stunt. I should have known. When I got back to my desk, I would just have to hold up my hands and admit that I'd fallen for it hook, line and sinker.

But it wasn't Tom from HR, or anyone else at Headrow for that matter. It was Beth, my flatmate.

"Mo, Fancy grabbing lunch at Reds?"

"I just got fired."

"Very funny. Can you do 12.30?"

"I can do any time you like. I. Just. Got. Fired."

"You crack me up. I'll see you there."

***

Beth and I had known each other a little over three years. When I'd quit uni and headed to London, my first order of business had been to find somewhere to live.

Having never ventured further south than Leicester until then, I'd had no idea just how expensive renting would be, and I was shocked that I couldn't afford a flat in central London. It turned out that I couldn't have afforded to rent a wheelie-bin there. Just before I landed in London, Beth's old flatmate had moved back home to Barnsley. If I'm honest, I'd never even heard of Deptford until I saw Beth's ad for a flatmate, but it was the only one that was within my price range. And the rest, as they say, is history.

I arrived at Reds at 12.20 and grabbed a table by the window, overlooking the forecourt and fountain.

"You're early." Beth did a double take when she realised that I'd arrived there before her. "You're never early. What's in the box?"

"The contents of my desk."

"What? You mean you really were sacked?"

"Yep."

"They can't do that, can they? Aren't they supposed to—?"

"They did. Twice, apparently."

"In that case, I guess lunch is on me."

"Thanks. And about the rent."

"I can cover it this month, but after that, I'm not sure."

"It's okay. It shouldn't take long for me to get something else and then I'll pay you back."

"You really are having a lousy month, Mo. What with what happened with—" She hesitated.

"It's okay. You can say it."

"Does Adam know you've been fired?"

Just hearing his name, brought back that hollow feeling inside. I'd had boyfriends before him, but nothing serious.

I'd honestly believed we had something special, which is why I'd asked him to move in with me. I'd been naive and worse than that, I'd been blind to what was going on behind my back.

"Why would he know?"

"I thought you might have messaged him."

"He dumped me, remember?"

"Yeah, but if he knew what had happened, he might feel sorry for you and come back."

"I think Adam has other things on his mind. Lily Baines for example."

"You don't know for sure that he's seeing her."

"Yes, I do. All that stuff about us needing our own space was rubbish. He'd been seeing her behind my back for at least a month."

"How do you know?"

"I've seen the emails."

"You read his emails?"

"I didn't intend to, but he left his laptop open one night, and there they were."

"How come you haven't told me any of this before?"

"Because I didn't want to talk about it. I still don't."

***

"Meow!"

As soon as I stepped through the door, Cat began to weave through my legs.

"Careful, you're going to trip me up."

Beth and I had spent so long arguing over what to call the cat, that in the end we settled on plain old Cat. He didn't seem to mind.

"It's not time for your food yet."

"Meow!"

"I know I usually feed you when I get home, but I'm back early."

"Meow!"

"I got fired." I held out the cardboard box as proof.

"Meow!"

"You'll just have to wait. And you'd better hope I get another job soon or it'll be Cheapo Catty Food for you."

After dropping the cardboard box on the kitchen table, I poured myself a glass of Coke. I'd just taken a sip when my phone rang.

Oh no! It was the last person I wanted to speak to.

"Hi, Mum."

"What did you do to get the sack?"

There was no need to ask how she'd found out. I'd have words with Beth later.

"I didn't do anything."

"Clearly you did, or they wouldn't have sacked you."

"It was more of a misunderstanding."

"Miriam next-door says they can't fire you until they've issued you with two written warnings."

"They did."

"Oh, Mo, when will you ever learn? You were just the same at school. I was always getting called in to see the headmistress because you'd been lippy to one of the teachers."

"It's fine, Mum, honestly."

"When are you coming home?"

"I'm not."

"You won't be able to afford rent without a job."

"I'll get one."

"That's easier said than done. Do you remember Harriet Black's son, Jeremy? He's been out of work for over a year."

"If I remember rightly, he was in prison for nine months of that time."

"That may be, but the job market isn't good at the moment. If you came home, I wouldn't expect you to pay board."

"I'm staying put. I've already put some feelers out for a new job."

"Really? Where?"

"Nowhere you'd have heard of. A couple of hi-tech start-ups. My skillset is in big demand."

"I never did understand what it is you do."

"I know. Sorry, Mum, there's someone at the door," I lied. "I'll have to go."

"If you change your mind about coming home, just let me know."

"I will. Thanks."

"Meow!"

"Okay, okay. Anything for a minute's peace." I grabbed the pouch of cat food and poured the slop into his dish. "Happy now?"

Judging by the speed at which he began to devour it, the answer to that question was a resounding *yes*.

I was eighteen when I'd moved out of the family home. That was seven years ago, and the prospect of moving back there, filled me with dread. I'd left home to go to uni, to study Philosophy, Politics and Economics. Why did I pick that particular degree? You may well ask. I'm sure I can't remember. After one and a half years of that purgatory, I'd quit the course and headed for the bright lights of London. Or to be precise, Deptford.

Even though I'd never had any formal training, I'd always had an aptitude for programming, and remarkably, I'd managed to secure a junior-level job at a small start-up in the city. The pay had been rubbish, and in the early days, I'd spent as much time running errands and making tea as I had doing any real work. But I'd learned a lot about app development during my time there; enough to land me a better paid and more senior role at Headrow two years later.

"Hey, Cat, why don't you come and give me a cuddle? I've had a lousy day."

He stopped preening himself just long enough to give me a look that conveyed total disdain.

"Come on, Cat. I need a hug."

His response was to turn his back on me and resume his preening.

"Thanks for nothing."

It was pointless feeling sorry for myself; it was time to start job-hunting, so I took out my phone and fired up one of the job search apps. Seeing the high number of vacancies for app developers lifted my spirits a little. I shortlisted six that were definite maybes. Now all I had to do was update my CV, which wouldn't take long.

Problem!

What was I supposed to say for the reason I'd left Headrow? If I said I'd been fired, that would put off a lot of would-be employers, but if I lied, I'd surely be found out when they sought references. I was still contemplating what to do when the door opened. Cat had obviously heard it too because he headed into the hall.

"Hello? Beth?"

It wasn't Beth.

"Hi, Mo."

"Adam? What are you doing here?"

Just seeing him again brought all the old feelings rushing back. I'd loved that guy so much it hurt, but that was nothing compared to the pain that I'd felt when he'd cheated on me.

"Sorry, I didn't think anyone would be here."

"How did you get in?"

"I still have the spare key. Don't you remember I got it cut after we got locked out that time?"

"When you moved out and I told you to leave your key, I meant all of them."

"Sorry."

"What do you want, anyway?"

"I came to collect the rest of my stuff."

"I burned it all."

"Not my Hugo Boss jeans." The look of panic on his face was priceless.

"Don't worry. Your jeans are safe. All your stuff is in a plastic bag in that cupboard. I was going to take it to the charity shop."

He walked over to the cupboard and retrieved the black plastic sack. "Thanks. How come you're home in the middle of the afternoon?"

"I—err—I've been a bit under the weather."

He glanced through the open kitchen door.

"What's all the stuff in that box?"

"Nothing."

Before I could stop him, he went through to the kitchen

for a closer look. "Did Headrow let you go?"

"They sacked me if that's what you mean."

"Why?"

"Why do you care?"

"Don't be like that, Mo. I thought we could still be friends."

"Me, you and Lily? Like a ménage à trois?"

"Let's keep Lily out of this."

"It's a pity you didn't keep her out of it while we were still together."

"I'd better be going."

"Hold on."

"What?"

"Key."

"Here, and I hope you find another job soon."

"Don't worry about me. I've already got one lined up."

As he closed the door, the memories came flooding back. Memories of the day I'd confronted him about the emails. How he'd denied it at first, but then admitted he'd been seeing Lily behind my back. How I'd cried as he'd packed up his things, and how I'd nearly cracked and told him not to leave.

Once I'd managed to compose myself, I refocussed my attention on how to word my CV in such a way that I wouldn't be automatically rejected.

"Come on, Cat, any bright ideas?"

He stared at me for a few seconds then curled up on the chair and went to sleep. A fat lot of use he was.

Chapter 2

Beth and I usually took turns making dinner and it was my turn. When I say, *making dinner,* what I really mean is opening a tin, or grabbing something out of the freezer.

We were overdue a trip to the supermarket, so the cupboards, fridge and freezer were all more or less bare. I was trying to decide between beans on toast or pizza when Beth arrived home.

"You're back early," I said.

"I wanted to make sure you were okay."

"I was until my mother rang. Thanks very much for that."

"I thought you might need someone to talk to."

"She's already talking about me moving back home."

"You're not going to, are you?"

"No way. Oh, and then just to make the day even more perfect, Adam came around."

"That was nice of him. Who told him what had happened?"

"No one had told him; he came around here to pick up the rest of his things. When he saw the cardboard box of the stuff I'd cleared out of my desk, he guessed I'd been fired. Why else would I have been here in the middle of the day?"

"What did he say?"

"That we should stay friends."

"He's right. You should."

"I don't think so. It's time for me to move on."

"Which is why you and I are going out tonight."

"No, we're not. I just want to crash in front of the TV and eat biscuits."

"Too late. I've already called everyone."

"Who's *everyone*?"

"The whole gang. Nicky, Jen and Carol. I called Mand too, but I couldn't get hold of her."

When I'd moved in with Beth, she'd automatically assumed that all of her friends would become my friends too, and that's how it had worked out.

"I suppose you've told them about me getting fired?"

"Obviously, and they're all determined to cheer you up."

"I don't need cheering up, thanks very much. And besides, I can't afford to go out."

"Don't be daft. We'll pay for all your drinks, and you never know, you might pull."

"I definitely *don't* want to pull. Have you forgotten that I've sworn off men."

"Don't talk daft. You need a fella."

"That's the last thing I need. I will go out, but only because you've already told the others. Just don't go trying to set me up with anyone because if you do, I'm coming straight home."

"Okay."

"Promise?"

"Cross my heart."

"Your heart is on the other side of your body."

***

"Seriously? Is that really what you're wearing?" Beth shot me that disapproving look of hers.

"What's wrong?"

"Jeans and a tee-shirt? You'll never pull in those."

"We've already had this conversation. I don't want to pull. Is that a new dress?"

"Yeah, I picked it up this afternoon."

"Where exactly are you planning on taking me tonight?"

"Jesters."

"You've got to be kidding. What's wrong with The Anchor?"

"If we go to The Anchor, we'll be the only people under fifty in there."

The Anchor was our local pub. Jesters was the newest bar in the city centre, which was always full of hipsters, and whose prices made your eyes water.

"We wouldn't need a taxi to get to The Anchor."

"We're going to Jesters, and that's final. Now, are you sure you don't want to get changed?"

"Nah, I'm good."

I was half-hoping that I might get turned away by the doormen at Jesters, so that I could get the next tube home, and spend a quiet hour in The Anchor, with a Coke and a chip butty. It was not to be because both doormen were too busy ogling Nicky to notice me. I could have been wearing a deep-sea diving suit and they would still have let me in. Nicky was one of those women who always looked like they'd just stepped off the front cover of Glamour magazine. She had the same effect on men wherever she went, and yet for the most part, she seemed totally oblivious to the attention she attracted.

"There's a table over there." Carol pointed. "You lot grab it while I get the first round. I assume it's the usual for everyone?"

The rest of us made a beeline for the one remaining empty table, but as we approached, two men in full-on hipster mode, were headed for the same table. They would have got there first if it hadn't been for Jen who practically leapt across the aisle and into one of the chairs. The taller of the two hipsters gave her a scowl, but they didn't make a scene.

"What are you going to do, Mo?" Nicky said.

"Sit here, drink Coke, and if I start feeling wild, maybe have a packet of crisps."

"I meant about a job?"

"She won't have any problem finding something," Jen said. "There's tons of jobs for computer geeks."

"I'm not a *geek*."

"You're doing your own app," Beth said. "That's pretty geeky."

"I'm not *doing* an app. I'm developing one, or at least I'm trying to."

"Will you sell it for like a bazillion pounds?" Nicky asked.

"That's not how it works, and besides I've got tons more work to do on it."

"Why did they sack you, Mo?" Carol had arrived with a tray full of drinks.

"Because they caught me working on my app in their time."

"Just the once?" Jen said. "That seems a bit harsh."

"It was a few times, actually, but I only ever did it when my own work had dried up and I was waiting for the next assignment."

Beth nudged my arm. "That guy is looking at you." She gestured towards a man, seated on a stool at the bar. He wasn't a hipster, so he had that much going for him, but he wasn't my type either. Tall, cleanshaven and handsome just didn't do it for me.

"Don't be stupid. He's looking at Nicky."

"No, he isn't. He's been staring at you for the last ten minutes."

"Whatever. I've already told you that I'm off the market."

"Hey, Carol," Jen said. "How did you manage to get a pass to come out with us tonight?"

"Very funny. I don't need permission to have a night out with the girls." We all laughed at that. "I don't know why you all think that Miles is controlling." The words were no sooner out of her mouth than her phone rang. "Hi, darling. Yeah, we're in Jesters. I told you: Jen, Nicky, Beth and Mo. I've only had one drink so far. I'm not sure what time. One o'clock probably. There's no need. I'll share a taxi with the girls. Okay, see you. Love you too." As Carol ended the call, she sighed. "Okay, maybe he is a *bit* controlling."

Although I'd originally been less than enthusiastic about the night out, I was glad I'd allowed Beth to twist my arm because if I'd stayed in, I would have become more and more down about the whole job situation.

Jen spent most of the night moaning about her in-laws, as usual. She was the only one of our little group who was married. Unfortunately, not long after she and Pete got hitched, the company he worked for went bust. At the time, they'd been on the verge of securing a mortgage for their own place, but that fell through with the result that they were currently living with Pete's parents. From all accounts, life with her in-laws wasn't working out too well.

"There's houseproud and then there's OCD." Jen took a sip of white wine. "I daren't put anything away in the kitchen in case it's in the wrong cupboard. Then yesterday, I was drinking coffee in the lounge, and when I went to pick it up, it had gone. *She* had swooped in and taken it away. I wouldn't have minded, but there was still half a cup left."

"How's Pete doing with the job hunting?" Nicky asked.

"He's got a second interview at the end of the week, so fingers crossed."

As always, Nicky was fretting about the amount she owed on her credit cards.

"You could always try going a week without buying more clothes," Beth said.

"That's rich coming from the woman who bought a new dress just to go out for drinks tonight," I chipped in.

"Yes, but I paid cash."

"What? As in actual money?" Carol looked nonplussed. "I didn't think anyone used that anymore."

"It'll be okay," Nicky said. "I've got a fancy new app that records all my outgoings, so I can't overspend from now on."

None of us commented, but we all knew the likelihood of her changing her ways was close to zero.

Beth talked mainly about her new boss.

"You fancy him, don't you?" Jen said.

"No, I don't. He's just a breath of fresh air after old Grimes. Leroy has got tons of new ideas and is much more forward-thinking."

"Is he married?" Carol asked.

"No. I mean, I don't think so."

"Engaged?"

"I've no idea."

"Does he have a girlfriend?"

"I'm not interested in him in that way."

"Of course you're not." I grinned.

Beth's only subject of conversation for the last few days had been her new boss. One sure sign that she had the hots for a guy was for her to state categorically that she *wasn't interested in him that way*.

"Have you actually started looking for a job, Mo?" Jen asked.

"I had a quick look at a couple of job websites this afternoon, and there's no shortage of positions that I should have a chance with, but the problem is my CV."

"Why's that a problem? You can create one online in no time at all."

"It's not that. Mine is already more or less up to date. What am I supposed to say about the reason I left Headrow? If I say I was fired, that's likely to put off most prospective employers."

"Just lie about it," Carol said.

"I'd thought about doing that, but any prospective employer is bound to request references, so they'll find out anyway."

"If they're going to find out, you might as well be honest about it on your CV," Beth said. "At least that way, if they do offer you an interview, they'll have done so knowing about the firing."

"I guess so." I shrugged. "But what if no one even offers me an interview? What if I never get another job?"

"Why all the negativity? You're always telling me

you're a glass half-full type of person," Beth said.

"I am usually, but this time I feel as though someone has taken the glass and smashed it into a thousand pieces."

They all did their best to reassure me that I'd be okay, and that I had nothing to worry about. According to them, I'd have a new job in no time at all, and probably one with a higher salary. Hopefully, they were right.

Although I wasn't in any position to pay for drinks, I did insist that they let me go to the bar to order the next round. The bar was heaving and despite the fact that there were five people behind the counter, they were struggling to keep up with demand.

After almost ten minutes, I finally saw my opportunity and was about to call out my order when someone behind me shouted, "A Coors Light, please."

"Coming up."

Livid, I spun around to find the guy from earlier standing there. The one who had, according to Beth, been staring at me. As if.

"Hey, it was my turn," I snapped.

"Sorry." He flashed me a smile. "I didn't see you there."

I may be only five-six, but there's no way he could have missed my hand waving in the air in front of his face. I knew his sort—thinks he's better than everyone else.

"Yeah, right. Invisible, am I?"

"Really, I'm sorry. Let me buy you a drink by way of an apology."

"No, thanks, I can buy my own drinks." Which, strictly speaking, wasn't true.

"I'm Rob."

"Good for you."

"This is the point where you're supposed to tell me your name."

"No, this is the point where you take your drink and get out of my sight." I turned back to the bar and after another five long minutes, managed to get served.

When I eventually made it back to our table, Beth practically leapt to her feet. I assumed she was desperate for a drink, but it turned out she just wanted to interrogate me.

"What did he say?"

"What did *who* say?"

"The good-looking guy at the bar who's been staring at you all night."

"First, he hasn't been staring at me. And second, he jumped the queue to get served ahead of me, so I wasn't much interested in what he had to say."

"He must have said something."

"Just that his name was Rob."

"And you said?"

"I told him to do one."

"You're hopeless, Mo."

Shortly after one o'clock in the morning, we called it a day. The others weren't exactly drunk but they were a few degrees north of merry. As usual, I was stone-cold sober. Nicky and Jen shared one taxi; Carol, Beth and I took the other.

We didn't have far to go to Carol's flat, which was in Chelsea. It was just after one-twenty when we pulled up outside.

"You're going to be in so much trouble." Beth tapped her watch and grinned.

"He might have gone to bed." Carol glanced up at the building. "Oh no, he's standing at the window." She got out of the cab. "See you, guys. Good luck with the job hunt, Mo."

"Thanks."

"She's in for it." Beth laughed as the taxi headed to Deptford. "Are you feeling any better than you were this afternoon, Mo?"

"Yeah, I am. I'm glad you persuaded me to go out. I needed that."

Cat greeted us at the door, hoping for a late-night feed.

"No chance, buddy." I gently nudged him away with my foot. "You'll have to wait until breakfast. Fancy a coffee, Beth?"

"It's a bit late."

"It's not like I have to get up for work, is it?"

"I'd better have tea, or I'll never get off to sleep."

We drank at the kitchen table while Cat kept up his vigil, just in case we had a change of heart.

"Oh, I almost forgot." Beth grabbed her handbag. "Rob gave me something for you."

"The idiot at the bar? When?"

"While you were in the loo, I had a quick word with him. I told him you weren't usually so grumpy, but that you'd just lost your job."

I almost spat out my coffee. "I wasn't being grumpy. I was annoyed at him because he'd jumped the queue. And you had no right telling him about me getting fired."

"He seemed really nice. Here you are." She handed me

a business card.

"Q-Ventures? What's that when it's at home?"

"I'm not sure, but that's his number. He said he might have a job for you, and that you should give him a call tomorrow."

"Sure thing." I ripped the card into small pieces and threw it into the bin.

"Why did you do that?"

"I'm not going to call some random guy who, by the way, has no manners, about some supposed random job. He probably hands those cards out to every girl he gets talking to."

"Please yourself." Beth shrugged. "But I liked him."

Chapter 3

The next morning, I was wide awake by six o'clock, but I didn't come out of my bedroom until I heard Beth leave for work. She wasn't a morning person at the best of times, but with a hangover, she'd be like a bear with a sore backside.

As soon as the coast was clear, I made for the living room where I found Cat sitting on the chair looking out of the window. He spotted me and began to meow.

"Do you want to go out?"

"Meow."

"Are you sure? It looks cold out there."

"Meow."

"Wouldn't you like to stay in here, in the warmth, and keep me company?"

"Meow."

Even with such a limited vocabulary, Cat had a way of making his feelings known. And that last meow was definitely the equivalent of him saying, *"I'd rather pull out my claws than stay in here and listen to you feeling sorry for yourself."*

"Please yourself, but don't expect me to give you a shoulder to cry on when you're feeling down."

Had I really just said that out loud? At this rate, if I didn't find another job soon, people would start referring to me as that crazy cat lady.

As soon as I opened the window, he leapt out and headed for the bushes in the communal garden. He no doubt had a hot date lined up.

I was ravenous and I would have killed for a bacon cob, but we had neither bacon nor bread, so I had to settle for no-brand cornflakes. I daren't check the best-before date.

As if that wasn't bad enough, when I opened the fridge, I discovered we were out of milk—great, just great!

Dry cornflakes it was, then. Washed down with a glass of water.

After I'd eaten breakfast, stacked the dishes in the dishwasher, and spent an hour pretending to tidy up, I could put it off no longer; I had to tackle my CV. Tempted as I was to lie about the reason that I'd left Headrow, I knew it would only come back to haunt me, so I decided to be truthful. Mostly. I said I'd been let go after a difference of opinion related to working practices. That was more or less accurate in that I'd believed it was okay for me to work on my app during office hours, and they'd disagreed. With the CV ready to go, I submitted an application for the six jobs I'd shortlisted the previous day. Now all I had to do was wait for the interview requests to come pouring in.

What to do with the rest of my day? Go back to bed? Watch Netflix? That would have been the first step down a slippery slope, so instead I decided to work on my app. I could have done it in the flat, but that would have meant having to put up with Cat trying to distract me when he returned.

The local coffee shops all had free wi-fi, but I would have been expected to fork out for their over-priced coffee, and in my current financial predicament, that wasn't an option. The local library was out too because their wi-fi was naff, so I took a tube ride into town to use one of the libraries there.

I'd no sooner left the flat than I bumped into our

neighbour from down the corridor. Mrs Potter was a widow in her seventies who always had a huge smile; she was one of the happiest people I knew.

But not today.

"Mrs Potter? Are you okay? Why are you crying?"

"It's Paxman."

"The guy off University Challenge? What's he done?"

"No. Paxman is my budgie. I nipped out to the bins and left the door open because I knew I'd only be gone a couple of minutes, but I'd forgotten that I'd let Paxman out of his cage."

"Are you sure he isn't hiding in your flat somewhere?"

"I've searched high and low. He must have managed to get out of the flat." She began to sob. "If something has happened to him, I'll never forgive myself."

"Why don't we go into your place, and I'll make you a nice cup of tea?"

"What about Paxman?"

"If you open all the windows in your flat, I'm sure he'll come home when he's hungry."

"Do you really think so, Mo?"

"Yes, I'm sure."

I didn't actually believe Paxman would return because he was a budgie, not a homing pigeon, but I hoped saying that might calm her down. It seemed to do the trick because, ten minutes later, Mrs Potter was telling me all about her great-grandson, Graham.

"He's nearly three." She handed me a framed photograph.

"He looks a cheeky little lad."

"Oh, he is." She beamed. "But I mustn't keep you, Mo. You'll be late for work."

"I'm not actually going into work today, but I probably should be making a move. Will you be okay now?"

"Yes, I'm fine. I'll just wait here until Paxman comes back."

"Okay, bye."

Poor old dear.

It was while I was at uni that I came up with the idea for my app. I'd always found that I studied better if I was working with someone who was doing the same subject as me. When I worked alone, my mind tended to drift off, but with a study partner, the two of us could push one another to do more, as well as bouncing ideas off each other. But finding a suitable person to study with had proved much more difficult than I'd expected. That's when I hit on the idea of Study-Ant, which I envisaged would be able to match students studying the same subjects across all the universities in the UK. The idea had been simple enough, but building it had proved much more difficult than I could ever have imagined.

The library was almost deserted, so I had no trouble locating a table near to a power point, but when I switched my laptop on, nothing. This could not be happening. It had been working fine only an hour before. I closed the screen.

"Come on, don't do this to me."

I hadn't noticed the young man who had taken a seat at the next table until he snorted with laughter. "Are you talking to that computer?"

"No."

"I heard you."

"So why did you ask?"

"Are you one of those crazies who come into the library out of the rain?"

"Be quiet. Can't you see I'm busy?" I opened the screen, hoping that the laptop might spring back to life, but my pep talk had been to no avail because the black screen was still taunting me.

"Any luck?" My annoying neighbour asked.

"Don't you have homework to do?"

A young woman with pigtails appeared and sat down next to the young man. He whispered something to her, and they both laughed. That was my cue to find another table, so I grabbed the laptop and headed to the opposite side of the room.

At a time like this, there was only one person I could call upon for help, so I grabbed my phone and found his name in my list of contacts.

"Laurence?"

"Mo? I thought you'd left the country. Or died."

"Sorry that I haven't been in touch for a while."

"That's okay. I imagine you're crazy busy at work. Same here."

"Actually, I'm kind of between jobs at the moment."

"What happened at Headrow?"

"Long story. Look, I need a massive favour."

"What's up?"

"My laptop just died."

"Have you switched it off and on again?"

"Very funny. Is there any chance you could take a look at it?"

"Sure. When?"

"Right now if you can. I'm kind of desperate."

"Okay. Can you meet me at Bean Shack?"

I'd walked past that particular coffee shop lots of times, but I'd never been inside; it was only a ten-minute walk from the library.

"Sure. I'll be there in fifteen."

Laurence and his then girlfriend, Sandra, had lived in the same block of flats as Beth and me. After Sandra had taken up with some Australian guy, and moved to Adelaide, Laurence had been forced to give up the flat, and he now lived somewhere in Barking. Since then, we'd barely seen one another, so it was a bit of a cheek to call him out of the blue, and ask him to repair my laptop. But needs must and no one knew more about hardware than he did.

When I arrived at Bean Shack, he was waiting outside.

"Hi, stranger." He gave me an awkward hug. "What did you do to your hair?"

"It was getting on my nerves, so I thought I'd try it short for a change."

"I meant the colour. Blue suits you."

"It's turquoise."

"If you say so. Have you been in this place before?"

"Nah."

"I love it here. The coffee is good and Jed, the owner, is a good laugh."

"Sounds good. What would you like to drink?"

"I'll get them," he offered.

"No, it's alright. This is on me. Will you take this stupid thing while I order the drinks?" I handed him the laptop. "What's it to be?"

"I'll have a cortado, please. While you're getting them, I'll grab a table and see what I can make of this."

I wasn't really in a position to be splashing out on coffees, but I figured it would be cheaper than paying to get the laptop repaired. I might be a dab hand at programming, but hardware was a complete mystery to me, so Laurence was my only hope.

By the expression on his face, I could tell the news wasn't good even before I reached the table.

"It's not looking good," he announced, as he took the coffee from me.

"What's wrong with it?"

"It's definitely not a power problem. It's most likely the motherboard."

"Can it be fixed?"

"Hopefully, but I'll need to take it home to have a proper look at it."

"Okay. Any idea how long it will take?"

"I can't do it tonight because I've got something on that I can't cancel, but I should be able to take a look at it tomorrow."

"Great. Thanks, Laurence."

"Are you going to tell me what happened at Headrow?"

I told him the reason I'd been fired and said I was worried I might struggle to get another job.

"Bummer. What was the app you were working on?"

"I call it Study-Ant. It matches up students who are studying the same subject."

"Why ant?"

There were definitely times when I wished I had come up with a different name for the app, but I gave him the same explanation I'd given a thousand others before him.

"Ants work together to get a job done. Plus, I've always

liked the little guys."

"You always were a bit weird."

"Thanks."

"Is it like a dating app?"

"Definitely *not* like a dating app."

"Talking of dating. Are you still with Adam, Mo?"

"No, he was cheating on me."

"What an idiot. Are you seeing someone else?"

"No, I'm taking a break from dating for a while."

"That's what I said too." He laughed. "But then I met Tonya."

"Is it serious?"

"We moved in together a couple of weeks ago, so I guess it must be."

"I'm really pleased for you, Laurence. What Sandra did to you was horrible."

"Talking of Sandra, she's back."

"Back in the UK?"

"Yeah, she came back a couple of months ago. Apparently, it didn't work out with the guy from down under."

"Have you seen her?"

"Yeah, I didn't know she was back until we bumped into each other. It was a bit awkward for us both."

"Where's she living now?"

"No idea. She didn't stick around long enough for me to ask; she made some excuse about a dentist appointment and shot off." Laurence checked his watch. "Speaking of which, I have to shoot off myself. Sorry."

"No problem. Thanks for doing this."

"No problem. I'll give you a call tomorrow."

"Please make it good news."

"I'll do my best." He picked up the laptop and hurried out of the shop.

As I still had three-quarters of a cup of coffee left, and no idea when I'd be able to afford coffee shop prices again, I sat back and savoured what was left of my drink.

The shop was busy and the guy behind the counter appeared to be working alone, so the queue kept building up. A couple of times, I heard people moaning about how long it was taking to get served.

I was just about to leave when I spotted a sheet of paper on the small noticeboard.

Help wanted: A few hours each weekday. Hours flexible. Apply at counter.

It said nothing about needing experience and it didn't mention what the job entailed. I had zero experience in the service industry, but I figured it was worth a try. If I could bring in a few quid while I looked for something more permanent, it would take some of the pressure off.

I nursed my empty cup for another twenty minutes until the queue had finally dispersed, and then I took my chance.

"Hi." I shot him my *please employ me because I'm desperate* smile.

"What can I get for you?"

"Actually, I was just wondering if the job on the noticeboard is still open?"

"It is, yes. Do you have any experience of working in a coffee shop?"

"None."

"Any similar experience?"

"No. None."

"Oh?" He sighed. Not a promising sign.

"I'm a quick learner, though, and I could start straight away."

"How soon is straight away?"

"Err, right now if you like."

He hesitated and for a minute I thought it was going to be a *no*, but then he asked my name.

"Maureen, but everyone calls me Mo."

"Okay, Mo. I'm Jed. Grab that apron and come behind the counter. We'll give it a couple of days and see how you go."

"Great."

"To start with, you'll just be taking orders and cleaning the tables."

"Okay."

"If I do decide to keep you on, I'll introduce you to Bertha."

"Does she work here too?"

"No. That's Bertha." He pointed to the huge coffee making machine.

"She looks scary."

"Don't worry about her. For now, you just need to know how to use the till."

"Okay. Where is it?"

"Right there."

"That thing?"

I'd been expecting some kind of modern point-of-sale terminal. What I got was something that looked like it had come in on the Ark.

"I was on a tight budget when I opened this place, so something had to give. I decided to spend the cash on the best coffee machine I could afford, and on the décor, but that meant I had to make do with this."

"How does it work?"

"It couldn't be simpler. You just press that button, but step back a few inches first."

I took a step back and pressed the button. A bell rang and the cash drawer flew open with some force.

"That thing is lethal."

"Why do you think I need a new employee? The last guy is still in ICU." He laughed.

Hopefully, he was joking.

"Is that all there is to the till?"

"Yeah, and most people pay by card, anyway, in which case you just need to enter the amount into this handset."

"That seems straightforward enough."

"And, regardless of how people pay, you need to keep a record of what they bought."

"Do you have a separate computer for that?"

"Not exactly." He reached under the counter and brought out a lined pad.

"You write it on there?"

"Yeah. Pretty old school, eh?"

"You could say that."

When I left, three hours later, I was dead on my feet, but quite pleased with how it had gone. More importantly, Jed seemed happy with me. He'd had the good sense to keep me away from anything complicated like making drinks. I'd spent most of the time taking the orders, clearing the tables and feeding the dishwasher. Even better, Jed had said he would pay me in cash at the end of each day, until such time as he decided if he was going to keep me on or not, which meant I left there with some money in my pocket.

I was starting to feel a little more optimistic.
Big mistake!

Chapter 4

On my way back to the flat, I called in at the local minimarket, and bought milk, bread, a pizza and a packet of chocolate digestives. That was tonight's dinner sorted.

When I walked into the living room, I heard Cat meowing outside. As soon as I opened the window, he leapt in and headed for the corner of the kitchen where we always fed him.

"It's not that time yet."

"Meow!"

"I know I'm back home, but that's because I haven't been to work. Well, I have, kind of, but not at— " Why was I explaining myself to the cat again?

"Meow!"

"You're just going to have to wait."

It had been hot work behind the counter at Bean Shack, and I was feeling a little grubby, so I decided to grab a shower before Beth arrived home.

Twenty minutes later, and feeling much refreshed, I headed back to my bedroom, wrapped in a large bath towel. I was almost at the door when I stopped dead in my tracks, and stared at the yellow feather on the floor.

"Cat! Come here!"

He didn't.

"Cat! Where are you?" I checked the kitchen but there was no sign of him. Had he gone back outside? Unlikely. I hurried to the lounge where I found him preening himself on the chair. "What have you done, Cat?"

He stopped what he was doing just long enough to glance at me, then picked up where he'd left off.

"I said what have you done?" I waved the yellow

feather in front of his face.

That caught his attention; he sprang to his feet and tried to swipe it from my hand.

"This isn't a game. Where's the rest of it?"

"Where's the rest of what?" Beth appeared behind me.

"Mrs Potter's budgie. This little monster has eaten Paxman."

"Who's Paxman?"

"I've just told you. He's Mrs Potter's budgie. Or at least he was." I held up the feather. "This is all that's left of him."

Then Beth did something totally unexpected: she began to laugh hysterically.

"It isn't funny, Beth. Poor old Mrs Potter was inconsolable when she discovered her budgie was missing. How am I going to tell her that Cat ate her darling Paxman?"

Beth was laughing so hard that she was unable to speak, but she did beckon me to follow her.

"Where are we going?"

She led the way into the kitchen.

"Beth, have you heard a word I've said? How am I going to tell Mrs Potter about Paxman?"

"Hold on." Beth pulled open the cupboard and took out a feather duster. A feather duster with yellow feathers identical to the one in my hand.

"Does that mean—?"

"That Cat hasn't eaten Paxman?" Beth wiped her eyes. "Yeah, you can relax. I bought this yesterday."

"Why?"

"You keep telling me that we should clean this place more often, and it was on special offer."

"I really thought Cat had eaten him."

"You really are priceless sometimes, Mo."

Thirty minutes later, we were in the lounge, eating pizza, when Beth's phone beeped. She read the message and laughed.

"Are you going to share?" I said.

"That was Jen. She sent me this." Beth held out the phone to show me a cartoon of a cat with a mouthful of feathers.

"You told her?"

"Of course I did. What did you expect? This is comedy gold."

"Who else did you tell?"

"Everyone."

"Thanks."

"No problem. What have you been up to all day, anyway? Lying in bed watching Netflix, I bet."

"And you'd be wrong. I've got myself a job."

"Wow, that was quick. Congrats."

"It's not like a *job* job. Just something to bring in a little money until I find something else."

"What is it?"

"Working in a coffee shop."

She laughed so hard that she almost spat out her pizza. "You? In a coffee shop?"

"What's so funny about that?"

"The last time you made me a cup of tea, you forgot to put the teabag in. You've got no chance of working out how to use one of those coffee machines."

"Thanks for the vote of confidence, but I'm not making the drinks yet, anyway. Just taking the orders, clearing the tables, that sort of thing."

"Which shop?"

"Bean Shack."

"That's miles from here. How did you hear about the job?"

"I was in there."

"How come?"

"My laptop quit on me this morning, so I gave Laurence a call."

"Laurence? You're a cheeky mare. You haven't spoken to him in months."

"I know. I felt a bit bad, but what choice did I have?"

"Did he sort it out for you?"

"Not yet. He's taken it home with him. Fingers crossed he can repair it. Anyway, after Laurence had left, I spotted the job on the noticeboard, so I asked the guy behind the counter about it."

"He must have been desperate to set you on."

"Thanks again."

"I meant because you have zero experience."

"I charmed him with my magnetic personality."

"It definitely can't have been that. I'm guessing he'd had no other takers. How did it go?"

"Alright, I think. He didn't send me home early or tell me not to come in tomorrow, so I reckon I must have done okay."

"What about the real job-hunting? Any luck on that score?"

"I checked the job websites just before I left the coffee shop, and I hadn't had any responses then." I took out my phone. "I'll have another look." I fired up the app and saw that there were two messages in my in-box: both rejections.

"Anything?"

"No. Nothing yet."

After our girls' night out the previous day, I'd assumed that Beth and I would have a quiet night in together, watching Netflix and eating digestive biscuits. It turned out I was wrong. I should have sensed she was up to something when she had a shower and then disappeared into her bedroom for thirty minutes.

"I'm off." She stuck her head around the door.

"Where are you going?"

"I'm just meeting up with some people from work. I thought I'd mentioned it to you."

"No, you didn't. Come in here."

"I'll be late."

"Come in here," I insisted.

Somewhat reluctantly, she stepped into the living room.

"Wow!" I stared at her dress in awe. "When did you buy that?"

"Today. Do you like it?"

"It's great, but it must have cost a small fortune. Couldn't you have worn the one you bought yesterday?"

"I spilled wine on it."

"Who exactly are these *people* you're meeting up with?"

"You wouldn't know them."

"It's your new boss, isn't it? What's his name? Leroy?"

"Sorry, I have to go, or I'll be late." And off she shot without answering my question, which more or less confirmed what I'd suspected: She was meeting her new boss.

The little minx.

Watching TV all on my own was pretty sad, but the chocolate digestives definitely helped. So much so that before I realised it the packet was empty. How had that happened? I could only assume Beth must have sneaked a few before she went out. And besides, it was only a small packet. If Beth spotted the wrapper in the morning, I'd never hear the end of it, so I took the rubbish outside to the bins.

On my way back in, a door opened, and Mrs Potter stepped into the corridor.

"Hello, Mo, I was hoping to catch you."

Oh no. She was probably recruiting people for the great budgie search party.

"Hi, Mrs Potter, I was just about to have an early night."

"Why would you want to do that? When I was your age, I was out painting the town red every chance I got. I could tell you some stories."

"I bet you could."

"I'm glad I've seen you because I wanted to tell you about Paxman."

This was it. I was about to be assigned my own search area.

"He's back home safe and sound."

"He is?"

"Yes, and I've given him a good talking to."

"Where did you find him?"

"After I'd finished my tea, I went into the lounge and there he was, in his cage."

"He came back by himself?"

"Yes, and I have you to thank for that. You said if I left the windows open, he'd come home when he was hungry, and that's just what he did."

"Great. I'm really happy for you."

"And remember what I said, Mo, you should be out having fun. You only live once."

To look at her now, it wasn't easy to picture Mrs Potter as a bit of a raver when she was my age, but apparently, she had the stories to prove it. Whereas, when I'm her age, I'll have stories about staying in alone, eating biscuits. Tragic.

I had almost nodded off when my phone rang.

"Laurence? I wasn't expecting to hear from you until tomorrow."

"I had a bit of free time, so I thought I'd take a quick look at it, and it's not good news."

"Please tell me you're joking."

"I'm afraid not. It would cost as much to repair it as for you to buy a new laptop. More probably."

"Okay." I sighed. "I'll just have to find the money to get another one. Luckily, I managed to land myself a temporary job at Bean Shack yesterday after you'd left."

"Good for you, Mo."

"Will you be able to transfer the data over for me?"

"No can do. The disk is a goner."

"But I thought you could always get data off a disk, even when it's dead."

"Ninety-nine times out of a hundred you can, but—"

"Let me guess. This is the hundredth time?"

"Correct. You're welcome to ask someone else to take a look at it, but they'll tell you the same thing. I assume you've got a backup of all the important stuff on cloud?"

"Err, yeah, of course."

"What do you want me to do with your laptop? I can probably drop it off with you this weekend."

"Don't bother. You can bin it."

"Are you sure?"

"Yeah, and thanks again for trying."

"No problem, and don't be a stranger. I'd love you to meet Tonya."

"I promise."

Great! Just great! When I'd told Laurence that I had a backup on the cloud, I'd been telling the truth. Unfortunately, it wasn't stored on *my* cloud account—I didn't have one. I'd always stored my stuff on Headrow's cloud.

My next call was to Ryan.

"Mo?"

"Hi. Have you been missing me?"

"You've only been gone for five minutes."

"You could at least pretend."

"They've passed most of your stuff on to me."

"You should ask for more money."

"Yeah, sure, like that would ever happen. Have you got yourself another job yet?"

"Kind of, but it's only temporary. Look, I need a big favour."

"I'm not spitting in Tom Powell's coffee if that's what you want."

"That's not such a bad idea, but that's not it. My laptop died today."

"You're not having much luck, are you?"

"No kidding. All my app stuff is on there and the disk is D.O.A."

"You've got a backup, though. Right?"

"Yeah, kind of. That's where the favour comes in."

"I don't understand."

"It's on Headrow's cloud."

"Are you crazy? Why did you put it on there?"

"For the easiest, I guess."

"Why didn't you put it in your own Dropbox? It's not like it costs anything."

"I know. I'm an idiot. The thing is I really need those files."

"Why don't you just log in yourself and get them. Don't tell me you've forgotten the password already."

"Of course not, but Headrow's security systems won't let me log in from offsite. But you can."

"If they catch me doing it, I'll be looking for another job too."

"They won't. It will literally only take you thirty seconds. Please, Ryan, I'm desperate."

"Okay." He sighed. "Give me your password, and I'll try and do it when there's no one around."

"Get back to me as soon as you can."

"Will do."

Chapter 5

I was beginning to get the hang of working behind the counter at Bean Shack. Jed had even suggested he might show me how to use Bertha in a couple of days.

The early morning rush had just reached its peak when who should walk in but the guy from Jesters. The one who had given Beth his business card to pass onto me. He was wearing a swanky suit.

"Hi again." He beamed.

"Are you stalking me?"

"Of course I'm not." He faked an affronted look. "I had no idea you worked here."

"You're pathetic. Do you really expect me to believe you just happened to be passing? Did Beth tip you off that I was here?"

"Hey, Rob," Jed shouted. "Your usual?"

"Yes, please, Jed."

Oh no! The guy must be a regular, and I'd just accused him of stalking me.

"Rob is one of our best customers, Mo," Jed said. "Make sure you take real good care of him."

"Sure."

By now, *Rob* was grinning from ear to ear. "Did you hear that, Mo? You have to take *real* good care of me."

"What can I get for you, *sir*?"

"That's quite a skill you have there."

"What is?"

"The way you managed to make the word *sir* sound like an insult."

"What do you want?"

"A cappuccino, please."

"What size?"

"Large. I always have large."

"Right."

"With chocolate sprinkles."

"A large cappuccino with sprinkles, is that it?"

"I'll have a chocolate twist too, please. Wait, no, make that a croissant."

"Are you sure?"

"No, I've changed my mind. I'll have a pain aux raisins. "

He was a *pain* in the backside.

"Anything else?"

"No, that's it, thanks."

"That'll be six-pounds, thirty-five."

"Thanks, Mo." He wafted his credit card over the contactless card-reader. His *platinum* credit card. What a poser.

"Thank you, *sir*."

"When did you start working here?"

"Yesterday."

"Why didn't you give me a call? Didn't your friend give you my card?"

"She did, but I accidentally ripped it into shreds and threw it in the bin. Whoops!"

"I thought you were looking for a job."

"I've got a job." I held out my arms. "See, I'm doing it right now."

"Judging by the look of terror on your face every time you walk by that coffee machine, I'm guessing this isn't your true calling. Your friend told me you were a computer geek."

"Beth talks too much."

"She said you were developing your own app."

"Why are you interested?"

"Everything okay, Mo?" Jed called from the other end of the counter.

"Everything's great. Rob was just telling me that he's in a hurry this morning."

"No problem. Your order is ready, Rob."

"Have a nice day, sir." I treated him to the falsest smile I could conjure up.

"I will, Mo. You too. I'm already looking forward to our little chat tomorrow morning."

"He's a nice guy that Rob," Jed said later when the early morning rush was over. "He's always polite, not like some we get in here. They ran an article about the company where he works in the Financial Times a few months back."

"What do they do?"

"Something hi-tech, but it's no good asking me. I can barely use my own phone." He pointed to the tables. "Will you clear those while things are quiet?"

"Sure. I'm on it."

I was on my break when I got a call from Ryan.

"Mo, it's me. I can't talk for long. It's not good news, I'm afraid."

"Don't tell me you've got cold feet?"

"No, I logged into your cloud account ten minutes ago."

"And?"

"There's nothing there. Someone has purged it."

"They can't have. Are you sure?"

"One-hundred percent. I'm really sorry, Mo."

"Maybe they can *un*-purge it?"

"How?"

"I don't know. I'm not a cloud expert."

"There's no need to snap at me. It isn't my fault."

"Sorry, Ryan, I'm just in shock. Who looks after cloud services?"

"I have absolutely no idea. I have to go now."

"Okay. Thanks." For a big fat nothing.

Just when I'd thought things couldn't get worse, they had. Ten-fold. Hundreds of hours of work—no, make that thousands—all up in smoke.

***

By the time I'd finished my shift at Bean Shack, I was shattered. After a bad start to the day with the Platinum Rob affair, things had gone from bad to worse. Jed had taken a call, after which he'd been in a foul mood. After he'd snapped at me for the second time in an hour, for nothing in particular, I told him he could stuff his job. To be fair to him, he apologised and admitted he'd been in the wrong. Apparently, the call had been from his bank; they wanted him to go in and discuss his loan payments. Reading between the lines, he'd fallen behind with them and they weren't best pleased. What with that, and the devastating news about my app, this day couldn't get any worse.

Or so I thought. Then I saw who was standing outside our block of flats.

"Mum?"

"You really ought to let me have a key. I've been standing out here for over an hour."

"What are you doing here?"

"I was just passing by."

"Leicester is a hundred miles away."

"Are you going to let me in, or do I have to wait here for another hour?"

Reluctantly, and because there seemed to be no viable alternative, I unlocked the door and led the way inside.

"Don't you girls ever tidy this place?"

"Don't start, Mum, I've had a terrible day. Why are you here?"

"A cup of tea would be nice. I haven't had a drink since I set off this morning."

"Why didn't you get one on the train?"

"I can't afford train prices. I came on the coach."

"There are plenty of coffee shops between the coach station and here."

"I'm not paying for one of their poncy coffees. Besides, I don't know what half of them are with their fancy-schmancy names. Are you going to make me a cuppa, or do I have to make my own?"

"I'll get you one."

She took one sip, pulled a face and said, "Very nice."

"What's wrong with it?"

"Is that milk in here?"

"Soya."

"What's wrong with ordinary milk?"

"We don't have any. You still haven't told me what you're doing here."

"I was worried about you."

"There's no need. I'm fine. See?"

"What's that you're wearing?"

"My uniform."

"What's Bean Shack?"

"A coffee shop."

"You're working in a coffee shop?"

"It's only temporary until I find something else."

"There's plenty of good jobs going in Leicester."

"I'm not going back there, Mum. If that's why you're here, you've had a wasted journey."

"You still haven't told me what happened to that other job you had. Beth said there was some kind of trouble."

"Beth's got a big mouth. Nothing happened. I just had a disagreement with the management."

"You were just the same at school. You never had any respect for the teachers."

"That's because most of them were too stupid to get toothpaste out of the tube."

"And, now you're making coffee?"

"Not yet, but I will be when I've had my training."

"*Training*?" She scoffed. "To make a cup of coffee?"

"What time is your coach back home?"

"Eight-thirty."

I glanced at my phone. "We've just got time for a takeaway and then I'll put you in a taxi."

"In the morning."

"Tomorrow? Where are you staying tonight?"

"I thought I'd stay here. Unless that's a problem?"

"No, it's okay. I can sleep on the sofa."

"There's no need to do that. We can share a bed like we did when you were a kid."

"We never shared a bed."

"Yes, we did. You used to come and climb into bed with me and your dad when you had a nightmare."

"I don't remember that."

"You were only three or four at the time. Anyway, I'm ready for a lie down after that awful journey. Which is your bedroom?"

Before I could answer, the door opened, and Beth walked in.

"Hello, Mrs Jackson. Did you have a good journey down?"

"Those bus seats are the wrong shape for my back."

"Why don't you go and lie down, Mum? Beth and I have a few things to discuss."

"Okay, dear. Don't go ordering in dinner. I can make do with whatever you two normally have. See you later, Beth."

"Okay, Mrs Jackson." Beth watched my mother disappear into my bedroom and then turned to me. "Why are you giving me that look?"

"Why didn't you tell me she was coming down?"

"I thought it'd be a nice surprise."

"Liar. You knew I'd kill you."

"I wish my mother cared as much about me as your mum cares about you."

"You can have her if you like."

"Are the two of you sharing your bed tonight?"

"No. You and I are sharing *your* bed. Have you got any money-off vouchers for a takeaway?"

"Your mum said not to bother ordering anything in."

"That's what she said, but if we give her what we'd normally have, she'll spend all night moaning about it. You must have an Uber Eats voucher somewhere."

***

Beth and I were in her bedroom. She'd just washed her hair and was looking through her wardrobe. I'd sought refuge in there just in case Mum woke up.

"Leroy asked me to have lunch with him tomorrow." Beth looked like the cat that got the canary.

"Have you found out if he's in a relationship?"

"He's never mentioned anyone, and anyway, it's just a business lunch."

"Oh yeah. What kind of *business*?"

"He said he wanted to talk strategy for the department going forward."

"Why couldn't he do that in the office?"

"He reckons we'll get a better run at it away from the distractions of the office."

"Where's he taking you?"

"The Beacon."

"Beacon *Hotel*?" I laughed. "Oh boy."

"What?"

"There's a hundred restaurants in a two-mile radius of your office. Why would he book one in a hotel?"

"It's not what you think."

"If you say so." I checked my phone. "The Uber guy will be here any time. Have you got any cash for a tip?"

"My purse is in my bag."

"I'll get it."

"No! I'll get—"

"What's this?" I held up the tiny pink carrier bag.

"I've been meaning to get some new underwear for ages."

"From Feel Chic? You must have more money than sense."

"Give it here."

"Oh boy. I'm not sure Leroy will be doing much strategizing when he gets an eyeful of you in these."

"I didn't buy them for Leroy."

"Of course you didn't."

"There's no talking to you, Mo." She turned on the hairdryer to drown me out.

I was trying to figure out how many shifts I would have to work at Bean Shack to be able to afford Beth's new lingerie when the bedroom door opened, and my mother appeared.

"Didn't you two hear the guy knocking at the door?"

"No, sorry." I gestured to Beth who was still drying her hair, oblivious to my mother's appearance.

"He reckons he had a takeaway for this address, but I told him we hadn't ordered one."

"Where is he now?"

"I sent him packing. He was obviously some kind of scam artist."

I jumped off the bed and legged it out of the flat. Fortunately, I caught the guy as he was about to climb onto his motorbike.

"That's our takeaway."

"It's supposed to be for flat number two."

"Yeah, that's me."

"The woman in that flat said you hadn't ordered it."

"Sorry about that. She's my mother."

"Say no more." He opened his insulated box and handed me the pizzas. "Enjoy."

"Thanks." It was only when I was about to tip him that I realised I'd never got around to taking any cash out of Beth's purse because I'd been too distracted by her lingerie. "I'll have to catch you next time."

"Sure you will."

"I told you not to order takeaway," my mother said. "What kind of food is Uber?"

"It's whatever you order."

"Are you sure it's okay?"

"It's fine."

"Did you know Mo was working in a coffee shop, Beth?"

"Yes. She did well to get a job so quickly."

"But it's a coffee shop."

"I'm standing right here. And, I've already told you that it's just a stopgap thing until I get something more permanent."

"What about the rent and other bills for this place? You'll never pay those with what you earn there."

"I'll manage, Mum. Can we please just enjoy this food?"

Chapter 6

After walking my mother to the local tube station, I joined Beth at the kitchen table.

"Do you think she'll find her way to Victoria coach park?" Beth said.

"Of course she will. She plays dumb sometimes, but she's whip-smart."

"You should have made her take a taxi."

"I tried but she wouldn't hear of it. She's given herself almost two hours to get there, so she'll be fine."

Beth was staring at her reflection in the mirror. "I don't know what Leroy will think when he sees these bags under my eyes."

"You don't have bags under your eyes."

"I do and it's your fault. I didn't get a wink of sleep last night with your snoring."

"I do *not* snore. And anyway, you can talk. At least I wasn't shouting in my sleep: *Take me, Leroy, I'm yours.*"

"You're hilarious. Do my eyes really look okay?"

"They look fine. And besides, I doubt Leroy will be looking at them once he clocks you in that Chic Feel combo."

"He isn't going to see them, but I must admit, they do feel good."

"You'll have to let me know how your *meeting* goes. And I want all the sordid details."

"Will do. I didn't get the chance to ask you last night. How did it go at Bean Shack?"

"Not bad, but I think Jed is having money problems, so knowing my luck, I'll get there this morning and the bailiffs will have boarded up the place."

"So says the *glass is half-full* optimist."

"That smarmy guy from Jesters came into the shop yesterday."

"The one who had the hots for you?"

"According to you. He's a smartass who is full of himself."

"You two have a lot in common, then. You should get on like a house on fire."

"Thanks."

"What happened? What did he say?"

"I accused him of stalking me, but then I discovered that he's actually a regular customer."

"Oh dear."

"He milked that for all it was worth. He's too smooth by half, flashing his platinum card around."

"He must be making some serious money if he's got one of those. Did he ask why you hadn't called him?"

"Yeah, and I told him I had a new job."

"At the coffee shop? That's just a temporary thing, isn't it? I thought you wanted to get back into whatever it is you do."

"I do, but not if it means working with that creep."

"What does his company do?"

"How would I know?"

"You could look them up on Google."

"I've got better things to do with my time. Anyway, I've already got my CV on all the main job sites, so it'll only be a matter of time until something crops up."

"I'd better get going. Wish me luck."

"You won't need it in that lingerie."

I waited until I was sure Beth wasn't going to come back—she had a bad habit of forgetting things: keys, phone, money—and then I logged into each of the job websites. I wasn't very hopeful because I hadn't received any email notifications.

Not a sniff. That didn't bode well. I had a decent skillset plus several years' experience, and according to the press, people in my line of work were in demand all over the country. So why no interest? There could be only one reason. Prospective employers must have seen through the double-speak I'd used to explain my reason for leaving Headrow. They must have figured out that *a difference of opinion related to working practices* actually meant I was a troublemaker who had been sacked.

Great! What now? What good was having the skills and experience if no one would touch me with a barge-pole?

I tried to remember the company name on the business card that I'd torn to shreds. It was *something*-Ventures. I was sure it was a single letter: G-Ventures? Maybe. I-Ventures? Neither of those produced any meaningful results. Q-Ventures—that was it.

It turned out they were a major player in FinTech who, according to their website, had a very impressive client list. My eyes were drawn immediately to the link marked *Join Us*. One click took me to a long list of their current vacancies, including several for app developers.

It was now official: I was a complete idiot. My stupidity at Headrow had potentially rendered me persona non grata with all prospective employers. And yet, when someone had offered me a lifeline in the form of an interview with one of the major players in the industry, I'd ripped up the guy's business card and, just for good measure, accused him of being a stalker.

I was done for.

***

Jed was in a much better mood when I arrived for work.

"Hey, Mo, I'm sorry if I snapped at you yesterday."

"Forget it. Sounds like you've got a lot on your plate."

"Even so, I shouldn't have taken it out on you. How about I give you your first lesson on Bertha before we open?"

Prior to taking this job, I'd never paid much attention to the coffee machines in my favourite coffee shops. Up close and personal, they were terrifying. Give me a block of C++ to debug any day of the week.

"Sure, if you think I'm ready." I tried to sound enthusiastic.

"Course you are. I reckon you're going to be a natural."

Ten minutes later, and I got the feeling that Jed's initial optimism had started to wane.

"Remind me again how many shots it is," I said.

"It's all on there." He pointed to the laminated A4 sheet that was stuck to the wall.

"Two shots?"

He shook his head. "What size did I ask for?"

"Large."

"So, how many shots?"

"Four."

"Correct." He checked his watch. "Time to open up. We'll call it a day on Bertha for now and pick up again another day."

"Okay."

I was relieved that the lesson was over, but disappointed that I'd not taken to it as well as Jed had expected me to. But then I'd always been better with my brain than my hands. I could write decent code when I was twelve years old, but ask me to change a plug even now, and I'd run a mile.

The morning rush had come and gone, but there had been no sign of Rob and his platinum card. I'd been debating all morning what I should do if he showed up. The logical approach would have been to apologise for my previous comments and ask if the offer of a job interview was still open, but the thought of having to grovel to him turned my stomach.

During the lull, I began to collect cups and wipe down tables.

"Hi, you must be Mo."

I'd been so lost in my thoughts that I hadn't heard the door open behind me.

"Err, yeah." I stared at the woman, trying to work out who she was and how she knew me.

"I'm Liz. Jed has probably mentioned me."

"Err—"

"Or not." She laughed and then shot Jed a look. "I'm his fiancée."

"Oh, yeah. Right. Of course. I remember now."

"It's okay, Mo, there's no need to cover for him. I know what he's like." She smiled. "I'm looking forward to working with you."

"Right, yeah. Great."

She had a quick word with Jed, gave him a peck on the cheek, and then disappeared into the back.

"You could have warned me your fiancée was coming in, Jed," I said.

"Sorry. I meant to, but I forgot all about it."

"She seems nice."

"She's great, but then I'm a tiny bit biased."

"How often does she work here?"

"Only when I'm really stuck because she has her own business to run. I have to visit the bank later and I didn't think you'd appreciate being left here by yourself."

He'd got that right. The thought of being left alone in charge of the shop terrified me.

Liz and I hit it off from the get-go. She was smart, funny and a whiz with the coffee machine.

"Jed said you're an app developer."

"*Was*. I think my career in app development may have come to an end."

"How come?"

"It's my own fault. I'd been working on my own app during company time."

"That was a stupid thing to do."

Normally, if someone had said that, I would immediately have gone on the defensive, but I knew she was right.

"In my defence, I only ever did it while I was waiting to be allocated other work."

"Still no excuse."

"I've learned my lesson, trust me."

"I'm sure you'll be able to get another job. In the meantime, you'll have time to work on your own project."

"I wish."

"What's stopping you?"

I explained that the only backup had been purged from Headrow's cloud. "So, in a nutshell, I'm a complete screw up."

"It definitely sounds like it." She laughed. "Still, there's always your burgeoning career as a barista."

"You wouldn't say that if you'd seen me earlier this morning when Jed was trying to show me the ropes on Bertha."

"It's really not that difficult. Why don't you make the next few orders that come through the door?"

"Me? Are you crazy?"

"I'll help you. Trust me, there's nothing to it."

And somehow, with Liz's guidance, I managed to make my first few drinks without totally messing up. The only one I really struggled with was the flat white.

As we approached the lunchtime rush, Liz took over the coffee making while I focussed on taking orders and clearing the tables. By two o'clock, the worst of the rush was over.

"What time will Jed be back?" I said.

"I thought he'd have been here long before now." Liz's smile had faded for the first time since she arrived. "I hope that's not a bad sign."

"He seemed really stressed yesterday."

"Did he tell you why?"

"He mentioned something about the bank being on his back."

"He's wanted to own his own coffee shop for as long as I've known him. Opening this place was a dream come true. I just hope it doesn't turn into a nightmare."

"I thought the shop was doing well. There's always a steady stream of customers through the door."

"There is, but it's taken longer than Jed anticipated to get to this point. In the early months, he was barely able to service the loan, but he managed it, mainly by drawing the minimum salary for himself."

"But if he got through the worst of it, what's the problem now?"

"The banks have suddenly become much more cautious. In some cases, they're demanding immediate and full repayment of loans. If they do that, the business will be sunk."

"Is that likely to happen?"

"I pray it won't, but we'll know soon enough."

Jed didn't need to say a word; his broad smile said it all. Liz rushed straight over to him, and without either of them saying a word, they hugged. While they were preoccupied, I made my first unsupervised coffee, and it went without a hitch. Okay, so it was only a black Americano, but still.

"Did I just see you make a drink for that customer?" Jed said when he joined me behind the counter.

"Yeah. Liz has been coaching me."

"I have to be making tracks," Liz took off her apron and handed it to Jed. "I'll see you tonight."

During the remainder of my shift, Jed seemed to be walking on air.

"I assume Liz told you about my problems with the bank."

"Just that they'd been giving you a hard time."

"To be fair, a lot of it was my fault. My cashflow projections for the first few months were miles out. Things are much better now, but I have a lot of catching up to do."

"But they're not going to pull the rug from under you?"

"No. Not yet anyway. I've got a reprieve for twelve months."

"I'm really pleased for you, Jed. And for Liz."

"How did you two get along?"

"Great. She's really nice. You mentioned she had a business too."

"She's a freelance interior designer. In fact, she more or less designed the interior of this place."

"She did a good job."

"You can go now if you like, Mo."

It was five o'clock and we'd just closed for the day.

"Are you sure? I don't mind staying to help tidy up."

"It's alright. I'll finish off here."

"Okay, thanks." I took off my apron and started for the door, but then hesitated. "Hey, Jed, you know that Rob guy."

"What about him?"

"You said he was a regular. Does he come in most days?"

"Two or three times a week, usually." He grinned. "Fancy him, do you?"

"Yuk, no."

"Right. You're just interested in his coffee drinking habits, I suppose."

"Goodnight, Jed."

I didn't need to ask Beth how her business meeting with Leroy had gone because her face looked like thunder.

"Engagement party!" She blurted out as soon as I walked through the door.

"Sorry?"

"That's what his business strategy meeting was really about."

"He's asked you to get engaged?"

"What? No, of course he hasn't. We barely know one another. He's getting engaged to *Deborah*."

Beth somehow managed to make the woman's name sound like a profanity.

"I've been on my feet all day and they're killing me. Why don't we sit down, and you can tell me all about it?"

Chapter 7

The next morning, I got up earlier than usual because I was hoping that I might get out of the flat before Beth stirred. I didn't think I could stand part two of the Leroy-Deborah engagement saga.

But it wasn't to be.

"Do you know how much that lingerie cost me, Mo?"

"Yeah, you mentioned it a couple of times last night."

"Seventy-five quid. Seventy-five. And they won't take them back for a refund, you know."

"I would hope not."

"He even showed me a photo of her."

"Deborah? Is she pretty?"

"What does that matter? What do you think I should do?"

"About the lingerie? I don't think you should try to return it."

"I meant about the engagement party?"

"Did you say you'd help to organise it?"

"I think so, but it's all a bit of a blur."

"Then, that's what you'll have to do."

"But it's all so unfair. You have the right idea."

"I have?"

"Swearing off men. I'm going to do the same."

"Right. Anyway, I'd better get going because I promised Jed I'd be in early this morning."

That was a lie; I hadn't made any such promise, but the thought of listening to Beth drone on about Leroy's engagement party for another hour was too much to bear. Instead, I decided to walk to work for a change. The exercise would do me good.

Forty minutes later, I was beginning to regret that decision. Not only was I exhausted, but it had started to rain, and of course I didn't have an umbrella.

"Want to share mine?"

I turned around to find Platinum Rob holding a large umbrella.

"No, thanks."

"Would you really rather get drenched than walk under this umbrella with me?"

"It's almost stopped now."

"It's pouring down. Jed won't thank you for turning up to work looking like a drowned rat."

"Fine." I moved nearer to him.

"You're still getting wet. Come a little closer."

I took another half-step closer.

"That's better. Do you always walk to work?"

"No, I usually take the tube, but I thought the exercise might do me good for a change."

"That explains it."

"Explains what?"

"Why you were wheezing just now."

"I was *not* wheezing. I was just clearing my throat."

"Sorry." He grinned that ultra-annoying grin of his. "My mistake. I like to walk to work and back every day."

Of course he did. He probably visited the gym every lunchtime too. And most likely took part in iron-man competitions at the weekend. All of which went to confirm what I already knew: The guy was a poser. But I had to put all of that to one side because, like it or not, he might be my only hope of getting back into the app development business.

I had to play nice. Or at the very least, try to be civil. What harm could a little small talk do? But what was I supposed to talk about?

"Do you live far from here?"

Why had I asked him that? It made it sound like I wanted to know where he lived.

"Not far. It's about fifteen minutes door-to-door on foot. What about you?"

"What about me?"

"You said you normally take the tube. Where from?"

"Across the river."

"Right." Another one of his grins. "Any chance of being a little more specific, or do you still think I might be stalking you?"

"Deptford."

"I used to live just down the road from there, in Greenwich, before I moved into the city. I should have stayed there and then we'd be neighbours."

By now I'd had quite enough of the meaningless chit-chat.

"Why did you give my friend your business card the other night?"

"She and I got chatting while she was waiting for you to come out of the loo, and I told her that I thought I'd upset you earlier."

"When you blatantly pushed in front of me, you mean?"

"I only did that to try and get your attention."

"Jumping the queue? Funny way to do it."

"I'd tried everything else, but you'd ignored me until then. It did the trick because you noticed me."

"Oh yeah, I noticed you, alright. But not in a good way."

So much for being civil. What was wrong with me? It was like I was determined to alienate him.

"On reflection, that probably wasn't one of my finest moves," he conceded. "As I was saying, your friend, Bess—"

"It's Beth."

"Sorry. Beth happened to mention that she'd taken you to Jesters to try and cheer you up because you'd lost your job that day. I asked what you did, and she said it was something to do with apps. We're looking for app developers, so I told her to give you my card. That's it."

"Why had you been staring at me before that?"

"I thought you looked—err—interesting."

"*Interesting*? Not attractive or sexy? Just *interesting*. Like a book, maybe? Or a vase?"

"Sorry, that came out all wrong. I really liked your hair; it's my favourite colour."

"Before you say it, it's not blue; it's—"

"Turquoise, yeah, I know. Look, I'm really sorry we got off on the wrong foot. I can see now that my attempt to get your attention at the bar was misjudged. Can we start again?"

"I suppose so." I felt as though I had him on the ropes now, so it was time to tell him that I would like to apply for one of the app developer jobs.

Before I could, he said, "I really do admire the way you've turned a negative into a positive. Most people would sit at home and brood if they'd been sacked, but you went straight back out there, and found yourself another job."

"But this is only—"

"Not just that. You've actually embarked upon a whole

new career. Kudos to you, that's what I say."

By now we'd reached Bean Shack, and my plan had so far gone horribly wrong. I needed to let him know that the job at the coffee shop was only a temporary measure, and that I was still very much in the market for one of his jobs.

"Have a good day, Mo." He opened the door for me.

"Aren't you coming in?"

"Not this morning. I have an early meeting. I might try to pop by later. Bye."

"Wow." Jed grinned. "You're a quick operator."

"Sorry?"

"It was only yesterday that you were asking about Rob, and this morning, you're walking to work with him. Did you have breakfast at his place?"

"What? No, I did *not*. I just bumped into him a couple of streets away."

"I'll believe you, thousands wouldn't. I thought I'd let you loose on the coffee machine this morning after the rush hour."

"I'm not sure I'm ready yet."

"Liz reckons you are and that's good enough for me."

"Okay, but you'll need to keep a close watch on me."

"Don't worry, I won't let you poison the customers. Oh, and there's something else I need to talk to you about later."

"Should I be worried?"

"Course not."

The morning rush was busier than ever, which just went to prove that, despite the problems Jed had been having with the bank, he was definitely doing something right. I was already starting to recognise many of the regulars.

I'd just taken an order from a sweet old lady when I happened to see Carol's boyfriend, Miles, standing right outside the shop. I'd only been in his company on a couple of occasions, and only then very briefly. He and Carol had been an item since long before I met her through Beth. They'd moved in together about six months ago, and she couldn't have been happier at the time. His possessiveness was something of a standing joke between the rest of us, but if we were honest about it, we were probably all a little jealous that she had found someone who cared so much about her.

Miles was holding two drinks, which he must have bought from a different coffee shop, and appeared to be waiting for someone. Carol worked in publishing on the other side of the city, so unless she had a day off, it was unlikely to be her. He put one of the coffee cups on the ground while he checked his phone; whoever he was waiting for was clearly running late. But then his face lit up and he held out one of the cups to a young woman who most definitely *wasn't* Carol. From what I could remember, Miles worked in banking, so he was probably on his way into the office, and the woman was most likely one of his work colleagues.

Then they kissed. Passionately.

Oh no!

"Mo!" Jed said. "There are customers waiting."

"Sorry."

I'd been so distracted that I'd allowed a queue to build up. By the time I'd served them all, there was no sign of Miles or the woman.

"What happened back there?" Jed said once the shop was quiet.

"Sorry, I saw someone I knew."

"You can't drift off like that when we're busy."

"It won't happen again."

"I wanted to let you know that I've placed an ad for a full-time assistant."

"Oh?"

"If you want the job, it's yours, but I figured you weren't looking to make a career of this."

"Not really. Will I be out of a job when they start?"

"No. You've seen how busy we get. We need more than two pairs of hands. In fact, if things carry on as they have been, I may well set two people on."

"Fair enough. Thanks for offering me the opportunity, anyway."

I took an early lunchbreak ahead of our own lunchtime rush. Earlier, I'd spent over an hour on the coffee machine, and I was becoming more and more confident. Rather than stay in the shop to eat lunch, I took a walk to the gardens just around the corner. I really wished I hadn't seen Miles and the unknown woman, but I had, which meant I had to decide what to do about it. Twenty minutes later, I was no nearer to making a decision, so I gave Beth a call. She was much better at this type of stuff than I was.

"Mo, you're such a good friend."

"I am?"

"Only you would be considerate enough to check on how I was doing after yesterday's—" She hesitated, trying to find the right words. "Traumatic experience."

"No problem. I thought I should make sure you were okay."

"Just about. Leroy has spoken to me a couple of times, and I've kept it very business-like. I don't want him to know how I really feel."

"That sounds sensible."

"Do you want to meet for lunch?"

"I can't. My lunchbreak is over in five minutes."

"It's only just turned half eleven."

"I know. Listen, I wanted to ask your advice about something. I saw Miles this morning, standing outside our shop. I thought he might be waiting for Carol because he had a couple of drinks in his hand." I hesitated.

"And?"

"It's probably nothing."

"What happened, Mo?"

"The other drink was for a woman who definitely wasn't Carol."

"Probably a work colleague."

"That's what I thought. Until they kissed."

"What kind of kiss?"

"Not the good type."

"Have you told Carol?"

"No. I called you to ask what you reckon I should do."

"I thought you called to check how I was."

"That too, obviously. So, what do you think *we* should do?"

"*We*?"

"Carol was your friend first. I only know her because you introduced us."

"We shouldn't rush into anything."

"Agreed."

"Let's talk tonight."

"Good plan."

Platinum Rob had said he might pop in later in the day, but by the time my shift was due to end, there had been no sign of him. Maybe I should just tell Jed that I'd take his job on a permanent basis. I was enjoying it more than I'd expected, and although the money wasn't even close to what I'd been earning at Headrow, I was confident that I could make my finances work.

"Hey, Jed."

"Are you off?"

"Yeah, but I— "

"I've got three people coming for an interview after we close tonight."

"That was quick."

"I know, and two of them are experienced baristas."

"That's great."

"Sorry, I interrupted you. What were you about to say?"

"Nothing. Just that I'll see you tomorrow."

"You won't. It's your day off."

"Oh yeah, right. See you the day after."

***

Dinner was a microwave ready meal.

"Did you check the eat-by date on this?" Beth said.

"I always check."

"This chicken is chewy."

"It's always chewy."

"Why doesn't it ever come out looking like the photo on the box?"

"Just eat it, and then we need to decide what to do about Carol."

"He wants a band."

"Who does?"

"Leroy. He wants a live band at his engagement party, and he wants me to book them."

"Can't you tell him to take a running jump? None of this is in your job description, is it?"

"I've got a much better idea."

"Don't go and resign. Job-hunting is no fun. Take it from me."

"I've no intention of resigning. I was thinking I might just put my own spin on this engagement party of his."

"What kind of spin?"

"Well, for example, he didn't specify what type of band he wanted for the party."

"You've got that same look in your eyes that you had the day you tipped a pint of lager all over Rory."

"What was the name of that guy you dated with the scorpion tattoo on his neck?"

"Griff? I didn't *date* him, exactly."

"What was that band of his called?"

"You can't be thinking of booking *them* for an engagement party."

"Why not? They got everyone dancing that night at the Bear Pit."

"And spitting, fighting and throwing up."

"They sound like just the ticket."

Chapter 8

It was Monday morning.

I'd worked all day Saturday, and on Sunday, Beth and I had spent most of the day discussing Leroy and Deborah's engagement party. Or to be more accurate, Beth had talked, and I'd been forced to listen. Whoever said Hell hath no fury like a woman scorned must have had Beth in mind. Our only other topic of conversation had been Carol and Miles, and what to do about what I'd seen.

And that particular conversation looked set to continue.

"I really think you should tell her," Beth said.

"Me? Why me?"

"It's your day off today, isn't it? I can't do it because I'm working."

"You don't actually have to go and see her. You could just phone her."

"The management frown on staff making calls during work hours. And, anyway, you were the one who saw Miles with someone else. Carol might need you to describe the woman."

"I only caught a quick glimpse of her."

"Sorry, Mo, I have to shoot off because I have an early meeting with Leroy." She headed for the door. "Call me and let me know how you get on."

"I thought you couldn't take personal calls during—"

Too late; she'd already left.

The thought of having to admit to Platinum Rob that I was interested in his job, stuck in my craw. But then, it occurred to me that I could apply for the job without asking for his help, by contacting Q-Ventures myself. The website specified that applications should be made online, but I disregarded that, and called the main phone number.

"Q-Ventures, how may I direct your call today?"

"Hi, I'd like to speak to someone about the app developer jobs you're advertising."

"All job applications must be submitted via our website. I can give you the URL if you like?"

"That's okay. I was actually approached by someone from your company who gave me their business card and said I should call."

"I see. Who was that?"

"I don't actually know his full name."

"But didn't you say they'd given you their business card?"

"Yes, they did."

"His name should be printed on that."

"The thing is, I had a bit of an accident with the card."

"What kind of accident?"

"I inadvertently tore it into pieces and threw it away. Obviously, I didn't intend to do that."

"Right. I'm afraid that without a name, I can't really help you."

"I know his first name. It's Rob."

"We have several Roberts."

"Do any of them work in HR or recruitment?"

"Let me just check." The line went dead for a couple of minutes. "No, sorry, none of them work in either of those departments."

"Are you sure?"

"Positive."

"Maybe I could speak to each of the Roberts in turn until I find the right one?"

"I'm afraid that isn't going to be possible. Maybe you could try putting the pieces of card together again, to find out his last name."

"They got thrown away."

"In that case, I'm afraid you'll have to submit your application via the website."

"But I—"

"Sorry."

So much for that plan.

Beth had really dropped me in it this time. What exactly was I supposed to say to Carol? Yes, we were friends, but only because of Beth. I wasn't sure we'd ever had what you'd call a serious conversation. What would she think if I turned up at her office and announced that her boyfriend was cheating on her? Would she even believe me? If I'd had my wits about me when I saw him and the other woman, I could have taken a photo of them, but it all happened too quickly.

Eureka! That was it! If I was going to be the one to give Carol the bad news, I would need to gather evidence first, and that meant getting a photo of Miles with his new girlfriend. I figured if he had another liaison planned it would most likely be during his lunchbreak. It was a longshot, but I had nothing else planned for the day, and if I failed, I would tell Beth that she would have to deliver the bad news herself.

I got to his offices by 11.45 and took cover in the doorway of a vacant shop directly across the road, which had until recently been a sushi bar. I felt like some kind of private investigator.

"There you go, love." A random stranger threw a

couple of pound coins into the doorway. "Buy yourself a hot drink."

"Err, I'm not—"

He'd already walked away, leaving me to question if it was time for me to invest in some new clothes.

Over the next hour, there was a steady stream of people coming and going from the office block where Miles worked. The majority of them were under thirty, and almost all of them had their phone glued to their ear. I was beginning to regret having that second cup of tea because the nearest public toilet was at least a ten-minute walk away, and I daren't leave my post in case I missed him.

Ten minutes and two crossed legs later, he appeared. He too had his phone to his ear and he was laughing. Was he speaking to Carol? Or to the other woman? With the phone still stuck to his ear, he set off at a lick down the street.

I followed at a distance, but I couldn't help wondering if this was all a colossal waste of time. He could be going anywhere. What were the chances he'd be meeting that woman again? Pretty slim. Still, I'd come this far, so I might as well see it through.

He took a left, and then a right onto Mountjoy Road. Halfway down that road, on the righthand side, he stopped and entered a coffee shop called Key Coffee. Was he meeting his girlfriend there? I needed to get closer, but I would have to be careful that I wasn't spotted. Ninja-like, I made my way down the road, and peered through the shop window. The place was clearly not as popular as Bean Shack because Miles was already being served. Once he had his coffee, he turned and headed towards one of the window tables. That was my cue to hurry across the road. Unfortunately, there were no vacant shops over there, so I was forced to lean against a lamp post, pretending to study my phone whilst watching his every move.

"Mo?"

I almost jumped out of my skin. "Carol?"

"What are you doing in this part of town?"

"I—err—I've just been for a job interview."

"Really?" She looked me up and down. "I guess it's a different dress code in your type of work."

"Yeah. Dungarees are kind of de rigueur in the app development world."

"How did it go?"

"Hard to say, but I'm hopeful."

"I'm meeting Miles across the road in Key Coffee. Why don't you join us?"

"I—err—"

"Come on. Miles often asks about you."

"He does?"

"Yeah. He would have liked to be a coder but he's not very good at maths."

"Doesn't he work in a bank?"

"Not in a bank with money. He's just a banker."

That made no sense, but now wasn't the time to request an explanation.

"Come on, Mo. It'll be fun."

"Okay, sure."

"Look who I found across the road, Miles," Carol said.

"Oh hi, it's Flo, isn't it?"

"Mo," I corrected him.

"Of course, yeah, that's what I meant."

"What would you like to drink, Mo?" Carol took her purse out of her handbag.

"Just an Americano, please."

"Are you sure? They do a fantastic Pumpkin Spice Latte in here."

"Americano's fine."

"What kind of milk?"

"None, thanks. I take it black."

"Okay. Do you want another one, Miles?"

"No, thanks, babe. I'm fine."

"So, Mo?" he said.

"So?"

"Carol said something about you losing your job."

"Yeah."

"That sucks."

"It does, yeah."

I could tell he was dying to ask why I'd been fired, but before he could, Carol returned with the drinks. "Black Americano for you, Mo. I don't know how you can drink that stuff. I need lots of syrup and cream. What have you two been talking about?"

"I was just about to tell Miles that I've found myself a temporary job in a coffee shop on Queensway."

"Really?" Carol gushed. "That's brilliant, isn't it, Miles?"

"Great."

"It's called Bean Shack. Do you know it, Miles?"

"Err, no, I don't think so."

"Pity. The coffee there is much better than this. No offence."

"How do you like the job?" Carol asked.

"It wouldn't be my first choice of career, but it's okay.

To tell you the truth, apart from the early morning and lunchtime rushes, I get plenty of time to just stand around and watch the world go by. I love to people watch, don't you two?"

"I do," Carol said. "Sometimes, I like to make up stories in my head about the people I see."

"Yeah, me too. What about you, Miles?"

"Nah. Not really."

"You're missing out. Only yesterday, I saw this couple standing right outside the window of the shop. He was a good-looking guy, not unlike yourself. They seemed really happy to see one another. I couldn't help but wonder what their story was."

Carol was smiling, clearly enjoying the imagery. Miles, though, looked like he'd just sucked on a giant lemon.

"Do you think they were husband and wife?" Carol asked. "Or boyfriend and girlfriend?"

"It might just be my overactive imagination, but there seemed to be something illicit about their assignation."

"Wow! Do you think they were cheating on their partners?" Carol said.

Before I could respond, Miles stood up. "Sorry, I have to go."

"What?" Carol glanced at her phone. "It's only a quarter past."

"I know. They called an emergency meeting for twelve-thirty. I have to be there."

"Why didn't you text me?"

"Sorry, I should have." He gave her a quick peck on the lips. "I'll see you tonight."

"Bye, Miles," I shouted after him.

"I'm really sorry about that, Mo." Carol looked

mortified. "I've never known him to do that before. It must be a really important meeting."

"I guess so. How long have you and he been together now?"

"Coming up for four years. Between you and me, I'm expecting him to ask me to get engaged on my birthday."

"When is that? Sorry, I'm hopeless with dates."

"In three weeks."

"And will you say yes?"

"Of course. Why wouldn't I? You've seen what Miles is like."

"That's true. It's a big step, though."

"Not when you've lived together like we have. I know the girls like to make out that he's controlling, but it's only because he cares about me so much."

"Sure. What about him? Does he get to go out on his own?"

"Of course. He usually goes out a couple of nights a week with his friends."

"Guys?"

"Yeah, they play pool or snooker—I can never remember which. And they sometimes play poker, but only for pennies. I wouldn't want you to get the idea he's a big gambler."

"Of course not. I have a friend who's into poker. From what he's told me some of those games can go on late into the night."

"Tell me about it. Some days, Miles doesn't get back until the next morning. When that happens, I always have a nice cuppa waiting for him."

I really wanted to tell her what I'd seen, but she was so besotted with him that I was sure she wouldn't believe me. Somehow, I had to get proof.

Chapter 9

"What do you mean you didn't tell her?" Beth said after I'd updated her on the day's events. "Why not?"

"Because I didn't think she would believe me. She thinks the sun shines out of his backside. And the worst thing is that she's expecting Miles to ask her to get engaged on her birthday."

"Poor Carol. She's going to be devastated when she learns the truth."

"Better to find out now than after she's engaged."

"Which is why you should have told her what you saw."

"I keep telling you: she's your friend. You tell her."

"I wasn't the one who saw him with the other woman."

"I wish I hadn't. I've got enough on my plate without having to worry about Carol's love life. Can we change the subject, please?"

"Okay, but it isn't going to go away. Sooner or later, someone will have to tell her."

"Fine, but I don't want to spend all evening discussing it. Did you book Griff's band for Leroy's engagement party?"

"No, I've had a change of heart. I was probably overreacting a little."

"You think?"

"And, anyway, Leroy said he would give me an invitation when the time comes."

"To the engagement party? You're not seriously thinking of going, are you?"

"Why wouldn't I?"

"Maybe because the guy you were lusting after is the

one getting engaged? I didn't think you'd be so keen to meet the future Mrs Leroy."

"Don't be daft. He's just my boss. Anyway, I've seen him with his friends and some of them are well fit, so I might be in with a chance there."

"What happened to joining me in swearing off men?"

"I was just joking about that. The invitation includes a plus one, so I thought you could come with me."

"No chance."

"Come on. It promises to be a good bash."

"*Bash*? Who even says that?"

"There'll be lots of single guys there. You might pull."

"I don't want to pull. And I definitely don't want to pull someone who works in marketing."

"Thanks."

"I didn't mean—you know what I meant."

"Please, Mo. I really want to go, but I'm not turning up there by myself."

"Take Carol with you."

"After what's happening with Miles? I don't think so."

"Nicky, then."

"No chance. If she's there, no one will give me a second glance."

"I see. So what you're saying is that you won't have to worry about that if I'm by your side."

"That's not what I meant. You know what it's like when Nicky's around."

"What about Mand?"

"She seems to have disappeared off the face of the earth. It's ages since I heard from her. Have you spoken to her recently?"

"Now you mention it, I haven't heard from her either. It

must be at least two weeks."

"That's not like her. I hope she's not dead."

"Beth!"

"I'm only kidding, but it wouldn't look very good if she was lying dead somewhere and none of us had been in touch, would it?"

"I'm going to call her now." I grabbed my phone from the kitchen table and gave her a call.

"It's ringing out."

"Do you think we should go around—"

"Hello."

"Mand, it's Mo."

"Oh, hi, Mo."

Mand had always been the loudest of our little gang, even before she'd had a drink. Today, though, she sounded like a tiny mouse.

Beth gestured for me to put her on speaker.

"I'm here too, Mand."

"Hi, Beth. I'm sorry I haven't been in touch for a while."

"What's up with her?" Beth mouthed to me.

I shrugged. "Are you okay, Mand? You don't sound great."

"I'm okay. It's just—" For a moment, I thought the line had dropped, but then I heard the sound of sobbing.

"What is it, Mand? What's happened?"

"It's my mum." She snuffled. "She died."

"Oh no. I'm so sorry. When—err—what—?"

"A couple of weeks ago. Heart attack. I was around at hers in the morning, then in the afternoon, I got a call from her next-door neighbour. She found Mum in the garden; she'd been hanging out the washing."

"When is the funeral?"

"It was this morning. Sorry, I should have let you know. Mum always did like you, Mo."

"That's okay. You've had enough to deal with. Where are you now?"

"At Mum's. I'm going through her stuff."

"Are you up to that yet?"

"Not really, but I don't know what else to do with myself."

"Do you fancy going out and getting wasted this weekend?" Beth blurted out.

I shot her a look. "Mand doesn't want to—"

"Actually, that sounds like a brilliant idea, but I have to go now because my aunty is at the door."

"Okay. Take care, Mand. What were you thinking, Beth?"

"What?"

"Her mum has just died and you're banging on about getting wasted."

"I was just trying to cheer her up."

"I can't believe her mum has gone. She was one of the good ones."

"She really was."

A knock at the door interrupted our thoughts.

"Are you expecting anyone?" I asked.

"Why would I be expecting anyone? Go and see who it is."

"What did your last slave die of?"

The guy at the door was so tall, I had to strain my neck just to see his face.

"Hi, I'm Toby."

"We're not in the market for any."

"For any *what*?"

"Whatever it is you're selling."

"I'm not selling anything. I've just moved in across the way." He pointed to the door across the landing.

"I didn't realise Vic had left."

"I don't suppose you have a key, do you?"

"I've got a keyring full of them. Did you have a particular key in mind?"

"For my apartment."

"Aren't you the one who's supposed to have that?"

"Yeah." When he smiled, he reminded me of the cartoon bear on the front of the cereal box. "It's inside the flat."

"You locked yourself out?"

"Yeah. I just nipped out to get some milk."

"I don't see any milk."

"When I got to the shop, I realised I'd left my wallet in the flat too."

"You're not having a good day, are you?"

"Not really. I thought maybe the previous tenant—err—"

"Vic."

"Yeah. I thought maybe Vic might have given you a key for his place."

"No, we barely knew the guy. Why would he give us a key?"

"That's what I did when I was at uni. Me and the guy in the flat opposite exchanged spare keys in case this sort of thing happened. Good job too, as it turned out."

"I take it you've done this before?"

"A few times, yeah."

"You're out of luck this time."

"I guess so."

"Okay, well—"

"Who is it?" Beth appeared behind me.

"It's the new neighbour from across the corridor."

"Hi, I'm Toby."

"I'm Beth."

"I was just telling—err—"

"Mo."

"Right. I was just telling Mo that I've managed to lock myself out."

"Don't stand out there, then. Come in. Let him past, Mo."

That was Beth all over; she was too trusting by half. This guy could be anyone. Just because he resembled a cartoon bear didn't mean he wasn't a mad axe murderer.

"Would you like a drink, Toby?" Beth offered.

"Do you have hot chocolate?"

"I'm not sure. Do we, Mo?"

"No. Just tea or coffee."

"I used the last teabag this morning," Beth said.

"In that case, it's coffee or coffee."

"Could I have a glass of water? Coffee doesn't agree with me."

"Sure." Beth had clearly taken a shine to our new neighbour because she couldn't get to the kitchen quickly enough.

"I don't suppose I could borrow your phone, could I?" Toby said.

"What's wrong with yours? Hang on, let me guess, it's in your flat?"

"Yeah, I didn't think I'd need it just to nip to the shop."

I unlocked my phone and handed it to him. "Don't go calling Australia."

"Do you know any locksmiths?"

Fifteen minutes later, Toby had managed to contact a twenty-four-hour locksmith who'd promised to be there within the hour. My earlier suspicions that Beth had already got the hots for our new neighbour were confirmed when she practically shoulder-charged me aside, so that she could sit next to him on the sofa.

"What do you do, Toby?" Beth said.

"I've got a couple of jobs. I work at a nursery during the day."

"Really?" Beth simpered. "I'm really into plants and flowers."

"Actually, it's a children's nursery."

"Right. Kids are great, too." Beth could pivot quicker than anyone I knew.

"What's your other job?" I thought I should at least pretend that I cared.

"I work on the door at Zodiac."

"You're a bouncer?" I said.

"They're not called bouncers anymore. We're known as door supervisors now."

"That's priceless." I laughed. "Nursery nurse by day, bouncer by night."

"Take no notice of her, Toby."

"That's okay. I'm used to a bit of ribbing." He shrugged those huge shoulders of his. "What do you two do, if you don't mind me asking?"

"I work in marketing," Beth said.

"I'm a barista by day and a couch potato by night."

"Ignore her, Toby. Everyone else does."

It was then that Beth asked the question she'd been

dying to ask since Toby had walked through the door. "Is it just you living across the way?"

"Yeah, just me." He would probably have left it there had he not felt Beth's laser glare encouraging him to tell her more. "I was in a relationship until recently, so when we broke up, I volunteered to move out."

"Break-ups are never easy, are they?" Beth said. "I've recently come out of a relationship myself."

"I'm okay. Once I've found my feet, I'll probably advertise for a flatmate to share the costs. Is the coffee shop where you work around here, Mo?"

"No, it's on the Queensway."

"Suzie and I lived just around the corner from there."

"Suzie's your ex?"

"Yeah."

"Moving here is a bit of a come down for you, isn't it?" I said.

"Suzie works in the city. It was her salary that paid most of the rent."

"A kept man, eh?" I grinned.

"Don't be so insensitive, Mo," Beth said. "It's never easy when a relationship breaks down, is it, Toby?"

"I guess not."

"But then I suppose it depends on the reason for the breakup." Beth was about as subtle as a sledgehammer. It was blatantly obvious she was dying to find out what caused the breakup. She put her hand on Toby's arm. "If you ever need someone to talk to, I'm a good listener."

I could take no more and felt obliged to come to his rescue. "Leave the poor guy alone."

"I'm just saying." She glared at me. "I'm here if he needs to talk."

"Thanks." Toby shuffled uncomfortably on the seat. "I appreciate the offer, but it's all a bit raw at the moment."

Saved by the bell. Or to be precise, by the knock at the door. The locksmith was short, spotty and looked young enough to have bunked off school. Toby thanked us for the drink and left.

"You are fricking unbelievable," I said.

"What? I was only being friendly."

"I bet he thought he'd walked into the Spanish inquisition."

"Unlike you, Mo, I'm able to empathise with others."

"Don't give me that drivel. You fancy him."

"He's quite a hunk. Did you see his arms?"

"I wasn't paying attention."

"You have to admit he's an improvement on Vic."

"That wouldn't be difficult. Every time I bumped into that slimeball, he tried to borrow money off me."

"I wonder if Toby will be having a housewarming party."

Chapter 10

It was a relief to get out of the flat the next morning because all Beth could talk about was our new neighbour. Speaking of whom, he came out of his door at almost exactly the same time as I stepped out of mine.

"Good morning, Mo."

"Before you close that door, are you sure you have your key?"

"Yep." He held it aloft as proof. "And my phone. I won't do that again in a hurry. It cost eighty quid for a new lock."

"Just think how much it would have cost if they'd sent a grown-up to fix it."

"I really do appreciate you letting me stay at yours until he came."

"You have Beth to thank for that. I was all for leaving you standing out here."

"Right." He smiled, and was obviously unsure if I was being serious or not. (For the record, I wasn't.) "Beth seems—err—"

"Nosey is the word you're looking for."

"I was going to say nice."

"She *really* likes you."

"Oh?"

"Oh yeah. She's hoping for an invitation to the housewarming."

"I wasn't—err—do you think I should have one?"

"Nah. Not unless you enjoy cleaning up beer, crisps and vomit."

"Are you on your way to work, Mo?"

"Yep. Another day, another latte."

"I'm going to Queensway because I have to pick up some stuff from my old place. Do you want to get the tube together?"

"I usually run there."

"Really?"

"I'm joking. Sure, we can travel together as long as you promise not to bore me to death with the details of your breakup."

"I wasn't going—oh, you're kidding right? I can't always tell with you."

Toby turned out to be good company; he made the normally tedious journey much more bearable. As we exited the tube station and began to walk towards Queensway, though, I sensed a change in his demeanour.

"Are you okay?"

"Yeah, I'm just a bit nervous."

"Why? Are you worried about seeing your ex again?"

"No, it's not that. Suzie said she'd be out."

"What then?"

"I reckon she's already moved her new fella in. If he's there, I'm worried I might do something stupid."

"Like, break his bones?"

"I would never do anything like that, but I might give him a gentle slap."

"Not a good idea."

"I know."

"Do you have a key?"

"Yeah. I'm supposed to leave it there today after I've collected my stuff."

"Why don't you tell me the address, give me the key, and I'll go and check if the coast is clear."

"I can't ask you to do that."

"I've got half an hour to kill before my shift begins. Give me your phone number and I'll call to give you the all-clear."

"Thanks, Mo. I really do appreciate this."

He handed me the key, gave me the address and his phone number, and off I went. I was hoping that the flat would be empty, and when no one answered the doorbell, I figured I'd lucked out, and I let myself in.

I was just about to phone Toby and tell him the coast was clear when I heard a male voice behind me.

"Who the hell are you?" The man appeared to be naked except for the towel wrapped around his waist. Judging by his wet hair, he'd just stepped out of the shower.

"I could ask you the same question," I said.

"This is my flat."

"Is Suzie home?"

"No. Are you a friend of hers?"

"I've never met her. I'm a friend of her ex."

"Toby? Why has he sent you here?"

"To save you a visit to A&E."

"What are you talking about?"

"Toby is coming around here in a few minutes to pick up the last of his belongings."

"So?"

"It would be a really good idea if you weren't here when he arrives."

"Are you telling me to get out of my own flat?"

"Not telling you, as such. Think of it as friendly advice. Have you ever met Toby?"

"Actually, no."

"Do you know what he does for a living?"

"Suzie said he was a child minder or something."

"Nursery nurse, actually."

"So what?"

"That's his day job. By night, he's a door supervisor. That's a bouncer to you and me."

"Oh. She didn't mention that."

"The thing is, sorry, I don't know your name—"

"Rupert."

"The thing is, Rupert, Toby is still finding the breakup quite hard, and although he's generally quite a mild-mannered individual, he does have something of a temper. I'm worried that if he was to find you here he may do something that he, and most certainly you, would regret."

"Right. Understood. Do you think it would be a good idea if I made myself scarce for a few minutes?"

"An hour would be ideal."

"Okay. I'll go and get dressed."

"Excellent."

I waited until Rupert was out of the door, and then called Toby. "All clear."

A few minutes later, when he stepped into the flat, it was as though all the air had been knocked out of him.

"Are you alright, big guy?"

"Yeah, I will be. It only seems like yesterday that Suzie and I moved in here. We were so happy."

"There's no point in dwelling on any of that now. If you'll take my advice, you'll grab your stuff, leave the key, and start the next phase of your life."

"You're right, Mo. Thanks. Do you want to wait, and I'll walk you to Bean Shack?"

"Nah, I'd better get going."

"Okay. Did you see him?"

"Who?"

"Her new fella."

"No, the place was empty when I got here."

"Mo, this is Christine." Jed was standing next to a young woman who was only marginally taller than me. She had what could best be described as a serial killer's smile. "Christine is joining us today."

"Nice to meet you, Mo," said the serial killer.

"Likewise."

"Christine is an experienced barista," Jed said. "When I interviewed her last night, I offered her the job on the spot. Luckily, she was able to start straight away. "I need to go into the back to sort out some paperwork, so I'll leave you two to it."

I'm not usually one for small talk, but I thought I should show willing. "Where did you learn to be a barista, Christine?"

"Nowhere you would have heard of. It's a boutique coffee shop in Kensington."

"Right. This must be something of a step down for you."

"That was ages ago. I've worked in a few places since then, but I've been travelling around Europe for the last two years."

"Nice."

Our riveting conversation was cut short by the appearance of the morning's first customers. To give Christine her due, she certainly knew her way around a coffee machine. All of the orders that morning were delivered in super quick time.

After a while, Jed reappeared and sent Christine on her

break. She'd no sooner stepped outside, than who should walk through the door than Platinum Rob.

"If it isn't my favourite barista." He grinned.

"I'm not actually a barista. I just take the orders and clean up around here."

"Still, it's nice to see your smiling face."

"I wasn't—oh, right. You're being sarcastic. Funny."

"Your usual, Rob?" Jed called from behind me.

"Yes, please." He took out his platinum card.

I couldn't allow this opportunity to pass me by because I might not get another one.

"Can I talk to you about the app developer jobs at your place? I might be interested."

"What about your career as a barista?"

"This is only a stopgap."

"Okay. Why don't you ask Jed to let you go on your break and we can discuss it?"

"I can't at the minute because Christine is on hers."

"Who's Christine?"

"She started here today."

"Is she as feisty as you?"

"Look, I just want to know if there's any point in my submitting an application or not."

"Why wouldn't there be? You've done that sort of work before, haven't you?"

"Yeah, and I'm good at it, but—"

"Excuse me. Is there any chance of getting served today?" The woman standing behind Rob was tapping her watch.

"If I give you another of my business cards, do you promise not to rip this one up?"

"I promise."

"Okay." He took out a card and pen, and scribbled on the back. "That's my personal mobile number. Call me on that after seven tonight."

"Seven? I get off at five."

"I'm going to be tied up all day, and I won't be done until seven."

"Okay, I'll call you then."

He picked up his drink and made his exit.

"If you've done chatting to your boyfriend, I'll have a hazelnut latte, please."

I pasted on my best smile and served the impatient woman. "Anything with that?"

"No, just the drink. I can't imagine how long I'd have to wait for something to eat too."

As soon as Christine had returned, I took my break. I normally stayed in the shop, but I needed some fresh air. Once I was outside, I took a proper look at Rob's business card, which was unusual in that it didn't show his job title. Maybe he didn't want anyone to know he worked in HR. It was a bit like admitting you were a tax inspector.

"Are you okay, Mo?"

I looked up to find Toby standing there; he had a large black sports bag in each hand.

"Yeah, I'm fine. I'm on my break."

"I thought I'd grab a coffee before I head back."

"Is that everything?" I gestured to the two bags.

"Yeah. Not much to show for twenty-six years, is it?"

"Come inside and I'll get us both a drink."

"Only if you let me pay. I owe you for helping me out last night."

Jed took my order but refused to take any money. "Another of your boyfriends?"

"No. Toby is my new neighbour."

"Big guy. Looks like he can handle himself."

"He's a bouncer."

"Figures."

"That's when he's not being a nursery nurse."

"Huh?"

"I'll explain later."

"How much do I owe you?" Toby said.

"Nothing. Jed let me have them on the house. He thinks you're my fella."

"How come? Hasn't he seen your real boyfriend?"

"What makes you think I have one?"

He shrugged. "I just assumed."

"I'm single at the moment, and I've sworn off men for the foreseeable future."

"Me too. Women, I mean."

"Beth will be disappointed."

"I doubt that. Something tells me she won't have any trouble finding a new boyfriend."

"Whereas I might struggle? Is that what you're saying?"

"No, that's not—I didn't mean—"

"It's okay. I'm just messing with you. While you're here, you might as well spill the beans."

"About what?"

"What happened between you and Suzie? It's not that I'm interested, you understand, but Beth is relentless. She'll be on your case until she knows every last sordid detail. Much easier to tell me and I can fill her in."

"You more or less know already."

"Rupert?"

"How do you know his name?"

Whoops! Busted. "You know earlier when you asked if

I'd seen your ex's new fella, and I said I hadn't?"

"Yeah?"

"I kind of lied."

"I didn't see him when I got my stuff."

"That's because I suggested it might be beneficial to his health if he made himself scarce for an hour."

"I wouldn't have hit him."

"I didn't want to take that chance. Not for Rupert's sake, you understand. If you were behind bars, we might have ended up with another Vic across the landing."

"Rupert works at the same place as Suzie."

"What kind of place would employ someone like Rupert?"

"They work at the same advertising agency. She started staying late at work more and more often, so one day I decided I'd wait outside her offices. I saw the two of them come out together, and I followed them to a bar. It was crowded, so I was able to watch them without being seen. After a couple of drinks, they were all over one another."

"I'm surprised you didn't drop him, there and then."

"I thought about it, but I was scared of what I might do. I confronted Suzie when she got home, and she admitted they'd been seeing each other for a couple of months. That spelled the end for us."

"How come she wasn't the one to move out?"

"I didn't really have a choice. I couldn't afford that place by myself, so it made sense for me to be the one to leave."

"And now Rupert has moved in."

"Sounds like it."

"Mo!" Christine called from behind the counter. "Those tables need clearing."

Cheeky mare. Admittedly, I'd overrun my break by a few minutes, but since when did she get to dish out the orders?

"Sorry, Toby, I have to get back to work."

"I hope I haven't got you in trouble."

"Nah, it's okay."

"Thanks again for this morning and last night," he said.

"Don't let anyone hear you say that. You'll set tongues wagging."

Chapter 11

"I can't believe you went to his old flat, but you didn't ask him why he'd split from his ex," Beth said.

We'd just finished our cordon bleu meal of fish finger sandwiches, and Beth had been on my case all the way through it. I could simply have told her what Toby had said, but sometimes it was more fun just to wind her up.

"That's because I have no interest in Toby's love life."

"Yes, but I do, and before I invest time in him, I want to be sure his ex isn't still on the scene."

"You'd be wasting your time because he told me that he isn't interested in getting into another relationship for a long time."

"Everyone says that, but no one means it."

"I do."

"Yeah, but you're—" She left the sentence hanging.

"I'm what?"

"You know what I mean."

"Not really."

"You're not like the rest of us, are you? And I don't mean that in a nasty way."

"Oh well, that's okay, then."

"I just mean that you speak your mind."

"What's wrong with that?"

"Sometimes it's best to keep your thoughts to yourself. That's all."

"Duly noted, thanks."

"Do you think I should go over there and see if he's okay? It must have upset him, having to clear out his stuff like that."

"Would there be any point in my saying that's a terrible

idea?"

"I'll just go and check on him. I'm sure he'll appreciate the company."

I felt sorry for Toby, having to put up with an inquisition from Beth, but I was pleased she'd left me alone because I was about to call Platinum Rob, and I really didn't want her eavesdropping on that conversation.

He picked up on the first ring.

"Rob Waites."

"Waits for who?"

"Who is this?"

"Mo from the coffee shop."

"I might have known. It's been a while since anyone made fun of my name. The last time was when I was at school."

"Sorry. It's just that I have a thing about people with funny names."

"Now would be a good time to stop digging that hole."

"Right, so you said I should call about the app developer jobs."

"When we spoke earlier, you ended on a *but*."

"Did I?"

"Yeah, you said you were good at the job, *but*—"

"Right. The thing is, I left my last job under a bit of a cloud."

"Did you kill anyone?"

"No."

"Were you sleeping with the boss?"

"Yuk, no."

"What then?"

This was the moment of truth. If he blew me off, my

career as an app developer would be over, but I had no choice but to come clean.

"They finished me because I'd been working on my own app during business hours."

"At the expense of the work you were being paid to do?"

"No, I would never do that. I only ever worked on it when I was waiting to be allocated more work. It was either do that or sit around twiddling my thumbs."

"What is your app?"

"I called it Study-Ant. It matches up students who are studying the same subject."

"Why ant?"

"Why not?"

"Fair enough. If Q-Ventures were to offer you a job, would you undertake not to work on any of your own stuff during office hours?"

"Of course. I've learned my lesson."

"Okay, here's what I want you to do. My email is on the card I gave you at the coffee shop. I assume you still have it, or have you ripped that one up too?"

"I've still got it."

"Good. In that case, send your CV to me at that email address, and I'll pass it on to our HR people."

"I thought you were HR."

"Not exactly."

"Do you think they'll consider my application?"

"Providing you have the sort of experience you've described, then I'm sure you'll hear from them shortly."

"Okay, I'll send it as soon as we end this call."

"Oh, and there's just one condition."

"What's that?"

"You have dinner with me."

"What?"

"Dinner. You know, it's that meal between lunch and supper."

"Why do you want to have dinner with me?"

"I'm a masochist. What can I say?"

"I'll have dinner with you, but only if I get the job."

"Deal."

"I'll send you my CV now."

What was I supposed to make of that? Did he have any real influence or was he just blowing smoke up my backside?

"I think I'm in there." Beth came charging back into the flat, grinning from ear to ear.

"Toby, I assume?"

"He's such a sweetheart. He made me a cup of herbal tea."

"You hate *herbal* tea."

"Rubbish. I've never said that. He told me all about his ex and that Rupert guy. How could she cheat on Toby like that?"

"Hmm, that's rich coming from you. What about you and Alan?"

"That was totally different."

"How was it different? You were going out with Alan and then you started to see Ricky on the side."

"I thought you might at least have washed the dishes while I was out."

"Nice change of subject there. And, anyway, it's your turn to stack the dishwasher."

"We should go to Zodiac this weekend."

"Isn't that where Toby works?"

"Is it? I don't remember."

"Liar. I don't want another night out. I'm still dealing with the fallout from the last one."

"What do you mean?"

"Platinum Rob."

"The guy who tried to give you a job?"

"Yeah, I just spoke to him on the phone while you were fluttering your eyelashes at Toby. He told me to send him my CV."

"That's good, isn't it?"

"I'm not sure. I hope so. He asked me to go out for dinner with him too."

"I told you he was keen. When? Where?"

"I said I'd only have dinner with him if I got the job."

"And you accuse me of being a schemer. That sounds a lot like blackmail to me."

"Let's hope it works because I reckon my days at Bean Shack are numbered."

"I thought you liked it there."

"I did. I do, but Jed set on a new woman."

"What's up with her?"

"I don't know. She just rubs me up the wrong way."

"That's not a difficult thing to do."

"I know she's a trained barista, but the way she talks to me, it's like she thinks I'm her personal skivvy."

"I'm sure you'll put her right. So, what do you think?"

"About what?"

"Going to Zodiac this weekend?"

"I'd rather chew glass."

"If you're not bothered, I'll give Mand a call."

"Are you sure that's a good idea?"

"You heard what she said on the phone when I

suggested a night out. She sounded well up for it."

"Please yourself, but don't go getting your hopes up about Toby."

I loved Beth to bits, but sometimes I needed the Beth-free zone that was my bedroom. After telling her I had a migraine, I'd grabbed some biscuits and a glass of milk, and I was now sitting up in bed, reading App Developer News. And yes, I do realise how sad that makes me sound.

When my phone rang, my first thought was that it was probably Beth calling from the living room, desperate to continue her Tobyathon. Unfortunately, it was much worse than that.

"Hi, Mum."

"Yes, I did get back safely, but thanks for checking."

"Is that why you rang? Just to have a go at me?"

"No, I called to tell you that I bumped into Sheila McAndrew today in Tesco. You remember Mrs McAndrew."

"Not really."

"Yes, you do. She's Trevor's mum."

"Still not ringing any bells."

"Trevor McAndrew was in your class at primary school."

"That's a bazillion years ago. Hold on, I do remember a Trevor. Does he have sticky-out ears?"

"He had them pinned some years ago."

"I'm still not sure what this has to do with me."

"Sheila McAndrew works for the council. In the council tax office, I think."

"I bet she's popular."

"She asked how you were doing, and I told her you were between jobs."

"I'm not between jobs. I told you when you were down here that I was working in a coffee shop."

"Sheila said there's a job going in their office. She did tell me what it was, but I can't remember. Data something, I think. I know it involves computers."

"Why are you telling me this?"

"I thought you'd want to come back and grab it while it's still available. Jobs at the council are like gold dust."

"I don't want to work for the council, and I'm not coming back to Leicester."

"There are worse places to live."

"I didn't say there was anything wrong with Leicester, just that I don't want to live there."

"What about the job?"

"I don't want a data-entry job."

"But it's computers, isn't it?"

"It's not the sort of thing I do. And, anyway, I may have an interview for an app developer job soon."

"That's good, I suppose. Shall I tell Mrs McAndrew to hold the council job open, just in case?"

"No. Tell her she can let it go."

"Okay, but I hope you know what you're doing."

I'd just finished on the call when Beth came through the door. "Who were you talking to?"

"My mother."

"I thought you had a migraine?"

"It's gone now."

"I called Mand, and she is well up for going to Zodiac on Saturday. Are you sure you won't change your mind and join us?"

"I'm positive."

"Please yourself. By the way, Carol will be here in twenty minutes."

"Did you tell her about Miles?"

"No, she called me while you were lying down. Miles has gone away on a work thing, apparently."

"A likely story."

"She's on her way over. I suggested she pick up a bottle of wine on the way."

"Why would you ask her to come here?"

"It's the perfect opportunity for you to tell her what you know."

"I'm not telling her. I've got a migraine."

"You just this minute told me it had gone."

"I can feel it coming back on again."

"Come on, Mo. We have to do this. You know we do. If the boot were on the other foot, you'd want Carol to tell you, wouldn't you?"

"I suppose so, but I'm not doing it by myself. You have to back me up."

"Of course I will."

Twenty minutes later, Carol showed up with not one but two bottles of wine and a family-size pack of Doritos.

"Beth said you had a migraine, Mo."

"I'm okay now." Apart from the nauseous feeling in the pit of my stomach.

"I'll get the glasses." Beth disappeared into the kitchen.

Carol put the wine and Doritos onto the coffee table, threw her coat over the back of the armchair, and took a seat next to me on the sofa.

"How are you enjoying working at the coffee shop?"

"It's okay, but I'll be glad when I get back to programming. I might have an interview lined up next week."

"That's great."

"Don't break any of those." Beth placed three mismatched wine glasses on the coffee table. "They're the last three we have."

"Mo just told me she may have an interview next week."

"I'll drink to that." Beth poured herself and Carol a glass of wine, then held up her glass. "To Mo's new job."

"You're a bit previous. I'm not even sure I have an interview yet."

"Okay, here's hoping Mo gets an interview and the job."

"Cheers!"

An hour later, and I was beginning to think that Beth had forgotten that we were supposed to be telling Carol about Miles because she'd done nothing but talk about our new neighbour.

"Me and Mand are going to Zodiac on Saturday night. That's where Toby works. You should come with us, Carol."

"I don't think so. I don't think Miles would like me going out again so soon after our last night out."

"But didn't you say he has gone away for a few days?"

"Yes, but that's different. That's for work."

Beth and I exchanged a glance. It was now or never.

"Are you sure about that?" I said.

"Yeah. He's had it planned for a couple of weeks."

"No, I meant are you sure it's a work thing Miles has gone away on?"

"What do you mean?"

"I—err—look, this isn't easy for me to say, but—"

"I need the loo." Beth stood up and hurried out of the room.

"Go on, Mo." Carol's face was like thunder now. "You've clearly got something you want to say. Why don't you just spit it out."

"Okay. It could be nothing, but the other day when I was working at Bean Shack, I saw Miles standing just in front of the shop. He was holding two coffees, so I assumed he was waiting for you."

"And?"

"He wasn't. Waiting for you, I mean. It was another woman."

"Probably a work colleague."

"That's what I thought, but then they kissed. It was a serious kiss."

I was half-expecting her to break down in tears. After all, I'd just told her the guy, who she thought was about to ask her to get engaged, had been kissing another woman. But that was not the reaction I got.

"Unbelievable!" She screamed at me.

"It's true. I saw—"

"I mean *you're* unbelievable. Miles told me but I didn't want to believe him. You really are a special piece of work, aren't you?"

"What are you talking about? Miles told you what?"

"That you'd come onto him, and when he said he wasn't interested, you said you'd wreck our relationship."

I laughed. I hadn't intended to, but the idea that I could in anyway be interested in Miles was too preposterous for words. "He's a liar!"

"You're the liar. I wish Beth had never introduced me to

you." She stood up and headed for the door. "I don't ever want to see or hear from you again."

She'd no sooner left than Beth reappeared.

"That didn't sound like it went very well."

"Thanks for running out on me."

"I was bursting for a pee, honest."

"You're a coward, Beth. You should have stayed to back me up."

"You're right. I'm sorry. It's just that I hate confrontations. You know that."

"As it happens, I don't think it would have made any difference if you'd been here. Miles had already poisoned her mind against me."

"You tried. There's not much more you can do."

Chapter 12

The next morning, Beth was up at some insane hour because she had to travel to a conference in Birmingham. She must have still been feeling guilty for having left me to face Carol alone the previous night because, before she left for the railway station, she'd popped her head around my door to say she'd made breakfast for me.

After I'd dragged myself out of bed and into the kitchen, I discovered that Beth's idea of making breakfast consisted of pouring cornflakes into a bowl. Still, it was the thought that counted.

I was still raging about that lying scumbag Miles when I arrived at work. It was a later start and finish for me today, so Christine was already behind the counter when I got there.

"Morning, Christine."

"Hurry up and get changed. Jed had to go out for an hour, so it's just me and you."

Yes, I'm fine, thanks. No, of course I don't mind starting ten minutes before my shift is due to begin, but thanks for asking, anyway.

That's what I was thinking, but what I actually said was, "Sure, no problem."

I was such a wuss sometimes.

I'd just changed into my uniform, and I was about to go out front when my phone buzzed with a call. It wasn't a number I recognised, so I ignored it. It was probably some idiot trying to get me to swap mobile networks, or someone eager to assist with my non-existent personal injury claim.

"Where's Jed gone?" I asked.

"How should I know?" She shrugged. "I don't get paid enough to run this place by myself."

Although I doubted the two of us were ever going to be BFFs, we did make a good team: Me taking orders and cleaning the tables, and Christine making the drinks.

"Where's Jed got to?" she said, during a lull. "It's well past time for my break."

"You can take it now if you like. I'll be okay."

"By yourself?" She scoffed. "I don't think so."

I was just about to tell her not to be such a cow when Jed appeared.

"Sorry, ladies. That took much longer than I expected."

"I'm taking my break." Christine took off her apron and headed for the door.

"How are you getting on with her, Mo?"

"Okay, I guess."

"She's a whiz on the coffee machine, isn't she?"

"Yeah, she is."

"You two haven't had words, have you?"

"Course not."

"I thought there was an atmosphere when I walked in just now."

"No. Everything's cool."

While we were quiet, Jed took time out to show me how to make a couple more types of coffee.

"You're definitely getting the hang of this," he said.

"I've a long way to go to catch up with Christine."

"She's been doing it for a long time. Talk of the devil, here she is. You go and take your break now, Mo."

The first thing I did was to check my phone. I had three missed calls, all from the same number, plus one voicemail. Those cold callers were relentless. After deleting the notifications, I checked voicemail, fully intending to erase that message too.

"Hi. My name is Rosemary Chance. I'm calling from Q-Ventures with regard to the application you submitted for the position of app developer. If you could call me on this number, which is my direct line, I would be most grateful. I look forward to hearing from you soon."

Although Rob had said I ought to hear something soon, I hadn't expected them to respond so quickly.

I was so eager, I tapped in the wrong number the first time.

"No, this isn't Q whatever you said. This is Alderley Funeral Directors."

"Sorry, I must have misdialled."

I had more luck with my second attempt.

"Rosemary Chance speaking."

"Hi. This is Mo—err—Maureen Jackson. You left a message on my voicemail about my application for the app developer job."

"Thanks for getting back to me. Is next Monday too soon for you?"

"Next Monday's fine. What time?"

"Nine o'clock, but after that it will be more flexible."

"Sorry?"

"Everyone at Q-Ventures is on flexi-time, but HR will explain that to you during your induction."

"I think there's been a mistake. I was expecting to come for an interview."

"Oh? Hold on while I double-check." The line went dead for a couple of minutes. "Hello, Maureen. I've checked and I was right the first time. Your employment with Q-Ventures will commence on Monday unless that's a problem. If so, I can ask if—"

"No, no. Monday is absolutely fine. Nine o'clock, you said?"

"That's right. Come into reception and ask for Sarah Godwin."

"Okay, thanks."

What had just happened? I would have been over the moon just to get an interview, but to be given the job without even attending one was nothing short of sensational.

I was still in a state of shock when my phone rang again. For a horrible moment, I thought they were calling back to say it had all been a mistake, but I needn't have worried because it was Platinum Rob.

"So, about that dinner you promised to have with me."

"How did you do it, Rob?"

"Do what?"

"They just told me I had the job."

"I know that. That's why I'm calling."

"But I didn't even have an interview."

"You're not trying to back out of our dinner date, are you?"

"No, but let's get one thing straight. It's definitely *not* a date."

"What shall we call it, then?"

"How about we call it *not-a-date*?"

"Not very romantic, but I guess I'll have to settle for that. Do you have a favourite restaurant?"

"Not really. I rarely eat in restaurants."

"Do you mind if I choose, then?"

"Sure."

"Why don't we meet at eight o'clock tonight on the corner of Chapel Street and Queensway."

"*Tonight*?"

"Do you already have plans?"

"Err, no, not really."

"Good. I'll see you at eight, then."

I'd no sooner finished on the call than Jed came through into the back. "You've not forgotten the time have you, Mo?"

"No, sorry. Can I have a quick word?"

"Sure, what is it?"

"I've just been offered an app developer job."

"Good for you. I didn't even realise you'd had an interview."

"They want me to start next Monday."

"Oh, I see. Well, if that's what they want, that's what you'll have to do."

"You don't mind?"

"I'd have liked more notice, obviously, but I know this is what you have your heart set on. Luckily, a couple of the other people I interviewed when I set Christine on were strong candidates. There's a good chance I'll be able to get one of them onboard. It would be really helpful if you could work until Friday, though. We should be okay at the weekend because Liz will be able to come in then."

"Sure, no problem."

"I'm really pleased for you, Mo. Now, get back in there and do some work."

"Yes, sir."

***

I was walking on air for the rest of the afternoon. Not even Christine and her snide remarks could bother me. And the tube ride home, which was normally something of an ordeal, passed in the blink of an eye.

"What do you mean you've got the job?" Beth said. "I didn't even know you'd had an interview."

"I haven't."

"They offered you the job without one? Who does that?"

"I was surprised too. I knew there was a shortage of people in the industry, but I had no idea it was as bad as this."

"We should celebrate tonight. Where do you want to go?"

"I can't. I'm having dinner with Rob."

"The guy with the platinum credit card? How come this is the first I've heard about it?"

"Because we only arranged it this afternoon. If you remember, he made me promise that I'd have dinner with him if I got the job at Q-Ventures."

"He is hot. I don't blame you for wanting to go on a date with him."

"It's not a date. We've agreed to call it a *not-a-date.*"

"O—kay." She laughed. "Where's he taking you?"

"I've no idea. He didn't actually say. Just that I should meet him on the corner of Chapel Street and Queensway."

"Let's have a look what's near there." She took out her phone and brought up a street map. "Oh wow!"

"What?"

"He must be taking you to Xquisite."

"Never heard of it."

"You must have walked past it, though. It's only a

couple of hundred yards from Bean Shack." She brought up street view. "Look, that's it."

"Oh yeah, I recognise it. Have you eaten there?"

"Me? No, and from what I hear, you need to take out a mortgage just to afford the starters."

"He can't be taking me there."

"Why not? You said he had a platinum card, didn't you? I bet he's minted." She looked me up and down. "You'll have to buy something new."

"I'm not buying something just to have dinner with him. There isn't time and I'm stony broke."

"You can't rock up in one of your usual outfits."

"Why not? What's wrong with them?"

"There aren't enough hours in the day to have that particular conversation. You'll have to borrow something of mine."

"Like what?"

"Let's go and take a look."

One hour and several changes of clothes later, Beth pronounced me suitably attired for Xquisite.

"I'm really not sure about this." I was staring at my reflection in the full-length wardrobe mirror. The black dress was a little on the long side.

"You look quite sophisticated." She glanced at my hair. "Except for that."

"I'm not dying my hair."

"There isn't time, anyway. You'll just have to wear a hat."

"I'm definitely not wearing a hat. I feel awkward enough as it is."

"That dress is beautiful. Do you know how much it cost me?"

"If memory serves me correctly, Ricky bought it for you."

"Are you sure about the hat?"

"I'm positive. If they won't let me in because of the colour of my hair, it's tough luck."

***

I was standing on the corner of the street waiting for Rob to arrive. My teeth were chattering because, like an idiot, I'd allowed Beth to persuade me to abandon my trusty parka; she'd said it wouldn't go with the dress. I hated getting dressed up almost as much as I hated eating in restaurants. My idea of eating out was fast food or, if I really wanted to push the boat out, a trip to the local Spoons.

I was half-hoping that Rob would call and say he couldn't make it, but he appeared from around the corner. He was wearing jeans, a polo shirt and trainers. He looked good, but it wasn't how I'd have expected him to dress for somewhere like Xquisite. He was probably a regular there, so was able to take a few liberties with the dress code.

"I wasn't one hundred per cent sure you'd show up," he said.

"A promise is a promise."

"Shall we go?" He held out his hand, but I ignored it.

"Sure."

He led the way down the road in the direction of Xquisite. I was desperately hoping that it wasn't one of those places where the menu was in a foreign language. My linguistic skills were practically zero and I didn't want to make a complete fool of myself.

To my surprise, when we reached the door of Xquisite, Rob walked straight past.

"Where are we going?"

"Nearly there."

Four doors down from Xquisite, he stopped outside Red Hot Wings, and held open the door for me.

"We're eating here?"

"This is my favourite food, bar none." He grinned. "But I doubt they get many customers as well dressed as you in here. Is this place okay or were you expecting something grander?"

"No, this is fine. I love chicken."

"I hope you like it hot and spicy. Something tells me you do."

"Sure."

We'd no sooner taken a seat at one of the Formica-topped tables than a waitress, wearing a costume with a cartoon-chicken logo, appeared and handed us each a laminated menu.

"I'll take the max-spicy wings and fries," Rob said.

"I'll have the same."

"Are you sure?" He grinned. "It's not for the weak-hearted."

"Positive." I handed the menu back to the waitress.

"You look amazing," he said. "But you really needn't have gone to so much trouble. I feel bad now for not taking you somewhere more upmarket."

"What, this old thing? I wear it all the time."

"Are you looking forward to starting your new job on Monday?"

"Yeah, but how did you manage to wangle it? I didn't even have an interview."

"I know they're eager to fill those vacancies, so they must have liked what they saw on your CV and decided to give you a chance. All new starters are put on a three-month probation period, so it isn't a big risk. What about your job at Bean Shack, though?"

"I feel really bad about letting Jed down, but when I told him about the job offer, he was very understanding. In fact, he couldn't have been more supportive."

"He's a good guy."

"He is. I just hope he's able to keep the bank off his back."

"The bank?"

"Yeah. I probably shouldn't be telling you this, but they've been giving him a hard time over his loan repayments."

"He needs to get that sorted ASAP, or he'll be in all kinds of pain."

"I think he has. For the time-being, at least."

"Good. So, what did your friend—what's her name again?"

"Beth."

"What did Beth say when you told her you were going on a date with me tonight?"

"This *isn't* a date, remember? It's a *not-a-date*."

"And did you tell Beth that?"

"I did."

"And what did she say?"

"She thought it sounded like a perfectly sensible arrangement."

"She laughed at you, didn't she?"

"Where's our dinner? I'm starving."

When I took a bite of the chicken wing, I felt like my

head was about to explode.

"I did warn you." He grinned.

"It's fine." I quickly sank almost half a glass of water.

"Are you sure?"

"Absolutely."

"So, why don't you have a boyfriend?"

"Who says I don't?"

"Do you?"

"Not at the moment, and I'm not looking for one either. Beth is, though. You should have tried hitting on her that night at Jesters, not me."

"She seems nice enough, but I've met a thousand Beths. And, anyway, I didn't hit on you. Beth mentioned you were out of a job, and the type of work you did, so I gave her my card to pass onto you. That was it. I was just trying to be nice, but that backfired big time."

"I wasn't exactly in the best of moods that night on account of just being sacked, so I was probably more of a bitch than I normally am. What exactly is it you do at Q-Ventures?"

"Do you mind if we don't talk shop? I like to forget about work when I clock off."

"Sure."

"What's that accent of yours?" he said. "You weren't born here in The Smoke, were you?"

"I'm from Leicester."

"Really? I was born in Derby, just up the road from you."

"You don't sound like you're from Derbyshire."

"That's because my parents moved down here when I was three. My grandparents still live in the midlands, though."

"Do you go up there to see them?"

"At Christmas usually. What about you? Do you get home often?"

"Not really."

"Any brothers or sisters?"

"An older sister, Zoe. She still lives in Leicester; she's married with a little boy. Do you have siblings?"

"No. I'm an only child."

"Figures."

"What does that mean?"

"I can just tell. There's something about an only child. Beth's one too. I told you that you should have hooked up with her."

Somehow, I managed to get most of the chicken down, but only after asking the waitress to refill the water jug three times.

"Would you like to go on to somewhere else?" Rob said once we were outside.

"Like where?"

"My place?" He grinned. "Just kidding. Maybe a club?"

"Thanks, but I'm dead on my feet. I think I'll head home."

"I can walk with you."

"I'm not walking. I'll take the tube."

"I wouldn't hear of it. We'll share a cab."

My feet were aching from a combination of standing up all day at work, and the uncomfortable shoes that Beth had insisted I wear, so I accepted his offer.

"Shouldn't he have dropped you off first?" I said, as the taxi headed towards Deptford.

"But then I wouldn't know where you live."

"You do realise that makes you sound like a stalker again. And, anyway, I might have given the driver a false address."

"I wouldn't put it past you."

When we arrived outside my flat, I got out of the cab, and through the open window, thanked Rob for dinner.

"My pleasure. You'll probably be able to feel your lips again in a few days."

"I hope so."

"Good luck with the new job on Monday, Mo."

"Thanks."

I had a feeling I was going to need it.

Chapter 13

Beth hadn't got back from her Birmingham trip until long after I was tucked up in bed, so it was at breakfast the next day that she learned of my night out at Red Hot Wings.

"I can't believe you wore that dress to eat in a fast food joint." She was in hysterics.

"It's your fault. You were the one who convinced me to wear it."

"Only because you told me that he was taking you to Xquisite."

"If I remember rightly, you were the one who jumped to that particular conclusion. I felt like a right idiot when he showed up in jeans and a tee-shirt."

"I wish I could have been there to see it."

"I'm glad you're enjoying this."

"The date went okay, though, didn't it?"

"I keep telling you, it was a *not-a-date*."

"I refuse to call it that. How was it?"

"Okay, I suppose. But I'll probably not be able to eat any solids for a week. I reckon those chicken wings have given me second-degree burns to the inside of my mouth."

"Was Rob good company?"

"Better than I expected. I assumed he'd spend all evening droning on about himself, like most men do, but he actually seemed interested in me."

"That's only because he wants to get into your—"

"He's out of luck, then. I made it quite clear that I'm not interested in a relationship with him or anyone else for that matter."

"You must fancy him a bit."

"Even if I did, which I most definitely do *not*, I'm not about to start a relationship with anyone who works at Q-Ventures. That could only lead to trouble, and I can't afford to lose this job because I might never get another chance. I did find out one thing about him that surprised me."

"Is he really kinky?"

"I wouldn't know. I discovered that he's originally from my neck of the woods. Derby."

"Which means you already have something in common. It was clearly meant to be."

"Enough about Rob. How was your trip to Birmingham?"

"Very eventful." She grinned.

"Something tells me you're not talking about the conference."

"Nah, that was every bit as boring as I'd expected it to be. I had to keep taking a walk outside to stop myself from nodding off."

"What happened, then? Please tell me you didn't make a play for Leroy."

"Of course I didn't. What do you take me for? And besides, he never stopped talking about Deborah and the engagement party. I have no idea what I saw in that guy."

"If it wasn't Leroy, what happened to make you look like the cat who got the cream?"

"Russell happened."

"*Russell*? I don't think I've heard you mention him before."

"That's because he's based in our Sheffield office."

"I didn't realise you had a Sheffield office."

"We have offices in Manchester, Sheffield and Glasgow."

"Am I to take it you've taken a shine to Russ?"

"Don't call him that; he doesn't like it."

"I'm pretty sure he can't hear me. Unless—you didn't bring him home with you, did you?" I glanced at her bedroom door.

"Don't be stupid. Of course I didn't. He is coming down next week, though."

"He must be keen."

"Not just to see me. He has a meeting at our office."

"And that's what got you breaking out in hot sweats?"

"He's staying over, and he suggested that we have a night out while he's here."

"Is he married?"

"No, of course not."

"What's he like?"

"Dreamy."

"That doesn't tell me much. How old is he? Tall or short? Fat or—"

"Six one and ripped. He's a bit younger than me."

"How much younger?"

"He's twenty. Soon."

"A toy-boy, then?"

"He's very mature for his age."

"What about Toby? I thought you had the hots for him?"

"Toby's obviously still in mourning for his ex."

"You realise you can't bring Russ back here, don't you? That would be against our seven-day rule."

"That rule is stupid."

"We both signed up to it. If you remember, the whole

idea was to stop either of us doing something on the spur of the moment that we might later regret."

"I vote we change the rule."

"No way. And, anyway, it was your idea in the first place after what happened with Dazzer."

"I've told you never to mention his name to me again. Just thinking about that guy gives me the creeps."

"That's precisely my point. You brought him home the same night you met him, and it took two weeks to get rid of him."

"Fair enough. The company will probably book a hotel for Russell anyway. What do you have planned for today?"

"I'm working."

"At the coffee shop? Why bother now you've landed yourself a job with Rob?"

"I promised Jed I'd work until the end of the week."

"It's not like he can sack you if you don't show up."

"Jed's a good guy, and he's been really fair with me, so I'm not going to let him down."

***

"Didn't think we'd see you today," Christine said.

The shop was deserted, and she was alone behind the counter, but I could hear Jed whistling in the back.

"I told Jed I'd work until tomorrow."

"Now you're here, don't think you can slack off, just because you're leaving."

"What exactly did I do to upset you, Christine? Just curious."

"You haven't upset me. I'm just not very fond of people

who think they're better than everyone else."

"And that would be me, would it?"

"You make out like this job is beneath you. What with you being a computer geek, and all."

"I've never suggested anything of the kind."

"Everything alright out here?" Jed popped his head out of the back office.

Christine got in her response before I had a chance to. "Everything's fine. Mo was just telling me about her swanky new job."

"I'll get my uniform on." I made my way through to the back before I said something I might have regretted later.

"Are you sure everything's okay, Mo?" Jed had followed me into the back.

"Yeah. Everything's fine. Have you managed to contact any of the other people who applied for the job here?"

"A guy called Charlie will be starting on Monday. It's a pity you're leaving because you and he have a lot in common. He's a computer nerd too."

The atmosphere behind the counter was rather frosty, but at least Christine and I didn't actually come to blows. She took her break first, and when it was time for mine, the shop was almost deserted, so Jed went through to the back to catch up on some paperwork.

I was reading everything I could about Q-Ventures, to try and get a feel for the work I might be doing there. They had developed a number of apps that had been taken up by some major players in the financial services industry, and judging by the reviews, they had been well received.

The bell over the door chimed, and in walked three of

our regulars. The guys, all wearing high-vis jackets, were from the building site just around the corner. They came in around the same time every weekday, and always ordered the same thing: Two Americanos: one black, one with soya milk and a flat white. They took turns to pay and always ended up arguing whose turn it was to foot the bill.

"I paid yesterday."

"No, you didn't. I did."

"Are you sure?"

"Yeah, because I had a sausage balm cake. Remember?"

"Oh yeah. Okay."

Moments later, the three of them were on the way out of the door. It was only then that it struck me: All of the builders always paid by cash, so how come I hadn't heard the till ding? I glanced across at Christine who was staring out of the window. Had she pocketed the cash? Surely, she wouldn't risk her job for a few quid, would she?

After that, I watched every customer who came through the door, to see what she did with the cash, but they all paid by card. When my break was over, I went back behind the counter, leaving Christine to work on the coffee machine. While she was busy making drinks, I stole a glance at the book that we used to record all the orders. There was no record of the drinks that she'd served to the builders.

What should I do? I couldn't simply stand by and watch her steal from Jed, who was already in financial difficulties, but I couldn't report her until I was one-hundred percent certain of what I'd seen. I elected to do nothing unless I saw her do the same thing again.

My shift over, I was headed for the tube station when I heard a familiar voice from behind me.

"Mo, can I have a word?"

Carol was the last person I'd expected to see, and I really wasn't in the mood for another confrontation.

"I don't want to argue with you, Carol. I'm sorry if I—"

"You were right." She began to cry. "About everything."

"Why don't we sit down, and we can talk?" I guided her to a seat at a table outside a cute little tearoom called The Polka Dot Teapot. I hadn't intended to get anything to eat or drink, but the waitress was already hovering.

"What can I get for you ladies?"

"Err, Carol?"

"A tea, please."

"Same for me."

"A pot of tea for two?"

"Yes, please."

Carol wiped her eyes and blew her nose. "I'm really sorry for the things I said to you the other day, Mo."

"Forget it."

"I was horrible to you."

"That's not important now. Do you want to tell me what happened?"

"I was supposed to go to our Exeter office today and travel back in the morning, but the meeting was cancelled. I thought it would be nice to surprise Miles by turning up at his office, so we could have lunch together. But when I got there, he was walking down the road with *her*. They were arm in arm."

"Do you know who she is?"

"She's his ex. They split up a few months before he and

I got together."

"What did he say when you confronted him?"

"I couldn't. I was too upset."

"So, he doesn't know you saw them together."

"I don't think so, no. I couldn't bear to go back to the office, so I called in to say I'd taken ill. I've been walking around and around ever since. Then I remembered the things I'd said to you, so I wanted to come and apologise. I really am sorry."

"So am I. For you, I mean. You didn't deserve this. What are you going to do?"

"I don't know. I can't think straight, but I know I can't go back there."

"To your flat?"

"Yeah. I simply can't."

"You can stay at ours tonight if you like."

"But you don't have room."

"We'll find room."

"One pot of tea for two." The waitress put the tray on the table.

While we drank, Carol did most of the talking, and I listened. For the most part, she was just rambling, but it seemed to help, so I didn't interrupt her.

"What about Miles?" she said.

"What about him?"

"What do I say to him?"

"Tell him to pack his bags and get out."

"But the flat is in his name."

"Not joint names?"

"No. He'd already bought it when we met."

"Did you contribute to the mortgage payments?"

"No. The arrangement was that I paid the utility bills

and he looked after the mortgage. I thought it was a sweet deal at the time because the mortgage payments were much higher than the other bills."

"Oh dear. That could make life complicated."

***

"Carol?" Beth looked horrified and for a moment, I thought she was going to bolt for the bathroom again.

Carol had once again dissolved into tears, so I brought Beth up to speed.

"She's seen Miles with that other woman."

"Oh, you poor love." Beth threw her arms around her, leaving Carol to sob on her shoulder.

"Is it okay if I go and lie down?" Carol managed eventually.

"Sure." Beth took her hand and led the way into the bedroom. *My* bedroom. When Beth reappeared, she said, "What happened?"

I brought her up to speed on Carol's aborted trip to Exeter, how she'd intended to surprise Miles, and how that had backfired.

"Poor girl. That guy wants stringing up by his—"

"I agree, but that'll have to wait. We need to decide what we're going to do tonight first."

"How do you mean?"

"She doesn't want to go back to her flat, so I said she could stay here."

"What about our seven-day rule?"

"*Seriously*?" I gave her a look.

"I guess that doesn't apply in this situation."

"And you'd be correct. Carol can have my bed. You and

I will have to share."

"Again? Couldn't you sleep on the sofa?"

"Couldn't you?"

"Okay, but what about Miles? What will he do when she doesn't go home?"

"He's not expecting her tonight because he thinks she's staying in Exeter. Carol will have to decide what she wants to do about him in the morning."

Chapter 14

When I woke up the next morning, Beth wasn't in the bed with me. I found her seated at the kitchen table looking half asleep.

"I could kill a cup of coffee." She yawned.

"And I suppose you've been sitting there, waiting for me to get up, so that I could make it for you?"

"It's the least you can do after the night I've just had."

"What do you mean?"

"Your snoring is ridiculous."

"You should have nudged me."

"I did. At least a dozen times, but each time you just stopped for a few minutes and then started again."

"Have you heard anything from sleeping beauty yet?"

"Not a sound. You don't suppose she crept out during the night, do you?"

"I doubt it. Take a peek while I get the coffee."

Beth tiptoed over to the bedroom door, cracked it open, and peeped inside. After closing it again, she shook her head. "Fast asleep. Do you think we should wake her?"

"No, let her sleep."

"But what about work?"

"I very much doubt she'll be going in today."

The knock on the door made us both jump.

"Do you think that's Miles?" Beth whispered.

"I doubt it. He thinks Carol is in Exeter."

"What if he's realised that she didn't go, and he's come looking for her?"

"There's only one way to find out." I gestured to the door.

"You get it," Beth said.

"Why me?"
"Because you're the nearest."
"Fine." I opened it a couple of inches, unsure what I would do if Miles was standing there. "Toby?"
"Morning."
"Shush!"
"Sorry. What's up?"
"Come in." I put a finger to my lips. "But be quiet." He followed me inside. "Do you want a coffee?"
"No, thanks."
I passed Beth her drink, grabbed mine, and then I joined them at the table.
"Is everything okay?" Toby whispered.
"A friend of ours is asleep in my room. We don't want to wake her."
"Okay. I came over to tell you that I've been thinking about Beth's suggestion that I have a housewarming party, and I've decided it's a good idea."
"Are you crazy?" I said.
"Ignore her, Toby. She's just a misery guts. When is it?"
"It'll need to be one of my nights off from Zodiac. I was thinking next Wednesday. Obviously, you two are invited."
"I'll be there with bells on," Beth said.
"You'll come too, won't you, Mo?" Toby said.
"I'll see."
"She'll be there if I have to drag her." Beth stifled a yawn.
The bedroom door opened, and Carol appeared; she was still wearing the clothes she'd arrived in the previous day. With her blotchy eyes, and streaks of makeup on her face, she was doing a good impression of the wicked

witch of the west.

"Why didn't you wake me up?"

"We thought the rest would do you good," I said.

"Has Miles been in touch?"

"No, but he'll think you're still in Exeter, won't he?"

"Oh yeah, I guess so."

"I probably should be leaving." Toby made to stand up.

"Don't go on my account," Carol said.

"Aren't you going to introduce yourself?" Beth gave Toby a pointed look.

"Sorry, yeah. I'm Toby. I've just moved in across the way."

"Nice to meet you. I'm Carol. Please excuse the way I look. I discovered my pig of a boyfriend is cheating on me yesterday, and these two were kind enough to offer me a bed for the night. Is there any coffee in the pot?"

"Yeah, it should still be hot."

She poured herself a cup and then joined us at the table.

"Toby was just saying that he's going to have a housewarming party next Wednesday night," Beth said. "You should come. That's okay, isn't it, Toby?"

"Sure, the more the merrier."

"I doubt Carol is in the mood for parties," I said.

"On the contrary." Carol brightened a little. "A party is just what I need. Wednesday, you said?"

"That's right." Toby nodded.

"Great, I'll be there."

"What are you going to do about Miles?" Beth asked.

"Cut his nuts off if I get the chance."

"But what about the flat? Can you get him out?"

"I doubt it. It's in his sole name."

"How come?"

"He said it would be too complicated to change it. And yes, I know. I'm an idiot."

"Where will you go?" Beth said.

I jumped in before Carol could reply. "She can stay here."

"I can't ask you two to do that. I'll find somewhere. Hopefully."

"You could crash at mine if you like," Toby said. "Just until you find somewhere permanent, I mean."

"Thanks. That's a very kind offer, but—"

"It's really not a problem. I have a spare room that's doing nothing. If you find somewhere else, then no worries, but if not, the offer stands."

"Thanks."

Carol showered, borrowed a change of clothes from Beth, and then went on her way. After Miles had left for work, she planned to get as much of her stuff out of the flat as she could carry. She also hinted that she might take the scissors to his designer suits.

"That Toby is a sly one." Beth grinned.

"What do you mean?"

"Asking Carol to shack up with him like that."

"That's not what he did."

"Sounded like it to me."

"That's because your mind is a cesspit. It was a genuine offer from a place of kindness."

"Sometimes your naivety astounds me, Mo. Who are you going to bring to the housewarming party?"

"He didn't say we could bring anyone else."

"He didn't need to. It's obvious. I might see if I can persuade Russell to stay on down here for a few days."

"Won't his mum be worried about him?"

"You're hilarious. Last day for you at Bean Shack, then?"

"Yeah, and I'm really not looking forward to it."

"I thought you liked working there."

"I do, but—"

"But what?"

"I didn't tell you last night because we got side-tracked by Carol, but I reckon Christine is stealing cash."

"The new woman?"

"Yeah."

"Did you see her do it?"

"Not exactly, but I know she didn't put the money in the till, and she didn't enter the order in the book. I can't think of any other explanation."

"Are you going to tell your boss?"

"I'm going to watch her today. If I see her do it again, then I'll have a word with Jed."

"Are you sure you want to get involved? These things have a habit of turning nasty."

"I have to. Jed's a nice guy and he's been good to me. And besides, the business is already struggling."

"Okay, but just make sure you're one-hundred percent certain before you go accusing her."

***

Christine made it really easy for me to dislike her; she'd started to snipe at me as soon as I walked through the door.

"You're late."

"I'm five minutes early."

"You should be on the floor by nine. By the time you've got your uniform on, it'll be at least five past."

"You won't have to worry about my timekeeping after today."

"Good. It'll be nice to work with someone who knows what they're doing."

"Good morning, Mo." Jed appeared from the back room. "You okay?"

"Yes, thanks. I'd better get changed. I wouldn't want to be late *on the floor*."

Jed was clearly confused by my comment, but he stepped aside to let me get past.

It was a shame that Christine had managed to take the shine off my last few days at Bean Shack. Until her arrival, I'd found the experience much more enjoyable than I'd expected. Being a barista definitely wasn't my calling in life, but I wouldn't hesitate to work in a coffee shop again if I ever found myself between jobs.

The time that I'd been dreading had arrived. I was on my break, and Jed had left Christine by herself behind the counter because the shop was really quiet. A part of me hoped that we wouldn't get any cash customers through the doors, but five minutes into my break, the same three builders appeared. They had their customary debate about whose turn it was to pay, before one of them handed a ten-pound note to Christine.

"Keep the change, love," he said, and the three of them left.

I pretended to study my phone, but in my peripheral vision, I was watching what she did. I was desperately hoping that the till would ding, to register the sale, but there was no such sound. And then I saw her stuff the bank note into her pocket. I considered going straight to Jed, but it was Christine's early finish, so I decided it would be better to wait until after she'd left.

Jed locked the door and turned over the 'closed' sign.

"I'm really sorry to lose you, Mo. You're sure you wouldn't consider a change of career?" He grinned.

"Thanks, but I'll have to pass."

"If you ever need to earn a few extra quid, just let me know. I'm sure I'll be able to find you a few hours' work."

"Thanks, Jed. For everything." I hesitated, dreading what I was about to do. "There's something I have to tell you before I leave."

"Okay?"

I told him what I'd witnessed yesterday and again today.

"Are you absolutely sure?"

"I really wish I wasn't, but yes, I'm positive."

He slumped onto one of the seats. "This is the last thing I need."

"I'm sorry."

"Don't be silly. I'm glad you told me, but these things are never easy to deal with."

"What will you do?"

"I don't know. It's not that I don't believe you, but I think I need to get Liz in over the weekend if I can. She's eagle-eyed. If she sees the same thing happen, it will put me in a much stronger position to act."

"Okay. I'll get going, then."

"Thanks again, Mo."

***

I'd no sooner arrived back at the flat than I got a phone call from Beth.

"It's me."

"I know it's you. It says so right here on my phone."

"Yeah, anyway, I'm just calling to tell you that I won't be home tonight. I didn't want you to worry and send out the search party."

"Let me guess. You're staying with Russell."

"He's taking me out on the town first, and then I'm going to stay in his hotel suite; he said that he'll take the couch."

"Sure."

"He did, honestly. He's a real gentleman. I think you'll like him when you meet him at the housewarming."

"You haven't forgotten that you've arranged to go to Zodiac with Mand tomorrow night, have you?"

"I had, yeah."

"You can't let her down. Not after the awful time she's had recently."

"I know and I won't. I'll sort something out. Anyway, I've got to run because Russell has booked a table for us."

"Okay. Enjoy your meal, and I hope you manage to get some sleep."

When I'd ended the call, I heard voices coming from out in the corridor. Moments later, there was a knock on the door. Just as on the previous day, my first thought was that it could be Miles.

In fact, it was Toby again. Standing next to him was Carol with a suitcase in her hand.

"Sorry to disturb you," Carol said. "I just thought I

should let you know that I've decided to take Toby up on his kind offer of somewhere to crash for a few days."

"Oh? Right. What about Miles? Does he know yet?"

"He will do as soon as he gets home from work. I've left him a little note on top of his pile of suits."

"You didn't—?"

"I did and I haven't had so much fun for years."

"Does he know where you are?"

"Not unless he's psychic."

"Right, okay, well good luck and I'll see you both at the housewarming on Wednesday."

Chapter 15

It felt strange to have the flat to myself on a Saturday morning. I hadn't heard any more from Beth since her call to say she wouldn't be home last night, so I assumed she must still be holed up with her toy boy in his hotel room. I'd had a much better night's sleep back in my own bed, even though I'd had a strange dream about being locked inside a giant till by Christine.

I was still deciding what to have for breakfast when there was a knock on the door. Had Beth lost her keys? It wouldn't be the first time. What if it was Miles? He would know by now that Carol had walked out on him. Annoyingly, we didn't have one of those peephole thingies.

"Who is it?"

"It's me. Carol."

I opened the door. "I thought it might be Miles."

"That's what I wanted to talk to you about. He's called me a thousand times and sent me a million messages, asking where I am, but I've refused to tell him. This will be one of the first places he checks, so I wanted to give you a heads up."

"How did he sound?"

"I only spoke to him the once; after that, I declined his calls. He was angry. Really angry."

"He's got a nerve. He was the one who cheated on you."

"That's what I told him, but he insisted it was all a big misunderstanding and that I'd got it all wrong."

"What did you say?"

"That he was a pathological liar and that I never wanted to see him again. He asked if we could meet up to talk things through. I told him to shove it."

"Good for you. I was just about to make breakfast. Why don't you stay and have some with me?"

"I'd like that. I haven't seen Toby yet this morning, so I assume he's having a lie-in."

"What would you like? I have cornflakes, toast or—actually, that's it: cornflakes or toast."

"I'll have toast, please."

"Tea or coffee?"

"Tea, please."

"What do you make of Toby?" I said.

"He seems really nice. A bit shy, though. Sort of like a gentle giant."

"Yeah, he's only been here a few days, but it feels like much longer. Any ideas where you're going to go?"

"Not really. I can't afford anywhere like Miles' place. I thought I might take a look online and see if I can find any suitable house shares. I've got used to living near the city centre, and I'd rather not have to move to the back of beyond."

"Like this place, you mean?"

"Yeah, no. I mean, I like this flat, but your commute must be awful."

"You get used to it. Actually, no you don't, but you do learn to live with it."

We'd finished our toast and were taking our time with the tea when there was another knock on the door.

"Miles." Carol's face dropped. "You can't let him know I'm here."

"Go in Beth's room. Quick."

I was just about to answer the door when I realised there were two plates and cups on the table. I grabbed them, shoved them in the dishwasher, and then cracked the door open.

For the second time that morning, it wasn't Miles.

"Toby?" I laughed. "What are you wearing?"

"I've just been for a run."

"In your underwear?"

"These are my running vest and shorts."

"You're all sweaty."

"So would you be if you'd just run five miles."

"*Five* miles? Are you insane?"

"I do it most mornings. I just wanted to check if you'd seen Carol. She isn't at my place."

"You'd better come in, and try not to sweat all over the floor." I walked over to Beth's bedroom and knocked on the door. "The coast is clear. It's Toby."

Carol stepped out, stopped dead in her tracks, and laughed. "Why are you walking around in your underwear?"

***

After Carol and Toby had gone back to his flat, I took a leisurely shower, and then got dressed. It was only when I picked out something from my wardrobe that it occurred to me that I hadn't considered what I would wear to my new job on Monday.

Headrow Tech had been very laid-back as far as any kind of dress code was concerned. Just about everyone had turned up in casual wear, and by that I don't mean business casual. I mean *casual* casual—as in, anything goes. I expected Q-Ventures to have a stricter dress code because they worked in the FinTech sector. If I'd been through the normal interview process, I'd have had a better idea of what was expected, but as that didn't happen, I would just have to use my own judgement—never a good thing.

I really couldn't be bothered to travel into the city. Doing that every day for work was bad enough. Instead, I took a walk down the local high street, to see what the shops there had to offer.

"Mo!"

Nicky was waving to me from the other side of the road. She was a sweet person, but I found it infuriating that she could throw on any old thing and look like a million dollars. If I were to wear exactly the same outfit, I would look like a bag of rags.

At the first gap in the traffic, she hurried across the road to join me.

"Where's Beth?"

"Holed up in a hotel somewhere with her toy boy."

"I didn't know she had one."

"His name is Russell, and he works in their Sheffield office."

"How old is he?"

"Nineteen."

"Good for her. Do you fancy getting a coffee?"

"Maybe later. I need to buy something to wear for my new job."

"I heard you'd landed one. Congrats. What sort of thing are you looking for?"

"That's just it. I don't have a clue. Will you help me choose something?"

"Me?"

"Yeah. You always seem to know what to wear for any

occasion, but I'm clueless."

"I can try, but you're going to have to give me at least some hint as to what you're looking for."

"I'm going to be working as an app developer."

"I thought computer nerds all dressed down?"

Ignoring yet another nerd reference, I said, "Normally, I'd agree, but this company works in the FinTech sector."

"The what?"

"Financial technology. That's banks and financial services, so its customers are big businesses. I feel like casual isn't going to cut it there."

"Something more formal, then?"

"Yeah."

"Okay, let's see what we can come up with."

An hour later, and Nicky had performed her magic. She'd picked out a black trouser suit and a white blouse that I wouldn't normally have given a second glance. They were formal without being too over the top.

"Thanks, Nicky. I would have taken all day and probably still come away emptyhanded."

"No problem. I quite enjoy shopping for other people. Do you fancy that coffee now?"

"Sure, and it's on me. I owe you for this morning."

The choice of coffee establishments on the high street was quite limited, but we settled on one that had only opened a couple of weeks earlier, called Java Flow.

"I hear that you're something of a barista now." Nicky grinned.

"Hardly. Though my stint at Bean Shack has given me a new-found respect for the people who do that for a living."

Once we had our drinks, we found a table outside on the pavement.

"What's going on with your love life, Mo?"

"In a word: nothing. And that's just how I like it."

"Aren't you missing Adam?"

"Who?" I forced a half-hearted laugh.

"What about that guy at Jesters? The one who gave you his business card. Did nothing come of that?"

"His name is Rob, and he was the one who got me the new job."

"Did he?" She smiled. "And?"

"And nothing. What about you? Who are you seeing at the moment?"

"No one."

"I find that hard to believe."

"I know you guys think I have it easy, but it's not true."

"Come on, Nicky."

"I'm serious. I know I get a ton of guys hitting on me, but the majority are only interested in one thing. I want a relationship that's built on something more than just sex. I want what Jen has."

It was strange to hear Nicky talking like this. I'd always assumed she was happy with her lot, but clearly, she had her problems just like the rest of us.

***

By the time I arrived back at the flat, I was already having doubts about the outfit that the two of us had picked out. What if it was too formal? Or not formal enough? Either way, it would have to do now because I couldn't bear the thought of another trip to the shops, and besides, I'd spent up.

"Where is she?" Miles demanded. He was seated on the landing with his back resting against my door, but he leapt to his feet as soon as he saw me.

"Have you lost someone?"

"Don't get smart with me, Mo. You were the one who told her, weren't you?"

"Actually, no, I didn't."

"Don't lie. What about all those not-so-subtle hints you kept dropping when the three of us had coffee?"

"It doesn't matter how she found out. What matters is that you were cheating on her, and my guess is you still are."

"It's none of your business. Just open this door so I can talk to Carol."

"She isn't in there."

"Liar! Where else would she go?"

"She could be anywhere. Maybe she's already found herself another fella."

"Are you going to open this door, or do I have to break it down?"

"Move out of my way, Miles."

"No."

"If you don't, how am I supposed to unlock the door, genius?"

"Oh, okay." He stepped aside.

"After you." I moved to one side to let him go first.

"Carol! I know you're in here," he shouted.

After a quick check of the kitchen, living room and bathroom, he looked inside each of the bedrooms.

"Where is she?" He was so red in the face that I thought his head might explode.

"I've already told you that I have no idea."

"I've had enough of your lies." He moved closer until he was in my face. "Tell me or else."

"Or else *what*?" Toby said. He must have heard the commotion and come to see what was going on.

"Who are you?" Miles took a step back.

"I'm Toby. Why are you threatening Mo?"

"I wasn't."

"It sounded like it to me. Who is this guy, Mo?"

"His name is Miles. He used to go out with a friend of mine."

"I still do. We haven't broken up." Miles protested.

"I think Carol might beg to differ," I said. "Seeing as how you've been cheating on her."

"Just tell me where she is, and I'll leave."

"Mo," Toby turned to me. "Do you know where your friend, Carol, is?"

"I have no idea."

"There you are, Miles. You heard what the lady said. She has no idea where Carol is, so I suggest you leave."

"But, I—err—"

"Right now." It was Toby's turn to get into Miles' face.

"Okay, but you haven't heard the last of this." He headed for the door.

"Nice to meet you, Miles," Toby shouted after him.

"Thanks, Toby," I said.

"My pleasure."

"Where is Carol?"

"In my flat. We heard the raised voices and she said it sounded like Miles, so I thought I'd better come over and have a word in his shell-like."

Chapter 16

It was Sunday, and for the second morning in a row, I woke up to an empty flat. While I was trying to decide whether to spread jam or marmalade on my toast, Beth phoned.

"Mo, it's me. Sorry, I meant to send you a message last night to say I wouldn't be coming home, but I kind of forgot. I hope you weren't worried."

"I wasn't. I figured that you'd be telling your toy boy all about the birds and bees."

"He already has a master's degree in that subject. I've never known anyone like him, Mo. He can go all night."

"Way too much information."

"But I mean, some of the stuff he—"

"Beth! Enough! I'm just about to eat breakfast."

"Okay, I'd better get back anyway. Russell will be getting frisky again."

"Before you go, don't forget that you promised Mand that you'd take her to Zodiac tonight."

"Do you think she'd be okay if I cancelled?"

"No, I don't. You heard the state she was in when we spoke to her on the phone. If you go and cancel on her, she'll be devastated."

"You're right. I'll be back in time to go clubbing."

"You better had."

"I will. I promise. Hang on; I can hear Russell. Morning glory is calling."

"Bye, Beth."

The nerves about my new job were really starting to kick in. I was quick enough to tell everyone what a badass programmer I was, but was I really? I'd never had any complaints about my work at Headrow, but then they were creating apps for the leisure sector, which was a whole different ballgame than FinTech. What if I simply wasn't up to it? What if they told me I hadn't made the grade after my probation period? What if I didn't even make it that far? What if they finished me after my first day?

"Meow!"

Cat was giving me that look of his that said *you forgot to feed me, didn't you*?

"Sorry, Cat, I was miles away. Do you think I'll make the grade in my new job?"

"Meow!" Which, loosely translated, means I neither give a fig about you or your new job. Just dish out the food.

To take my mind off things, I did something very out of character, and took a walk to the park. By the time I'd walked through the park gates, I was in need of a sit down, so I grabbed the nearest bench.

"Want to join me, Mo?"

I looked up to see Toby, running on the spot. He was dressed in his underwear again, or as he insisted on calling them: his running vest and shorts.

"I need a rest. I've just walked all the way here."

"It's only just over a mile and a half."

"Are you sure? It felt like ten."

"I'm going to do a few circuits of the park. Why don't you join me for a couple?"

"Thanks, but no thanks. I think I'll just sit here and enjoy the view."

"Is it okay if I join you for a few minutes before I start my run?"

"Sure, but didn't you already run here from the flat?"

"Yeah, but I don't count that."

"O—kay. Be my guest." I tapped the bench.

"I love the view from here. It's much better than where I used to live," he said.

"Me too. I should make the effort to come here more often."

"Do you do any sports, Mo?"

"Do e-sports count?"

"Not really."

"Then no."

"You really should. Spending all day in front of a computer screen isn't good for you."

"That's what I hear."

"You're welcome to come running with me anytime."

"Would I have to dress like you?"

"I'm serious. If ever you fancy it, just let me know."

"Okay, but I'm probably going to be really busy for a while with the new job. By the way, how's Carol? Did she get upset after Miles' visit yesterday?"

"No. In fact, I think she enjoyed the way I gave him his marching orders."

"That guy is such a creep. Carol is well shut of him. What about you?"

"What about me?"

"I've seen the way you look at Carol. You like her, don't you?"

"She's really nice. And gorgeous, obviously. But she's way out of my league."

"Don't do yourself down."

"I'd better get going. Those five miles aren't going to run themselves."

The more I saw of Toby, the more I liked the guy, and I couldn't help but feel that he and Carol would make a great couple.

I was contemplating what to do about my lunch when there was a knock on the door. Surely, even Miles wasn't stupid enough to risk Toby's wrath.

"Who's there?"

"It's me. Jen."

Her eyes were red, and her mascara had smudged a little.

"Come in. Are you okay?"

"I'm fine."

"You've been crying."

"Is it still obvious? No wonder I got so many funny looks on the tube ride over here. Any chance of a cuppa?"

"Sure. Tea?"

"Yes, please. Where's Beth?"

"Getting Karma Sutra lessons from her toy boy."

"Beth has a toy boy? Tell me more."

"Not until you tell me why you've been crying."

"It's nothing. I'm just being stupid."

"I'll be the judge of that. Remind me, how do you take your tea?"

"Milk, two sugars, please."

"Okay, there you go. Now, spill the beans."

"It's Sheila again."

"Who's Sheila? Oh, hang on. Is that your mother-in-law?"

"None other. She's driving me insane."

"Hasn't that always been the case?"

"Yes, but it's getting worse. Yesterday, she tried to give me instructions on how to iron Pete's shirts."

"Why doesn't he iron his own shirts?"

"That's not the point. If I choose to do them, I don't need her to critique me."

"Fair enough."

"I'm afraid I flipped out on her and said a few things I shouldn't have."

"Oh dear."

"That's not the worst of it. Pete took her side and said I shouldn't have thrown his mother's kindness in her face. *Kindness*? The woman is a total control freak."

"You said that happened yesterday. Did something else happen this morning?"

"She's been giving me the silent treatment. Even after I apologised."

"Why on earth did *you* apologise?"

"Pete convinced me that it would clear the air, but now I wish I hadn't bothered. If we don't get out of there soon, Mo, I'm not sure our relationship will survive."

"How did Pete get on at his second interview?"

"He thought it went well, but he hasn't heard back yet. If he doesn't get it, I'm afraid we'll be stuck in that hellhole forever."

"I'm sure he will. I can feel it in my water."

"I hope you're right."

"Do you fancy getting lunch, Jen?"

"I'd love to, but I'm broke."

"Me too, actually." I laughed. "There's a pizza in the freezer. We could have that."

"Sounds great. Anything to delay going back there."

"Pizza it is, then."

"You promised to tell me about Beth's toy boy."

"His name is Russell, he's nineteen, and by all accounts he's a dynamo in the sack."

"Nineteen? Where did she find him?"

"He works in their Sheffield office. He came down here a few days ago for a meeting, and Beth has had him handcuffed to a hotel bed ever since."

"How the other half lives. I'm jealous."

"No, you're not. You and Pete were made for one another."

"I know, but it's easy to forget that on days like yesterday."

"You'll be alright when you have your own place."

"If we ever do."

Half an hour later, we were getting stuck into the pizza.

"This is just what the doctor ordered." Jen wiped tomato from the corner of her mouth.

"I haven't told you about Carol, have I?"

"What's happened?"

"She's left Miles, and she's staying just across the landing."

"How come I never get to hear the gossip anymore? Why did she leave him?"

"He's been cheating on her."

"I never did like him. His nostrils are too big. How come she's living across the way?"

"A new guy called Toby moved in there a few days ago. He offered to let Carol stay in his spare room until she can sort out something more permanent."

"What's he like?"

"He's a really nice guy. He works as a nursery nurse."

"Aww. That's sweet."

"Then at night, he works as a bouncer."

"Are you kidding?"

"No, honestly."

"What a combination."

"Miles came around here looking for Carol yesterday, but Toby sent him packing."

"Good for him. How's Carol bearing up?"

"Better than when she first walked out on him."

"Poor, Mo. You're becoming everyone's agony aunt."

"I don't mind. It takes my mind off my own problems."

"I didn't think you had any."

"I'm just kidding. I'm okay now I've got a new job."

"When do you start?"

"Tomorrow morning and to tell you the truth, I'm bricking it."

"You'll be fine."

"I hope so. This is probably the last chance saloon for me."

By the time Jen left, she seemed much happier than when she'd arrived, but that would probably be short lived. Things were unlikely to improve until such time as she and Pete found a place of their own.

***

It was almost eight o'clock and there was still no sign of Beth. She'd arranged for Mand to come to our flat, so they could share a taxi from there. I'd tried to phone Beth several times, but all of my calls went straight to voicemail.

"This is the fifth voicemail I've left you. If you don't get back here before Mand arrives, you'll have me to answer to."

"This is the sixth voicemail. Where are you?"

My messages had gone unanswered too. In fact, as far as I could tell, she wasn't even checking them.

Then, at eight on the dot, there was a knock at the door.

"Mand, come in."

"Hi, Mo." She glanced around the room. "Is Beth getting changed?"

"She isn't here."

"Was I supposed to meet her at Zodiac? I'm such a klutz." She took out her phone. "I'd better give her a call."

"You didn't get it wrong. You were supposed to meet here."

"I don't understand. Where is she?"

"I'm not sure," I lied.

"I've been stood up a couple of times in my life, but not by one of my girlfriends." She sighed. "She must have forgotten that we'd arranged to go out."

"I think she must have."

"I'd better call a cab to get me home."

As I was starting my new job the next day, I had intended to have an extra-early night, to make sure I was wide-eyed and bushy-tailed in the morning, but I could see how disappointed Mand was.

"I'll go with you to Zodiac if you like."

"Really?"

"Err, yeah, why not?"

"Okay, but I—err—"

"What?"

"To tell you the truth, Mo, I was going to try and

persuade Beth to change our original plans. I'm not sure I'm up to going out clubbing just yet. I was going to suggest to Beth that we just go down the pub."

"The Anchor?"

"Yeah. Unless you really want to go to Zodiac, Mo?"

"Definitely not. I start my new job tomorrow morning and to be honest, the last thing I need is to turn up there half asleep."

"The Anchor it is, then."

At less than a quarter of a mile from our flat, the Anchor was within easy walking distance. The pub had been bought by one of the big chains about three years ago, when it was transformed from a drinkers' local to a slightly more up market gastropub.

"Did you want to get something to eat, Mand?"

"Not really. Unless you're hungry."

"Nah, a bag of salt and vinegar crisps will do me."

"What do you want to drink, Mo?"

"I'm going to stick with Coke, but don't feel you have to hold back on my account. If you end up tipsy, you can stay at our place. We have a spare bed, apparently."

As the evening wore on, Mand began to loosen up a little, due in no small part to the white zinfandel rose, but then the black clouds seemed to gather again.

"I still can't believe she's gone." She stared down into her half-empty wine glass. "I know it's daft, but I sort of expected her to be around forever."

"Your mum was a lovely lady."

"I was supposed to make a start on clearing out her house yesterday, but I couldn't bring myself to go around there again just yet."

"What are you going to do about her house? Will you move in there?"

"Me? No way."

"I just thought as you're renting at the minute that you might want to live there."

"I wouldn't be able to handle it. I know I wouldn't. I'll probably end up selling it. Or I could rent it out, I suppose. I really haven't given it much thought yet."

"If it would help, I'll gladly go around there with you sometime, to help you clear it out."

"Would you? That would be great. I might find it easier if I'm not there alone."

"Sure. It would have to be on a weekend, though. Just give me a couple of days' notice."

"You're a good friend. Are you sure you don't want something stronger? I feel guilty sitting here getting merry while you're drinking Coke."

"I'm positive. This is fine for me."

"Can I ask you a question, Mo? You can tell me to mind my own business if you like."

"Ask away. I'm an open book."

"I've often wondered why you hardly ever go back home to see your family. Not even at Christmas. I know your dad died some years ago, but what about your mum and sister. Did you have some kind of falling out?"

"I—err—it's complicated."

"Sorry, I shouldn't have asked. Forget I mentioned it."

"No, it's okay. And, in answer to your question, I love my mum and sister to bits. They drive me mad occasionally, but that's the same for any family. It's that house that's the problem."

"What's wrong with it?"

"When I do go home, which isn't very often, Mum naturally assumes I'll want to sleep in my old bedroom." I could feel the tears beginning to well up, so I took a drink to allow time to compose myself. "My dad died of cancer. He was just about okay for the first year, but then things started to go downhill quickly. He was determined not to go into hospital, and Mum asked if he could move into my room, so that they could set up all the equipment in there. Obviously, I said yes, and I moved into Zoe's bedroom with her. Every day, when I went into that room to see him, he looked a little worse. It was like he was fading away right in front of my eyes. I could see the pain he was in, even though he did his best to put on a brave face. Until one day—"

"I'm so sorry, Mo." Mand was in tears now too.

The two of us hugged for several minutes.

"Well, isn't this a jolly night?" Mand laughed.

"Beth doesn't know what she's missing." My tears soon turned into laughter too.

Although it had been very painful opening up to Mand, it had also felt cathartic. It was probably the first time I'd admitted to myself, let alone to anyone else, the real reason I didn't like to return to the home where I'd grown up.

At the end of the evening, I told Mand she was welcome to crash in Beth's room for the night, but it would have meant a horrific commute for her the next morning, so instead, she took a taxi home.

Chapter 17

I'd thought the anxiety of knowing I was starting a new job in the morning might mean I didn't sleep, but in fact, I slept like a log. As soon as I did wake up, the nerves kicked in straight away, but after a long shower, I felt a little better. That was until I took the trouser suit and blouse out of the wardrobe. They were truly awful. What had Nicky been thinking? What had I been thinking?

I'd just slipped them on when I heard a noise; Beth must be back. The last thing I needed before I left for my new job was a shouting match with her, but I couldn't ignore the way she'd treated Mand. I hurried out of my bedroom and charged into hers.

"What were you—?" The words died on my lips when I saw a young man standing next to Beth's bed.

"Hi," he said, quite casually.

"Who the hell are you?" I took a couple of steps backwards, ready to make a run for the door.

"You must be Mo."

How did he know my name? "Who are you?"

"Russell."

It took me a moment to register that he was Beth's new guy; he looked several years older than I knew him to be.

"Where's Beth?"

"In hospital."

"What?"

"She's okay."

"Why is she in hospital, then?"

"She was in an accident last night, but she's alright, honestly."

"You'd better tell me what happened." My legs were

feeling a little wobbly, so I sat on the edge of the bed.

"Beth wanted to get back here because she'd promised to go out with one of her friends."

"Mand, yeah."

"She was worried she'd be late, so she called a cab. I'd just seen her into the taxi when someone shunted it from behind. Luckily, it wasn't too bad because the car was only crawling at the time."

"How did they manage to hit a stationery cab? Never mind. If it was only a minor knock, how come Beth ended up in hospital?"

"She hadn't had the chance to put on her seat belt, so she was thrown into the dividing screen. She took the full impact on her face, and lost consciousness for a few seconds."

"Is she badly injured?"

"She's got a black eye and she's broken one of her front teeth. They kept her in for observation last night because she was knocked out. Just in case she has concussion."

"Are you sure she's okay?"

"Yeah, she was more worried about letting her friend down than she was about her injuries."

I felt terrible now for jumping to the conclusion that she'd just blown Mand off.

"Why didn't she call me?"

"Her phone was smashed in the crash."

"She could have used yours."

"I suggested that, but she didn't know your number because she usually just calls you from her contact list. She asked me to pop over here to get her a change of clothes because the ones she was wearing have blood on them. I'm not really sure what I should take, though. Can you help?"

"Of course. Are you certain she'll be coming home today?"

"That's what the nurse said. She just has to wait until the doctor does his rounds."

"Okay, move out of the way, and I'll pack her a bag."

"Thanks. What shall I do?"

"Do you know how to make a cup of tea?"

He grinned. "Beth said you were funny."

"Go and make us both a cuppa. I take mine with milk, no sugar."

Once I'd packed everything I thought she'd need, I joined Russell in the kitchen, and took a sip of tea. "Not bad."

"For a toy boy, you mean?"

"She told you I'd said that, did she?"

"I've been called worse things."

"I called Beth some horrible things too last night when I thought she'd let Mand down. I feel bad about that now I know what happened."

"You weren't to know." He yawned.

"Where did you sleep last night?"

"On a chair in the A&E waiting room. They wouldn't let me stay on the ward."

"Why don't you grab a few hours in Beth's bed before you go back to the hospital."

"No, I want to get back. She'll be keen to get out of there as soon as the doctor has seen her."

"I wish I could go with you, but it's my first day in a new job this morning."

"That's why you're dressed like that."

"What do you mean, *like that*?"

"I—err—I just meant you look really smart."

"Hmm. Are you going back to Sheffield today?"

"I was supposed to be back in the office this morning, but I called them to say I'd have to take a few days' holiday. I'll go back once I know Beth's okay."

"I like you more than I thought I would."

***

This was not the start to the day that I would have wished for, but I was relieved to hear that Beth was doing okay. I'd been very impressed by Russell who seemed way more mature than his years. He clearly cared about Beth because a lot of guys, finding themselves in that position, would have made for the exit at the first opportunity.

As I walked towards the steel and glass office building that housed Q-Ventures, my nerves began to rattle. It was only when I approached the huge reception desk on the ground floor that I realised I'd forgotten the name of the person I was supposed to ask for. I was such an idiot. Why hadn't I made a note on my phone?

"Hi, I'm starting a new job at Q-Ventures today, but I can't remember who I'm supposed to ask for."

"They're based on the fourth, fifth and sixth floors. They have their own reception on the fourth floor. I'm sure someone there will be able to help you."

"Right, thanks."

The reception on the fourth floor was smaller than the one downstairs, but much more impressive; the desktop was marble.

“Hi, my name is Maureen Jackson. I’m due to start work here today, but I’m afraid I’ve forgotten who it is I should ask for.”

“Sarah Godwin is expecting you. I’ll give her a call.”

“Thanks.”

I was just about to ask if I should take a seat when a woman, dressed in jeans and a blue tee-shirt, appeared from a door to my left.

“Maureen? I’m Sarah. Welcome to Q-Ventures.”

Ignoring the sinking feeling in the pit of my stomach, brought on by the realisation that I was tragically overdressed, I shook her hand. “Nice to meet you. Please call me Mo.”

“HR will want to run through all the usual induction stuff sometime today, but I imagine you’d like to see where you’ll be working and to meet your team leader, Chelsea.”

“That’d be great.”

“Okay, follow me.”

I was desperately clinging onto the hope that Sarah Godwin might be a rebel who ignored the formal dress code, but that illusion was soon shattered when I followed her into a large open-plan office. Everyone in there was dressed casually, and judging by some of the looks I attracted, they clearly thought I was an inspector from HMRC.

As we approached my team leader’s desk, it felt like her eyes were burning a hole in my forehead. Even before the introductions were made, I had a bad feeling about this.

“Chelsea, this is Maureen Jackson, but she goes by Mo. I’ll leave her in your capable hands.”

“Hi.” I conjured up my brightest smile and offered my

hand. "Nice to meet you."

Ignoring my outstretched hand, Chelsea gestured towards an unoccupied desk. "That's yours."

"Err, okay." I was expecting her to say more, but she turned away, and began to type.

On the assumption that I'd been dismissed, I made my way over to the empty desk, and took a seat.

"Sorry for your loss," said the man at the desk next to mine.

"Pardon?"

"I thought you must be going to a funeral later." He laughed.

"Funny."

"I take it you didn't get the dress code memo."

"What does it say?"

"That there isn't one. Nakedness is frowned upon, but apart from that, more or less anything goes."

"I wish I'd known that before I spent this month's rent on this lot."

"Classic. I'm Gary, by the way."

"Mo."

"I know. We've heard all about you."

"You have?"

"Oh yes, and then some. Why do you think Chelsea is giving you the silent treatment?"

"I assumed she was like that with everyone."

"No, she's usually quite nice."

"What did I do to upset her?"

"Do you really not know?"

"I don't have a clue."

"How did you land the job?"

"I submitted my CV."

"Through the company website?"

"No, I gave it to—wait a minute, is this about Rob?"

He nodded. "Bingo."

"But all I did was send him my CV to pass on."

"Hmm."

"What does that mean?"

"What did you expect to happen when the CEO personally hands a CV to HR?"

"CEO? Rob?"

"Oh boy. You don't know much about your boyfriend, do you?"

"I know he *isn't* my boyfriend. And I'd assumed he worked in HR."

"Don't worry. Most people won't hold it against you provided you know your stuff. Chelsea just doesn't like someone else picking her team members."

"Great."

Gary went back to his work, leaving me to stare at the screen and twiddle my thumbs. Normally, I would have approached my team leader to ask what I should be doing, but I was afraid Chelsea might pitch me straight out of the window.

By ten-thirty, I'd had enough.

"Hey, Gary."

"Yeah."

"Where is Rob's office?"

"On the sixth floor. Why?"

"Thanks." I got up from my desk and headed to the stairs. As I passed by her desk, I got the distinct impression that Chelsea wanted to say something, but she remained silent.

On the sixth floor, large glass-fronted offices stretched

the length of all four walls. I walked past each one until I eventually spotted my quarry.

"Excuse me," said a woman, wearing cat's eye glasses, seated at a desk outside Rob's office. "You can't go in there."

"Just watch me."

Before she could stop me, I was through the door.

"I'm sorry, Mr Waites, I tried to stop her."

"That's okay, Beverly, I'll see to this." Rob waited until his PA was out of the door before saying, "What are you doing, Mo?" Then he did something that I wouldn't have thought possible—he made me even angrier by saying, "And what's that you're wearing?"

"Shut up."

"What's wrong?"

"*What's wrong*? I'll tell you what's wrong."

"Why don't you sit down first?"

"I don't want to sit down. I want to stand up."

"As you wish."

"Why didn't you tell me you're the CEO?"

"I didn't think it was important."

"Maybe not to you, but how do you think I feel, knowing that everyone thinks I only got the job because of my boyfriend?"

His face lit up. "I didn't realise I was—"

"You're *not*. Obviously. But all of your staff seem to think you are. And can you blame them? I would never have agreed to apply for the job if I'd known you were going to push my application through without even an interview."

"That's not what happened."

"Yes, it is. I gave you my CV one day and was offered

the job the next."

"I assumed they'd made their decision to offer you the job immediately based on the strength of your CV. I definitely didn't instruct them to treat your application any differently to anyone else's."

"How on earth did you manage to become CEO when you're so naïve?"

"I really don't see the problem. You wanted the job. You've got the job. Unless, of course, you aren't up to it?"

"Of course I'm up to it. It's what I do, and I'm very good at it."

"Then why are you standing in my office, yelling at me, when you should be downstairs doing whatever it is that you geeks do? Unless what you're really telling me is that you want to quit already?"

"I'm not a quitter."

"Good. Then I suggest you get back downstairs and do some work."

"I will, but do me a favour, would you?"

"What's that?"

"Don't do me any more favours." I started for the door.

"Mo, just one last thing."

"What?"

"I really am digging that outfit."

"Get stuffed."

Chapter 18

Judging by the looks I got from some people when I returned to my floor, word had obviously reached them about my confrontation with Rob. Not that I cared. I was so done with that man.

"Are you okay, Mo?" Chelsea asked, like we were suddenly best buddies.

I knew her game; she was desperate to find out what had happened between me and Rob, but she was stone out of luck because I had no intention of telling her what had taken place.

"Can I have something to be working on, please?" I said.

"You haven't had your induction with HR yet, have you?"

"No, but what's the point of me sitting here, twiddling my thumbs?"

"Err, okay. You're going to be working on the Omega project with Baz. Why don't you ask him to bring you up to speed?"

"Which one is Baz?"

"Over there, behind Gary."

"Right."

"You're my hero," Baz said, before I'd even taken a seat.

"What are you talking about?"

"I heard you just ripped the CEO a new one."

"You heard wrong. Can you bring me up to speed on this Omega thing?"

"Sure. It's pretty routine stuff."

He wasn't wrong. I'd expected the work involved on FinTech applications would be much more complex than what I'd been used to, but this looked very straightforward.

Thirty minutes later, and I'd completed the section of code Baz had asked me to write.

"What next?"

"You need to doublecheck it."

"I already have."

"And test it."

"Done."

"Are you sure?" He clearly wasn't convinced. "Let me take a look." He spent the next twenty minutes checking the code, line by line, and then tested it. "Yeah, that looks okay."

"What now?"

"You'll have to wait a while until I've finished what I'm working on. I've been trying to sort out this section of code for a couple of days, but I'm getting nowhere."

"Why don't I take a look at it?"

"I appreciate the offer." He practically scoffed at the suggestion. "But this is really very complicated stuff."

"A fresh pair of eyes can't hurt, surely?"

"I don't think so, Mo." He stood up. "I have to nip to the loo, but when I get back, I have some documentation that needs checking. You can work on that."

I waited until he was at the other side of the office, then wheeled my chair over to his desk, and took a look at the code he'd been working on. By the time he was back, I'd found a workaround, and I had the module working.

"What did you do, Mo?" He stared at the screen.

"Fixed your code."

Baz studied it for several minutes. "You really shouldn't go messing about with other people's projects."

"Don't mention it. You're welcome."

To show his gratitude, he dropped a huge user-manual on my desk. "Proofread that, will you?"

It took me the rest of the day to check and markup the manual. "All done." I dropped it onto his desk on my way out.

I'd been checking my phone all day in case I received a message from Russell, but there had been nothing. Hadn't they released Beth from hospital as expected? Or had he forgotten to let me know she was out? Once I was outside on the street, I checked again, but there was still nothing, so I fired off a message to him.

What's happening with Beth?

Moments later, he called me.

"What's going on, Russ? You promised to keep me updated."

"Sorry, but she was only discharged about an hour ago."

"Is she okay?"

"She's fine. I wanted to take her straight to the flat, but she insisted on buying a new phone first. We're in the shop now."

"Can I speak to her?"

"It's Mo. She'd like to speak to you. Sorry, Mo, she's shaking her head. Her mouth is still quite swollen and she's finding it hard to talk. We'll see you back at the flat in a couple of hours."

"Okay, give her my love."

As Beth wasn't home yet, I decided to head over to Bean Shack, which was only a couple of streets away.

Jed greeted me with a huge smile. It was nice to see a

friendly face after the day I'd just had.

"Look at you. How come you never got dressed up like that when you were working here?"

"This outfit is going straight in the bin when I get home."

"It sounds like you need a drink."

"I really do. Could I get an Americano with an extra shot?"

"Sure, and you can put your money away. This is on the house."

"Don't be daft. I can afford to pay my way now I'm working."

"Keep your money. I owe you, anyway."

"What for?"

"You were right about Christine."

"You caught her at it?"

"I didn't but Liz did. Twice, so I sacked her sorry backside."

"How did she take it?"

"Not well. She denied it of course, and then threatened to hit me with a complaint for unfair dismissal."

"Do you think she will?"

"I doubt it. She's all mouth that one. Here you are. Enjoy."

"Thanks. I've been drinking something masquerading as coffee from a vending machine all day. It tasted like dishwater."

"I'm getting the vibe that your first day didn't go well."

"It was beyond terrible and that's mostly down to that idiot Rob."

"Our Rob?"

"He's not *my* Rob, but just try telling that to everyone in my office. They think I only got the job because he's my boyfriend."

"Is he?"

"Of course he's not. He passed on my CV, that's all. I had no idea he was the CEO."

"I didn't realise that either. He's very down to earth for a guy of his age in that position."

"He's an idiot."

"Apart from the Rob angle, did the job itself live up to your expectations?"

"It's too early to say, but I did manage to upset the guy I'm supposed to be working with."

"How did you manage that?"

"I sorted out the code he'd been struggling with for days."

"Isn't that a good thing?"

"I thought it was until he showed his gratitude by giving me a job more suited to the office junior."

"I'm sure it'll get better."

"It can't get worse."

***

As soon as I walked into the flat, I could hear Russell's voice coming from the kitchen. He was making a cup of tea, and Beth was seated at the table, fiddling with her new phone. She looked worse than I'd expected, with a black eye, swollen lips and grazing to one cheek.

"How are you?"

She shrugged, but then inexplicably burst into laughter. I thought at first that it might be the side-effects of the medication they'd given her, but then I realised that I was the source of her amusement.

"What are you wearing?" She managed to mumble.

"This is the all new me. Don't you like it?"

She laughed again, but then winced and held her jaw. "Is Mand angry at me?"

"Of course not. As soon as I found out what had happened to you, I sent her a message to explain. She was just concerned about you."

"I really don't think you should be talking, Beth," Russell said.

"He's right." I nodded. "I'll go and get changed, and then I'll order in something for dinner. What do you fancy?"

She frowned and pointed to her mouth.

"Oh yeah, sorry. Soup it is, then."

It felt so good to get out of those ridiculous clothes and put on jeans and a tee-shirt. When I went back into the kitchen, Russell was at the table by himself. He put his finger to his lips and whispered, "She's having a lie down."

"Okay. What do you want to do about dinner?"

"I have to get back to Sheffield. I'm already in trouble at work for not going in today. I've explained to Beth and she's okay with it. I'm going to try and get down again at the weekend. Will you keep me posted on how she's doing?"

"Sure."

He stood up and tiptoed to the door. "Bye, Mo."

"See you, Russ."

It was pointless ordering takeaway just for me, so I made do with the last of the pot noodles. I'd managed to let Mand, Jen and Nicky know what had happened to

Beth, but I hadn't been able to get hold of Carol, so I took a walk over to Toby's flat.

There was no answer, and I was just beginning to think that no one was home when the door opened, and Toby appeared, wearing a bath towel tied around his waist. Bumping into half-naked men was becoming a habit.

"Sorry, Mo, I was in the shower."

"So, I see."

"Come in and I'll get dressed."

I almost told him not to bother on my account but thought better of it.

Toby's flat was incredibly tidy and put ours to shame. I knew that couldn't be Carol's influence because she was an even bigger slob than me and Beth.

"That's better." Toby reappeared, wearing a green and red striped rugby shirt. "Would you like a drink?"

"What have you got?"

"Hot chocolate."

"What is it with you and hot chocolate?"

"I've loved it ever since I was a kid. I did try to get into coffee or tea, but they just don't do it for me."

"I actually popped over to see Carol. I take it she isn't here?"

"She's gone to look at a couple of house shares."

"I wanted to let her know about Beth. She was in a bit of a car accident last night."

"Is she okay?"

"Yeah, more or less. She's back home already. She has a black eye, a swollen mouth and she's broken a tooth."

"Poor Beth. What happened?"

"Apparently, she'd just stepped into a taxi when it was shunted from behind."

"Nasty. But you're sure she's okay? Did she get checked out?"

"Yeah. They kept her in hospital last night for observation."

"What do you think I should do about the housewarming party?"

"How do you mean?"

"I'm not sure I can cancel it now because I've already invited lots of people."

"Why would you even think of cancelling it?"

"Because of Beth's accident."

"Don't be daft. She wouldn't want you to do that, and besides, if I know Beth, she'll be there broken tooth or no broken tooth. Anyway, how about you? How are you settling in?"

"I really like it here."

"Has Carol heard any more from Miles?"

"I don't think so. If she has, she hasn't said anything to me. She certainly seems much more relaxed than when she first moved in. I've told her that she can stay here as long as she needs to."

"I assume you'll be looking for a flatmate too."

"Yeah, as soon as Carol is sorted, I'll put up an advert."

"Why don't you just ask Carol if she wants to move in here permanently?"

To my surprise, he blushed. "I—err—don't think I could suggest that to her."

"Why not?"

"She might think I was coming onto her or something. And besides, she's already made it clear that she doesn't want to live this far out."

The door opened, and in walked Carol.

"Why do I get the feeling you two were talking about me?" She grinned.

"Toby was just telling me that you were checking out some house shares."

"And a complete waste of time it was." She took off her coat and threw it on the nearest chair. "They were both dumps." She made a show of sniffing the air. "Is that hot chocolate?"

Toby was on his feet in a flash. "Would you like one?"

"That would be lovely, thanks."

"Since when did you like hot chocolate?" I said.

"Toby has got me into it. I get through so much coffee in the day at work it's nice to have something different."

"I came over to tell you that Beth has had a bit of an accident."

"Is she okay? What happened?"

I repeated the same story that I'd told Toby a few minutes earlier.

"Poor Beth. I'd better go over there and say hello."

"You can't at the moment. She's having a lie down and it wouldn't surprise me if she sleeps through until the morning."

"Okay, but tell her I asked about her, won't you?"

"Sure."

Chapter 19

Just as I'd predicted, Beth didn't emerge again until the next morning, and when she did finally make an appearance, she was in a foul mood.

"Why didn't you wake me so I could say goodbye to Russell?"

"Because you were fast asleep. Besides, he was the one who said I should let you sleep."

"And he's definitely coming down at the weekend?"

"He said he would try. Why don't you call him to check?"

"I already have. A dozen times, but it goes to voicemail."

"I'm sure he'll call you back when he can. It's obvious he really likes you."

"Did he say so?"

"Not in so many words, but he didn't need to."

"What did you think of him?"

"I reckon when he comes through puberty, he'll be a looker."

"I'm being serious. Did you like him?"

"More than I expected to. I've dated guys ten years older than him who weren't half as mature."

"I had a really weird dream last night."

"That'll probably be the drugs they gave you."

"I dreamt that you were dressed like a funeral director." She laughed.

"Very funny."

"What were you thinking, wearing that awful outfit?"

"It was your fault for not being here. I had to rely on Nicky to help me choose something."

"That explains it. She can wear anything and get away with it. I can't wait to see you in it again."

"You're bang out of luck, then. I'm handing it in to the charity shop on my way to work."

"Pity. I didn't even get a photo of you in it." She touched her swollen lip and winced. "If I ask you a question, Mo, will you give me an honest answer?"

"Sure."

"Does my face look really bad?"

"It does, yeah."

"Thanks for nothing. I should have known better than to ask you."

"You said you wanted me to be honest."

"I didn't want you to be *that* honest."

"The swelling around your eyes and mouth will have gone down in a few days."

"What about this, though?" She pointed at her broken tooth. "I can't go back to work looking like this. It's bad enough that Russell saw me."

"Have you called the dentist?"

"Yes, but he can't fit me in for a week. I'll have to go private."

"That'll cost."

"My dad says he'll lend me the money."

"*Lend*?"

"Yeah. I can't expect him simply to give it to me."

"Right. He's *lent* you money before, hasn't he?"

"Yeah, a couple of times, but only when I've been really up against it."

"How many times have you actually repaid him?"

"I can feel a headache coming on. Do you think you could get me a couple of tablets?"

Beth had always been a past master at avoiding awkward questions, but I didn't labour the point. When I returned with the tablets, I told her about my conversation with Toby.

"He can't cancel the party. I need something to cheer me up."

"He isn't going to. I told him I thought you'd still want to go."

"I do. It's just a pity Russell couldn't stay for it."

***

The people at work would be in for a surprise because I'd reverted to my usual work-attire, which consisted of faded jeans plus tee-shirt. And I felt so much better for it.

By the time I'd attended to all of Beth's demands, I had to run to catch the tube. I could definitely understand why Carol was so averse to moving out of the city. Tube travel during the rush hour was about as much fun as sniffing someone's armpits after they'd just finished a workout—and not that much different, actually.

After dropping off that awful outfit at the charity shop nearest to Q-Ventures, I made my way once again into the lion's den. As I walked through the open-plan office towards my desk, I got exactly the kind of reaction, including a few double takes, that I'd been hoping for. Before I reached my desk, Chelsea beckoned me over, and told me to take a seat next to her.

"Baz won't be in for at least the rest of the week."

"What's up? Isn't he well?"

"He says not. He has a fever, apparently, so we're going to need you to stand in for him at FinDev."

"Isn't that the exhibition in Manchester?"

"Correct. Q-Ventures has a stand there. Baz and a few others were supposed to attend, so you'll have to go instead."

I loved going to exhibitions, mainly for all the freebies, but the thought of being put straight onto the front line, after only being with the company for a couple of days, terrified me.

"I'm not sure that's a good idea. How am I supposed to answer questions from the attendees?"

"Don't worry about that. You'll mainly be handing out leaflets and collecting business cards."

"Right. What day is it on?"

"*Days*. It's open to visitors on Thursday and Friday. You'll travel up there tomorrow morning to help set things up, and return on Saturday after everything has been tidied away. The train and hotel rooms have already been booked."

"Okay, sounds good."

She handed me a sheet of paper. "That's a list of all the other people from here who'll be attending the exhibition."

I glanced down the list, but didn't recognise any of the names. That came as something of a relief because for a horrible moment, I'd thought Rob's name might be on there.

"Did you finish work on that module yesterday?"

"Yeah, all signed off. I also proofread the manual."

"What manual?"

"The one Baz told me to check."

"Why would he ask you to do that? We have a pool of proof-readers who do that kind of stuff. You didn't upset him, did you?"

"I might have done. He'd been struggling with a piece of code, and I came up with a workaround."

"That explains it." Incredibly, Chelsea smiled. An *actual* smile. It was a good job I was sitting down, or I might have fallen over from the shock. "Okay, in that case, you'd better team up with Hannah today." She pointed to a woman, in her early thirties, who was wearing a tee-shirt with a zombie on the front. "Tell her I said she should bring you up to speed on project Epsilon."

"Will do."

Hannah had her head down and was typing frantically, so she didn't see my approach.

"Hi."

She jumped so much that she almost fell out of her chair. "Oh, hi. You scared me to death."

"Chelsea said I'm to work with you. I'm—"

"I know who you are." She smiled. "Everyone does."

"O—kay?"

"Grab a seat and tell me all about it," she said. "And don't spare any of the gory details."

"I think you must have got me mixed up with someone else."

"You're the one who told our CEO to go stuff himself, aren't you?"

"Oh that."

"So, what happened? Before you arrived yesterday, everyone had been saying you and he were a thing."

"We're definitely *not* a thing."

"You mean since you had that blazing row?"

"We never were a thing." I hesitated, wondering how much I should share, but then I figured it might be best to tell Hannah the full story. I had a hunch that doing so would probably save me the bother of having to explain it to everyone else.

"There's not much to tell, really. My friend got talking to Rob in Jesters about a week ago."

"Jesters? Rob was in Jesters?"

"Yeah. Anyway, my friend likes to talk. A lot. Somehow, she got around to telling him what I did for a living and that I'd just got fired."

"What did you get fired for?"

Whoops. Perhaps I should have left out that part of the story. "Nothing. It doesn't matter. Anyway, Rob mentioned that Q-Ventures were looking for app developers and that I should submit my CV. That's pretty much it."

"I heard he'd ordered HR to take you on without an interview."

"Then you heard wrong."

"You're not like boyfriend, girlfriend, then?"

"Definitely not."

"And you've never been on a date with him?"

I quickly weighed up whether or not I should mention the not-a-date but decided against it.

"No, I haven't."

"What was the big bust-up about?"

"It was nothing. I just made it crystal clear that I didn't want any help from him, and that I wanted people to judge my work on its own merits. That's it."

"Fair enough." She leaned back in her chair. "You'll do for me."

"I think I saw your name on the list of those going to the Manchester exhibition."

"Yeah. Are you going too?"

"Apparently. I'm taking Baz's place."

"That guy's never here. If you ask me, he's got some kind of side-gig going on."

"That's terrible."

After what had been an awful first day at Q-Ventures, my second day there was a vast improvement, and I was actually beginning to enjoy myself. The project that Hannah was working on was much more challenging than the work I'd been doing with Baz. In fact, I was so into it that I worked through half of my lunch-break, and I didn't even realise when it was time to call it a day.

"Don't you have a home to go to?" Chelsea said.

It was only when I looked around, and saw that most people had already left, that I checked my phone and realised it was almost six-thirty.

"I lost track of time."

"Can I have a quick word before you go?"

"Sure." What had I done wrong now?

"I was a bit of a cow to you yesterday," she said.

"You were."

She laughed. "I was hoping you might tell me not to be silly."

"Oh sorry. Don't be silly, Chelsea, you weren't a cow at all." I grinned. "Except you were."

"I was ticked off because I like to pick the people who will work under me, so when they told me that you were joining my team, I wasn't a happy bunny."

"I get it. I didn't realise that's what had happened until I walked in yesterday morning."

"I've been going through the work you did with Baz."

"Oh?"

"I'm impressed. Very impressed. Particularly with the workaround you came up with to resolve the problem he's been struggling with for weeks now."

"Thanks."

"I'm going to be absolutely honest with you, Mo. I thought the only reason you'd been given the job was because you and Rob were a thing."

"We're not. I can promise you that."

"I believe you. I heard what really happened."

"From Hannah, I assume?"

"Yeah. She's a great coder, but you should never tell her anything you don't want to go any further."

"I was kind of hoping she *would* tell everyone, to save me having to do it."

"If it's okay with you, I'd like to think we could make a fresh start."

"Fine by me. I've really enjoyed myself today."

"There's just one thing I need you to promise me."

"What's that?"

"That you'll never come to work wearing that awful outfit you had on yesterday."

"You can bank on that."

"Great. Okay, I'd better let you get going. I'll see you tomorrow."

"Before I go, can I just ask you one question?"

"Shoot."

"If you pick your own people, how come Baz is on your team?"

She rolled her eyes. "We all have our off-days. He was mine."

***

As soon as I walked into the flat, Beth came hurrying over, and gave me a toothy grin.

"You got that repaired quickly."

"Yes, and it cost me a small fortune."

"Cost your dad one, don't you mean?"

"What do you think of it?"

"They did a great job. I never would have known it had been broken."

"I just wish the bruising would disappear. I've tried my best to conceal it, but you can still see it."

"You look fine. It could have been so much worse."

"I know. I managed to get hold of Russell too. He's coming down on Friday night, and you know what that means, don't you?"

"I suspect you're going to tell me."

"It'll be more than seven days since I met him, so he can stay the night."

"Fair enough, but I'd appreciate it if you two could get all the pent-up lust out of your system on Friday night while I'm away."

"Away where?"

"I have to go to an exhibition in Manchester tomorrow. I'll be back on Saturday."

"What about the housewarming party tomorrow night?"

"There's nothing I can do about that. I'll nip over and apologise to Toby later."

"Who else is going to Manchester with you?"

"There's a few of them from my office."

"I bet Rob will be there. Rob and Mo, sitting in a tree, K-

I-S-"

"Grow up. He isn't even going."

"How come?"

"How would I know? Or care?"

Chapter 20

I'd been told not to bother going into the office, but instead to meet the others at Euston Station. As I didn't need to be there until eleven, I'd planned to treat myself to what I considered to be a well-deserved lie-in. But it was not to be.

I would have recognised that laughter anywhere. Mand had one of those laughs that grated like fingernails on a blackboard, but after what she'd been through recently it was music to my ears.

"Morning, Mo." She was seated at the kitchen table with Beth.

"Morning." I yawned. "Isn't it a bit early for wine?"

"I brought it around for the invalid here, but I hadn't intended for us to drink it this morning."

"That was my idea." Beth picked up her glass and took a swig. "I figured I deserved this after what I've been through."

"I don't suppose you want a glass, do you, Mo?" Mand held up the bottle.

"No, thanks. I'll make do with a cup of tea."

"*Mand* reckons my face is almost healed," Beth said pointedly to me.

Mand, who clearly had more sense than I did, had apparently told Beth what she wanted to hear.

"Yeah, she's right," I said. "It's looking much better this morning."

"What we need is another girls' night out," Beth said.

"You can count me out." I took a sip of tea. "Three a year is my limit."

"You're such a killjoy. What about you, Mand? I

promise not to stand you up again."

"Sure, I'd be up for it."

"Now that Carol has dumped that loser, Miles, she'll definitely want to come," Beth said. "What about Jen and Nicky?"

"I'm not sure about Nicky," I said. "And I doubt Jen will be interested. She came around here the other day, and she was in a terrible state."

"Why? What's the matter with her?" Mand, the mother hen of our little gang, was quick to enquire.

"The usual. She'd had another bust up with her mother-in-law."

"Jen and Pete need to get out of that place and get their own home," Beth said.

"I'm sure they'd love to, but until Pete gets another job, there isn't much prospect of that. And they'll probably have to reapply for a mortgage. That stuff takes forever."

"Do you think they might consider renting?" Mand asked.

"I've no idea." I shrugged. "Why?"

"I've been wondering what to do about Mum's place. I'm not sure I can handle all the hassle of trying to sell it just yet. Do you think Jen and Pete might be interested in renting it?"

"I'm sure Jen would snatch your hand off at the chance to get away from her mother-in-law. Whether they could afford it is a different matter."

"I think I'll give Jen a call and see what she says. Anyway, Mo, how come you aren't at work? You haven't gone and got yourself fired from your new job already, have you?"

"Not yet. I'm going to Manchester later this morning. Q-

Ventures have a stand at an exhibition up there."

"Mo has to dress up like a bunny and hand out drinks," Beth said.

"Don't listen to her. That knock on the head has sent her funny. I'll just be handing out leaflets and collecting business cards. And no, I won't be wearing a bunny costume."

At least, I hoped not.

***

Euston station was rammed, and I was trying to figure out which platform I needed when I heard someone call my name.

"Mo, over here."

I looked around to find Hannah waving to me. "We're all in the first-class lounge."

"We're travelling *first class*?"

"Yeah, we always do."

"Neat."

"Come on. We've just got time to grab a drink and something to eat."

I had no idea that travelling first class entitled you to free refreshments. After filling my pockets with an assortment of snacks, I joined the others, most of whom I recognised from the office.

"Have you been to one of these exhibitions before, Hannah?"

"Yeah, this is my third. The London one is the biggest and best, but Manchester is usually good too."

"Chelsea said that I would just be handing out leaflets."

"Hmm."

"What does that mean?"

"When they see you're wearing a Q-Ventures badge, people will assume you can answer all their questions, but don't worry, you can refer them to me. And I'll tell them I don't have a clue either." She laughed.

I was really beginning to like Hannah. I'd seen what a talented coder she was, but unlike Baz (who couldn't hold a candle to her), she didn't take herself too seriously.

The seats in the first class carriage were wider than those I was used to in standard class, and once again all the drinks and snacks were free. I could get used to this.

"Where are you from originally, Mo?" Hannah said in between mouthfuls of salt and vinegar crisps.

"Leicester. What about you?"

"Can't you tell?"

"Not really. I've never been very good with accents."

"I'm from Bath. I moved here five years ago."

"To work for Q-Ventures?"

"Not initially. I was at one of their competitors for a year first. Q headhunted me." She giggled. "Who'd have thought someone would headhunt little old me?"

"Based on what I saw yesterday, I'm not surprised at all. You know your stuff."

"Thanks. Chelsea told me that you'd sorted out Baz's code."

"I thought I was doing him a favour, but I realise now it was a mistake."

"Don't lose any sleep over him. He's a liability."

"What exactly will we be doing today?"

"Setting up all the software and making sure that—" Her phone buzzed with a message, which she scanned quickly. "Oh no!"

"Something wrong?"

"It sounds like there'll be fireworks at the exhibition."

"I love fireworks."

"Not *real* fireworks, you nit. I meant there's going to be trouble."

"Why? What's happened?"

"Edward is going to be there."

"Who?"

"I take it you haven't heard about him yet? Edward Black co-founded Q-Ventures with Rob. They met at uni and started the business in their last year there. About two years ago, they had some kind of big bust up, and Edward left the company."

"What happened?"

"No one really knows. He still owns ten per cent of the business and he turns up at the offices every now and then. Whenever he does, there's always trouble."

"Why is he coming to the exhibition?"

"According to my sources, he'll be on one of the other stands. He recently launched another business in direct competition to Q-Ventures."

"Do you think Rob knows he'll be here?"

"You can bank on it."

***

I'd assumed that the day before the exhibition opened to the public would be quiet, and that I'd be able to take it easy. I couldn't have been any more wrong. I'd attended a few exhibitions in my time, but I'd never given any thought to how much work went into installing and preparing all the stands.

It was total madness. There were lots of people running back and forth, all giving out orders. I'd no sooner finished on one task than I had to start on another. To be fair, I wasn't the only one who was run off their feet. Everyone on our team was hard at it, stopping only for the occasional refreshment or loo break. We eventually called it a day at just turned nine o'clock, by which time we were all well and truly exhausted.

Fortunately, the hotel where we were staying was only a ten-minute walk from the exhibition centre. I'd assumed I'd be sharing with someone, but the company had booked individual rooms for us all. Everyone else stopped off at the hotel restaurant for supper, but I was way too tired to eat, and besides I'd already overdosed on crisps and chocolate, so I headed straight to my room. All I wanted was a nice hot shower and a comfy bed.

My room was on the fifth floor and there was no way I was tackling the stairs after the day I'd just had, so I headed straight to the bank of three lifts. I was just about to press the button for my floor when someone stepped inside.

"Mo?"

"Rob? What are you doing here?"

"I heard there was an exhibition going on." His fingers hovered over the buttons. "Which floor are you on?"

"Five."

"Pity." He grinned that annoyingly sexy grin of his. "I'm on six."

"Your name wasn't on the list."

"Wasn't it? I'd better get back to London, then."

"Very funny. I just meant that—"

"I hadn't intended to come, but something happened to

change my plans."

"Edward?"

"How do you know about him?"

"The office grapevine."

"You look like you could do with a nightcap. Why don't you come up to my room? We can raid the mini-bar."

"Yeah, that's never going to happen."

Before he could come back at me with some clever remark, my phone rang with an unknown number.

"Hello?"

"It's me."

"Beth?" She must not have been able to transfer her old number to her new phone.

"This is your floor, Mo," Rob said.

I stepped out of the lift and the doors closed behind me.

"Who was that?" Beth said.

"No one."

"Liar. It was Rob, wasn't it?"

"Yes, but we're not here together."

"You said he wouldn't even be there." She snorted.

"I didn't think he would be. And before you ask, our rooms aren't even on the same floor."

"Sure."

"Did you actually call for a reason?"

"I called to tell you about the housewarming."

"How was it?"

"It's still going on. Toby invited a few of his friends."

"Bouncers?"

"No, more's the pity. They work with him in the nursery. To be honest, the whole thing is a bit lame. I've seen more action on a visit to the library."

"I hope he can't hear you."

"Nah, I'm in the loo. I do have one piece of gossip, though."

"What's that?"

"Toby definitely has the hots for Carol."

"What happened? What did he do?"

"Nothing. It's just the way he looks at her. I can tell."

"Look, I have to go. I'm absolutely shattered."

"Has Rob worn you out?"

"The first time I saw him was five minutes ago. Not that I expect you to believe me."

"You're right. I don't."

"Please yourself." I unlocked the door to my room. "I'm going now because I need to shower and then I'm going to bed."

"With Rob, I hope."

"Goodnight, Beth."

Chapter 21

Thankfully, there were no more calls from Beth that night, so I'd managed to get a good night's sleep. I'd set an alarm on my phone because we had to be at the stand by nine-thirty, and Hannah had said we should meet in the restaurant for breakfast at eight.

I was a little apprehensive that Rob might be in there, but there was no sign of him. After a trip to the breakfast buffet, I joined Hannah at a table near the door. My plate was piled high with fried everything—enough calories to sink a ship. Hannah had only a bowl of cereal and an orange.

"Is that all you're having, Hannah?"

"It's all I can face after last night."

"Heavy session?"

"You did the right thing, having an early night. I wish I'd done the same."

"What time did you all call it a day?"

"I don't remember, but it was the wrong side of midnight. I'm not sure I'll be much use on the stand today."

"You'll be fine. By the way, I saw Rob last night."

"I heard he was here. If you take my advice, you'll stay out of his way. Edward brings out the worst in him."

"Don't worry. I plan to keep my distance."

At nine-thirty on the dot, the doors to the exhibition hall were opened and the crowds started to roll in. We had all been given red and green Q-Ventures tee-shirts, and name badges. I'd also been given a box full of glossy flyers. As is always the case, the majority of people who found their way onto our stand were only there to see what freebies were on offer. Quite a few of them took one of my flyers, and by midday, I'd taken a dozen or more business cards from people requesting that a detailed info pack be sent to them. Much to my relief, I'd been asked very few technical questions, and when I had, I'd been able to hand them over to Hannah who was looking a hundred times better than she had at breakfast.

"Could I get a leaflet?" A man with pencil-thin eyebrows snapped at me.

"Certainly, sir. And if you'd like more detailed information, I—"

"When is version three-point-two being released?"

"I'm—err—not sure, but I can—" I glanced over at Hannah, but she was already talking to another visitor.

"Are you telling me you don't know when your own software is going to be upgraded?"

"Actually, I'm just—"

"The current version has got enough bugs to sink a battleship. Are they all addressed in the new release? Whenever that may be."

"I—err—" Hannah showed no sign of finishing with her current visitor.

"Did you hear me?" The man demanded. "Or are you deaf?"

"That's enough." Rob appeared from nowhere, grabbed the man by the arm, and practically dragged him away from the stand, in the direction of the nearest exit.

"Are you okay?" Hannah said. She must have seen what had happened and abandoned the visitor she'd been talking to.

"That guy was having a real go at me, but then Rob

bundled him outside."

"That was Edward."

"His ex-partner?"

"Yeah."

"He was asking me all kinds of questions that I couldn't answer. I tried to pass him over to you, but you were tied up."

"Sorry."

"It's not your fault. The man is obnoxious." I glanced towards the fire exit. "Do you think Rob will be okay?"

"I'm sure he'll be fine." She laughed. "Didn't you know he has a black belt?"

"Karate?"

"No, it's just a black belt that he likes to wear."

"Seriously, do you think I should go and check on him?"

"No, he'll be fine."

We'd been allocated staggered times for our lunchbreaks, and mine was scheduled for one o'clock. I'd seen no more of Rob, and despite what Hannah had said, I was a little concerned that he might have been hurt after coming to my rescue. There wasn't anything I could do, so I headed for the large food-hall.

I'd loaded my tray with pizza, chips and Coke, and I was trying to find a free table when I heard a familiar voice.

"Mo! Come and join me."

"Looking none the worse for his earlier altercation, Rob was seated alone, eating a salad.

"I see you went for the healthy option." He eyed my tray.

"I'm starving. Are you okay?" I took a seat opposite him.

"Yeah, I like salad."

"I meant after what happened earlier."

"I'm fine. I'm sorry you had to put up with that nonsense."

"That's okay. I take it that was Edward?"

"The one and only. It's hard to believe he and I were once best friends."

"He was asking about the next version of the app. He said something about the current version being full of bugs."

"He's full of *something* and it isn't bugs. He's just trying to generate bad publicity for us. There's nothing in what he says. Just ignore him."

"Which is his new company's stand?"

"It's at the opposite end of the hall from ours. It's called Quest Ventures."

"Isn't that suspiciously like—"

"Q-Ventures? Of course it is. He's hoping the confusion might drive some unsuspecting clients to his joke of a product. There are no depths to which that man won't sink. Anyway, never mind him. How about you? How are you finding life at Q-Ventures?"

"I've only been here five minutes, but so far, so good, I think."

"You'll be fine. I have total confidence in you."

"Thanks."

"So, how about dinner tonight?"

"I might have known there would be a motive behind your flattery."

"I was being sincere, but I'd still like you to have dinner

with me. What do you say?"

I wanted to say yes because I'd enjoyed our *not-a-date,* but I knew it would be a mistake.

"No."

"Why not?"

"I've just about convinced the people I'm working with that you and I aren't a thing, and that you aren't the only reason I landed the job. If I go on a date with you now, I'll be back to square one."

"Okay, in that case, how about we go on another not-a-date?" Cue sexy grin.

"It doesn't matter what you call it, the answer is still no."

"What if I ask you again? Say in a month's time when you've had time to prove your worth to everyone?"

"The answer will still be the same."

"I'll ask anyway."

When I got back to the stand, Hannah ushered me into the tiny room where we kept our belongings.

"Come on, Mo, spill the beans. What's the real story with you and Rob?"

"There's nothing to tell."

"A couple of people saw you having lunch with him."

"And that's all it was. He asked me to join him at his table, and I could hardly say no after he'd rescued me this morning, could I?"

"You're not seeing him, then?"

"No. Look, I'm going to be honest with you. He did ask me out to dinner, but I told him no. I said I didn't want everyone to think I was only in this job because of him."

"Pity."

"What do you mean?"

"Everyone likes Rob, and he's had a rough time. He deserves to be with someone nice like you. You're nothing like the ones he usually dates."

"In what way?"

"You know the sort. Tall, slim, beautiful with big boobs. They all look as though they fall out of bed every morning, ready for a photo-shoot."

"Let me see. *Tall, slim, beautiful with big boobs.*" I looked myself up and down. "Are you telling me that I'm not all of those?"

"Your boobs are bigger than mine if that's any consolation." She laughed. "We'd better get back out there before they send the search party to find us."

***

Even though the day had been full-on, I was feeling much less tired that evening than I had the previous day. So, after dinner, when Hannah suggested I join her and the others in the bar for drinks, I readily agreed. By now, I knew almost everyone's names, and I was beginning to feel like one of the team, rather than an outsider.

"Why don't you have a real drink?" Hannah said when she saw my Coke.

"I don't drink."

"Never?"

"I'm not teetotal. I do occasionally have something stronger at weddings and the like, but I've always preferred soft drinks. I think it's because on the few occasions I've had too much to drink, I don't get merry—I get sick. I'm surprised you're drinking after the state you were in this morning."

"That was then; this is now. I feel fine." Her gaze suddenly shifted to the other side of the room. "Don't look now, but—"

Why do people say that? If anything is guaranteed to make you look around, it's being told not to. I followed her gaze and saw Rob sitting by himself.

"Why doesn't he join us?" I said.

"I'm not sure. He usually does on occasions like this. You should go and see if he's okay."

"Me? Why me?"

"Do you really need to ask? He's been staring at you ever since he sat down."

"Rubbish."

"Go on. Ask him to come and join us."

"Okay, but only because I feel sorry for him sitting all alone."

Rob spotted me walking across the room and his face lit up.

"Hi. I've been sent to ask you to join us."

"I don't think that's a good idea."

"Why not?"

"Because I don't trust myself to be so close to you."

"Very funny."

"I'm being serious. If I spend too much time in close proximity to you, I will have to kiss you."

"How much have you had to drink?"

He held out his glass to me. "Take a sip."

"I don't drink."

"Then you have nothing to worry about. Try it."

"Lemonade?"

"Yeah."

"What shall I tell the others why you won't join us?"

"Tell them the truth. That I don't trust myself not to kiss you."

"I'm not telling them that."

"You'll have to make up a lie, then."

"I don't get it. Why me? From what I hear, I'm hardly your type."

"*My type*?" He half-laughed, half snorted. "And what, pray tell, is *my type*?"

"Tall, slim, beautiful with big boobs. Like a model."

"Says who?"

"Never mind. Is that right?"

"It's true that I've been out with a few women over these last few years, but none of the relationships have gone anywhere."

"Were any of them like me?"

"Feisty, fun and hard work? Definitely not."

"That's not what I meant, and you know it. Did any of them look like me?"

"This is stupid. I like you, Mo. I like you a lot. And, I have a sneaking suspicion you might like me too—if only a little."

I should have jumped straight in and contradicted him, but instead I said, "It's not that I don't like you."

"So, you do like me?"

"I didn't say that."

"If you don't *not* like me that must mean you like me."

"It means I'm neutral on the subject of liking or not liking you."

"You see, that's what I love about you. You're so complicated."

"Not the greatest compliment I've ever had."

"Am I at least in with a chance?"

"No."

"Why not?"

"I've already told you why. I've just about managed to persuade the people I work with that I didn't get the job just because of you. If I was to date you now, I'd look like a liar."

"How long, then?"

"How long until *what*?"

"You *will* feel comfortable going on a date with me."

"Never."

"Come on, that's not fair. How about a month from now?"

"Definitely not."

"Three months."

"This isn't some kind of business negotiation."

"Six months."

"One year," I countered.

"Done. One year it is. I'm beginning to think we hired you to do the wrong job. You should be negotiating contracts with our suppliers. So, to recap, when you've been working at Q for a year, I'm going to take you on the best date you've ever been on."

"That's if you haven't forgotten all about this silly little arrangement by then."

"I won't forget. You can bank on that. And on that first official date, I'm going to kiss you."

"We'll have to see about that when the time comes." Despite my best efforts not to, I couldn't help but smile. "So, will you come and join us over there now?"

"Okay, but you have to promise not to sit anywhere near me because if you do, I might not be able to resist stealing a kiss."

"Don't worry. I'll keep my distance."

Chapter 22

That evening turned out to be one of the most enjoyable I'd had for months. Everyone, including Rob, let their hair down and had a good time. Every now and then, I caught him looking at me, and a couple of times he patted the seat next to him and beckoned me to go over, but I ignored him. I'd be lying if I said I wasn't tempted.

By eleven-thirty, people had started to drift back to their rooms, and I was just beginning to think I should do the same when my phone rang. As soon as I saw my sister's name on caller ID, I knew something was wrong.

"Zoe? What's up?"

"It's Mum."

"Oh no."

"It's okay. It isn't serious. Well, it is but—"

"Just tell me what happened."

"She slipped coming down the stairs and turned her ankle over."

"How is she?"

"I'm at the hospital with her now. They thought at first she might have broken something, but it turned out to be a bad sprain."

"What are they going to do?"

"They've bandaged her ankle and told her she has to stay off it as much as possible, and they're going to give her crutches. We're just waiting for the doctor to say she can leave."

"Did she injure anything else?"

"No, but it's shaken her up a bit."

"Okay, thanks for letting me know."

"I didn't call just to update you. Me, Jim and Ben are

going away tomorrow for a week. We've had it booked for months. If I cancel, it will break Ben's heart. I need you to come and babysit Mum until I get back."

"Me?"

"You're her only other child unless you know something I don't. And besides, from what I hear, you're in-between jobs."

"But I've just—"

"Come on, Mo, I don't ask you a favour very often. I'm worried if Mum is by herself, she might try and get up and fall again."

"Okay. I'll try and get there early tomorrow."

"Can't you come up tonight? Our flight is at seven in the morning."

"I'm not sure what the trains are like at this time of night."

"They run from St Pancras every hour, even I know that."

I didn't tell her I was in Manchester because then I'd have had to tell her about the new job. Knowing Zoe, she'd have told me to stay put, and not to risk losing my job. That would have meant them having to cancel their holiday. My young nephew would be devastated.

"I'll get there as soon as I can. Are you taking her back to your place?"

"No, she insists on going back to her own home."

"Okay. I'll see you there later."

I was just about to check the train times when…

"I'll take you." Rob had taken a seat next to me. I'd been so engrossed in my discussion with Zoe that I hadn't seen him come over.

"Where did you spring from?"

"I could tell that something was wrong, so I came over to see if you were okay."

"You heard everything, I take it?"

"Most of it. I couldn't really help it. Your sister is not exactly softly spoken."

"That's true."

"Get your things together, and I'll drive you to Leicester."

"Don't be daft. I'll get a train."

"At this time of night? It'll take ages. Let me drive you there."

"But you've been drinking all night."

"Lemonade, yeah. While you're sitting here arguing, we could be on the road. Go and get packed and meet me in the car park."

In less than twenty minutes, I was standing in the car park, looking for Rob. Out of the semi-darkness, two headlights appeared, and moments later, he pulled up alongside me.

"I thought you'd have some brand new, swanky, top of the range motor." I threw my bag into the backseat (what there was of it) and climbed in beside him. "Not this old thing."

"I'll have you know this is not old. It's a classic motor."

"Will it get us there? Maybe I should have taken the train."

"It's okay, Cindy, she doesn't mean it."

"Who's Cindy?"

"The motor of course."

"You've given your car a name?"

"She came with it."

"O—kay."

"Do you want to listen to some music?" He tapped a strange box-shaped thing that was hanging under the dashboard.

"What's that?"

"An eight-track stereo."

"A what?"

"Open the glove compartment."

I did as he said. "What are these?"

"Cartridges. You put them into the player. Pick one you like."

I spent a few minutes going through them and then closed the glove compartment.

"What's wrong?" he said.

"I've never heard of half of them, and the rest are plain awful. Have you always had such terrible taste in music?"

"There are some classics in there."

"What's wrong with Spotify?"

"It has no soul."

"The last time I looked, there was plenty of soul. Lots of R&B too."

"That was funny. Almost. Do you see now how well we get on? We'd be great together."

"Is this why you offered to drive me? To give you a chance to try and wear down my resistance?"

"Absolutely."

"You'll have had a wasted journey, then. I'm really sorry I have to skip out of the exhibition."

"Don't give it a second thought. Family comes first."

"Is this going to affect my three-month appraisal?"

"Absolutely not. Don't worry about any of that stuff. Just make sure your mum is okay."

"Thanks."

The rest of the journey passed mostly in silence because I was thinking about my mum and wondering how she would be when I got there.

"It's the next road on the left. You can drop me on the corner."

"Don't be daft. I'll take you to the house. Which one is it?"

"It's on the left."

"The one with the woman on crutches, standing in the doorway, by any chance?"

"What's she playing at?" As soon as the car had stopped, I hurried up the driveway. "You should be in bed, Mum."

"Zoe said you were coming, so I decided to keep a lookout for you. That's not a taxi, is it?"

"No, it's—"

"Good evening, or I suppose I should say good morning, Mrs Jackson. I'm Rob Waites. I work with Mo." He had my bag in his hand.

"It's nice to meet you, Rob, and you must call me Shirley. Come on inside and I'll make us all a nice cup of tea."

"You'll do no such thing, Mum. I'm taking you up to bed."

"Not until I've had a cup of tea, you aren't. Come on inside. You're letting all the warmth out."

Rob deposited my bag in the hallway and then the two of us followed her into the kitchen. To say she'd only had the crutches a matter of hours, she was already quite proficient on them.

"Shirley, please sit down and let me make the tea," Rob said.

"What a gallant young man. Thank you." She took a seat and patted the one beside her. "Come and sit with me, Mo."

"What happened, Mum?"

"It was nothing. I just had a bit of a tumble."

"Zoe told me the doctor said you have to rest in bed for a few days."

"And I will, but I can't spend every minute there, can I? I have to eat and go to the loo."

"I'll take care of that while I'm here."

"I'm not using a bedpan."

"I meant your meals. Where is Zoe, anyway?"

"I made her go home. She didn't want to, but they have an early flight this morning, and I wanted her to get at least a little sleep. It will be nice to have you here for a few days, although I'm surprised you remember where the house is."

Rob started to laugh, but soon stopped when I shot him a look.

"Milk and sugar, Shirley?" he said.

"Just a drop of milk, please. I'm sweet enough."

"Just like your daughter."

My mum's eyes lit up. "Are you two seeing one another?"

"No, we aren't," I got in before Rob could say something he'd live to regret. "He's just messing with you, aren't you, Rob?"

"Mo's right. We're just work colleagues." Then he turned to me, so my mother couldn't see, and mouthed, "For now."

Ignoring him, I tried to get Mum to tell me more about what had happened at the hospital, but she'd clearly lost all interest in that particular subject.

"How long will you be staying, Mo?"

"Until I'm sure you're okay to be left alone or until Zoe gets back from her holiday, whichever is the soonest."

"It could take a while to heal." She winced dramatically. "I did quite a number on my ankle."

When Rob had finished his tea, he stood up. "I'd better be making tracks."

"You'll do no such thing, young man," my mother said. "There are bad storms forecast. You don't want to be driving all the way back to London in that kind of weather."

Rob threw me a puzzled look, and it was only then that I realised I hadn't told my mother where I'd been when I got the call from Zoe.

"We didn't come from London, Mum. We were at an exhibition in Manchester when Zoe called me."

"That's even worse. It will be terrible over the tops tonight. Rob, you must stay here and travel back tomorrow when it's light."

"But, Shirley—"

"I won't hear another word about it. If you drive back tonight, I won't get a wink of sleep for worrying about you. You wouldn't want that, would you?"

"Err, no, of course not."

"It's settled, then. Mo, you can sleep in your old room. Rob, you can take Zoe's old room."

"Thank you, Shirley." Rob had clearly warmed to the idea.

"Now, can one of you give me a hand to get up the

stairs? I'm starting to get weary."

Rob offered to help her, but I waved him away. "I'll do it." Once she was tucked up in bed, I gave her a kiss and I was just about to turn out the bedside lamp when she said, "I like him."

"Rob? Yeah, he's okay."

"He likes you too. I can tell."

"I told you. We're just work colleagues."

"Hmm."

"What does that mean?"

"He has that same look in his eyes that your father had when we first started seeing each other."

"Goodnight, Mum."

"Don't let him get away or you'll regret it."

"Sleep tight."

I crept downstairs to find Rob on the sofa, with a huge grin on his face.

"I like your mum."

"She seems to have taken a shine to you too, although I can't think why. Look, you really don't need to stay. She'll be fast asleep in a few minutes, so she'll be none the wiser if you go."

"I can't do that. It would be rude."

"What about the exhibition?"

"If I set off early in the morning, I won't miss much. And besides, your mother is right, it will be a better journey in the morning when the storms have passed. So, are you going to show me to my room?"

"Follow me." I led the way upstairs, but then hesitated as I reached the door to my old room.

"Is this it?" Rob said.

"Err, no. This is mine."

"What's wrong?"

"Nothing."

"You're crying."

"I'm not." I wiped away a tear.

"Tell me what's wrong."

"It's nothing. I'm just being silly."

"Come with me." He took my hand and led the way back downstairs where we both took a seat on the sofa. "Now tell me what's wrong."

"It's that room—" That's when the floodgates opened, and I began to sob.

"It's okay." He put his arm around my shoulder. "Take your time."

Eventually, I managed to compose myself enough to tell him about my dad being moved into that room in the last few weeks of his life.

"I'm really sorry, Mo, that must have been awful."

"Ever since then, whenever I step into that room, I see Dad, lying there, in pain. Dying."

The tears came again, and this time it was several minutes before I managed to pull myself together.

"It's okay, Mo. You take your sister's old room."

"What about you? I can't bear the thought of you being in that room either."

"That's alright. I'll sleep down here."

"You can't do that," I snuffled. "I'll sleep on the sofa."

"This is your boss speaking now. I'm sleeping down here, and that's final."

"You haven't even got a change of clothes."

"That's true, but that's no different to my old uni days when we used to crash at each other's places. I'll be fine. Now, go to bed before we wake your mum."

"Okay." I stood up and for a moment considered giving him a peck on the lips, but common sense got the better of me, and I made my way upstairs.

Chapter 23

Even though I hadn't gone to bed until the early hours of the morning, I was wide awake by a quarter to six. No matter how hard I tried, I couldn't get back to sleep, so I decided I might as well take my bath before the rest of the house stirred. And when I say bath, I really do mean *bath*. Mum had refused point blank to have a shower installed, not even one of those over the bath. According to her, you couldn't get properly clean in a shower.

First, though, I opened Mum's bedroom door and poked my head inside; she was still out like a light. Next, I tiptoed to the top of the stairs, and listened for any movement below. It was silent except for the ticking of that awful clock in the hall. At least Rob was getting some sleep.

I couldn't remember the last time I'd taken a bath, and it turned out to be much more relaxing than my usual three-minute shower. So much so, in fact, that I topped up the hot water a couple of times, so I wouldn't have to get out.

Eventually, I had to make a move, or I would have shrivelled up like a prune. I'd just stepped out of the bath and grabbed the towel when the door opened, and Rob stepped inside.

"Get out!" I clutched the towel to my body for dear life.

"Sorry, but the door wasn't locked."

"There isn't a lock."

"Who doesn't have a lock on their bathroom door?"

"My mum doesn't. Are you going to get out or do I have to kick you out?"

He grinned. "You have lovely feet."

"Get out!"

Incredibly, Mum hadn't heard my little outburst and was still fast asleep. Rob had disappeared into the bathroom as soon as I'd done in there. After I'd dressed, I headed downstairs and checked the cupboards to see what there was for breakfast. I was still trying to decide between cornflakes or scrambled eggs on toast when Rob made an appearance—his hair was still wet.

"There isn't a shower in there."

"Ten out of ten for observation."

"Who doesn't have a shower?"

"The same person who doesn't have a lock on the door. Mum doesn't believe in them: showers or locks."

"I can see where you get your quirkiness from."

"Did you sleep okay on the sofa?"

"Like a log."

"Do you want breakfast?"

"Is there any muesli?"

"In this house?" I laughed. "My mum wouldn't allow it through the door. We have cornflakes or toast."

"Any jam?"

"I'll check. Yes, there's strawberry or strawberry."

"Toast with strawberry jam sounds great. How's your mum? Have you checked on her yet?"

"Still dead to the world."

"Sleep is probably the best thing for her. Why don't you brew the tea and I'll make the toast?"

"Do you know how?"

"You have a remarkably low opinion of me, don't you?" He grinned.

"I just figured that you've probably always had someone who did that sort of stuff for you?"

"Like a sexy maid?"

"Just make the tea."

Ten minutes later, we were both tucking into strawberry jam on hot, buttery toast.

"What time are you going back?" I asked.

"As soon as I've finished breakfast. I'll need to call in at the hotel to get changed before I go to the exhibition."

"I really do appreciate you bringing me here last night."

"Enough to do away with that silly pact to wait for one year before we go on a date?"

"No."

"You're a hard woman."

"I've explained the reason for the wait. I have to prove myself at work first."

"Fair enough, but before I go, there's something I want to show you."

"What?"

"Come with me." He held out his hand.

"Where are we going?"

"Just for once, will you do as I ask without a million questions?"

"Okay." I took his hand, and he led the way upstairs, stopping outside the door to my old bedroom. "What are you doing?"

"I told you, there's something I want you to see." He took hold of the door handle.

"Rob, no! I can't go in there."

"It's going to be okay." He pushed open the door.

"Why are you doing this to me?" The tears began to well in my eyes.

He pulled me gently into the room. "Look at the bed."

"I can't." I closed my eyes tight shut.

"Mo, please. Will you please trust me and open your eyes."

All my instincts were telling me to turn around and run out of the room, but instead I opened my eyes and stared at the bed.

"What are those?"

"What do they look like?"

"Photos."

There were about a dozen of them lined up across the bed. Rob picked up the first one and held it out for me to see. "Tell me about this one."

I studied the photo that I hadn't seen in more than a decade.

"I was poorly. Flu, I think. Dad was trying to make me laugh by wearing that stupid green wig."

"It looks like it worked."

"Yeah, it did. I was trying my hardest not to laugh at him, but I couldn't help myself."

"Who took the photo?"

"Mum. She took all the photos. Where did you get all of these from?"

"When I told you that I'd slept like a log, I lied. That sofa is full of lumps."

"You should have let me sleep downstairs."

"While I was lying there, wide awake, I noticed all the photo albums on the bookshelf, so I took a look through them."

"Without asking permission?"

"Who was I supposed to ask? You and your mother were dead to the world."

"Why did you choose these particular ones?"

"Look at that photo again. Where was it taken?"

"In this room."

"Look at the others."

I picked up each one in turn. Every one of them had been taken in that room.

"That's Christmas day." I smiled. "Zoe and I used to take turns opening our presents. She would open hers in her bedroom while we all watched and then I'd do the same in here."

"That shows remarkable restraint on your part. Most kids would want to get stuck into opening their own presents straight away."

"You said I was quirky."

"That's true."

"What's going on in this one?" Rob held up another one of the photos.

"That's when me and Zoe both decided to dye our hair for the first time. Mum wasn't thrilled but Dad thought it was great, and he insisted Mum take a photo of him with us."

"Seems like he was a bit of a character, your dad."

"He was. He was the best." As I looked at each of the photos, the memories came flooding back. Happy memories, every one of them. "I still don't understand why you did this."

"I thought that seeing them might bring back the good memories you shared in this room. I suppose I was hoping it might help to dispel the bad memories that have been haunting you. I'm sorry if I've made things worse."

"You haven't. I needed to see these. We did have some great times in here. I'd just forgotten about them because of what happened at the end."

"This is just a thought, but why don't you make a

collage of these photos? You could frame it and hang it above the bed. That way, every time you come into this room, you can focus on them. On the good times you had with your dad in here."

I took his hand. "Thank you for doing this."

"No problem."

"But Mum will probably kill you when she finds out you've been ripping photos out of her album."

"In that case, I'd better get going before she wakes up." He grinned. "I do have one question before I go, though."

"If it's about the no-date pact, it still stands."

"It wasn't. I wanted to ask you why the bird cage in the living room has a framed photo of a budgie in it."

"That's Timmy." I laughed. "He was supposed to be mine and Zoe's pet, but we soon got bored with him. Mum loved that little bird to bits. When he died, she wanted to have him stuffed, but we all managed to persuade her that was a terrible idea. As a compromise, she decided to keep his framed photo in the cage where he used to live."

"How long ago did the budgie die?"

"It must be at least fifteen years ago now."

"O—kay. And on that crazy note, I'll get back to Manchester."

"I'm not sure when I'll be back at work."

"Don't worry about it. Take as long as you need."

"Okay. And, Rob, thanks again."

"All part of the service."

I was still sitting on the bed, going through the photos, when Mum hobbled into the room.

"That's where you are. I thought you'd all deserted

me."

"Sorry. I didn't hear you get up."

"What are those you're looking at?"

"Photos of me and Dad in this room."

"Let me see." She sat down on the bed next to me, and I handed them to her one at a time. "I remember that one." She laughed. "That was when we'd just come back from our holidays. You and Zoe insisted on bringing home those silly toy donkeys."

"I loved that donkey. Whatever happened to it?"

"I threw them both out after you and Zoe had moved out. When did you take these photos out of the albums?"

"I didn't. Rob did."

"What was he doing looking through our photographs?"

"He couldn't get to sleep on the sofa, so he looked through the albums."

"I thought he was supposed to be sleeping in Zoe's room?"

I spent the next few minutes, telling Mum about the problem I'd had going into my old bedroom, and how I'd been haunted by the memories of Dad's final days in there.

"I'm so sorry, Mo."

"What for?"

"I should never have suggested your dad move into your room. It was just that with all the fitted furniture in our bedroom, there wasn't enough room for all the stuff he needed."

"I knew why you did it, and I didn't mind, honestly. It's just that whenever I come in here now, it all comes flooding back."

"I still don't understand why Rob took these photos out of the album."

"He thought they would help to bring back happy memories I'd shared with Dad in this room, and that it might help me to forget the bad ones."

"Has it worked?"

"I think so. The fact I'm still in here with you now kind of proves that. He suggested we could make some kind of collage with these, frame it and hang it above the bed."

"That's a brilliant idea. That guy of yours isn't just a looker, he's smart too."

"He's not my guy."

"Not yet, but I have a feeling he will be soon."

"How are you, anyway?"

"My ankle is still painful when I walk, but I think it's improving. Slowly."

"Good. What would you like for breakfast?"

"A couple of slices of buttery toast would go down a treat. That's if you've learned how to make it without burning it."

"I'll have you know my toast is second to none now."

"Good. Before you go downstairs, I just want to say that I'm really happy you told me what's been bothering you these last few years. I just wish you'd told me before. I thought I'd done something to upset you."

"Don't be silly. You've always been there for me."

"Does this mean you'll be visiting us more often?"

"When I can, yeah, but I'm going to be busy with the new job for a while."

"Just don't be a stranger."

"I won't. I promise."

While Mum was eating her toast, which she conceded had improved a little since I'd last made it for her, I gave Beth a call.

"How's Manchester?" she asked. "Or more to the point, how's Rob?"

"I'm not in Manchester. I'm at my mum's house."

"What's wrong?"

"She had a bit of a fall. She's okay, but I'm going to stay with her for a few days."

"What about the exhibition?"

"It's okay. I cleared it with Rob. He said I can stay here as long as I need to."

"He seems like a solid guy."

"He is. He drove me over here."

"Did he now?"

"I might as well tell you because, knowing you, you'll find out anyway. He stayed over and went back this morning."

"This is getting juicier by the minute. I hope you two didn't wake your mum up."

"Not that it's any of your business, but he slept downstairs on the sofa, and I slept in Zoe's old room."

"And he didn't creep up to join you in the night?"

"No, he didn't. He's not like that."

"You've changed your tune. It's not five minutes since you couldn't bear the sight of the guy, and now you're sticking up for him. He's getting to you, isn't he?"

"Don't be ridiculous. Look, I'd better get going because I need to help Mum with her bath."

"When will you be back?"

"I'm not sure. I'll keep you posted."

"Just a heads-up. Russell will be staying the weekend,

and he definitely *won't* be sleeping on the sofa."

Chapter 24

About three months later.

"Happy birthday to you, happy birthday to you." Beth jumped onto my bed. "Happy birthday dear Maureen, happy birthday to you."

"*Maureen*?"

"It has two syllables and sounds better than *Mo-oh*. Come on, open your cards." She dropped them onto my bed.

"It's Sunday. I was planning to have a lie-in."

"It's almost eleven o'clock. I would call that a lie-in."

I picked up the cards. "That's from Carol. That one's from Jen. That's from you—"

"How did you know? I tried really hard to disguise my handwriting this year."

"Because no one else in the world does their Js like that. That's from Mand, and that one is Nicky's. That's from my mum and that's from Zoe." I was left holding two cards. "Who are these from?"

"Here's a crazy idea. Why don't you open them and find out?"

I tore open the smaller of the two. "It's from Toby. Did you tell him it was my birthday?"

"I didn't. It was probably Carol."

"Are those two still in touch with one another?"

"Yeah, she's popped over to see me a couple of times recently. When she leaves, she always nips across the way, to say hello to Toby. And she's always in there an awfully long time. Just saying."

"You're not suggesting there's anything going on with

those two, are you?"

"I'm not suggesting anything, but I do know she's regretting moving into that house share, so maybe's she's missing chez-Toby."

"How come I don't know any of this?"

"Because you're hardly ever here. You work until all hours of the night. I don't know why you put up with it."

"No one forces me to do it. I'm just really into what I'm doing at the moment."

"Would that be Rob that you're *doing*?"

"No, it wouldn't. I barely ever see him."

"Are you going to open that other card or not? I'm dying to know who it's from."

"Okay." I tore open the flap. "How dare he?"

"How dare *who* do *what*? Who's it from?"

"Rob."

"The guy that you barely ever see? Let me have a look."

"No." I pulled my hand back so she couldn't reach the card.

"What's really going on with the two of you?"

"Nothing. We just exchange the occasional '*hi*' when we bump into one another in the corridor or the lift."

"In the lift, eh?" She grinned. "Get stuck between floors, did you?"

"Watch my lips. Nothing. Is. Going. On."

"Hmm, and yet he obviously still has the hots for you."

"This is an outright liberty, that's what it is."

"Sending you a birthday card? That's harsh, even by your standards."

"How did he know it was my birthday? That's what I'd like to know."

"Perhaps someone told him."

"Or he's been reading my personnel file."

"You can't possibly know that."

"It's obvious that's what's happened. It's an invasion of privacy. It's probably against the Data Protection Act too."

"It's *a birthday card*. What does he say in it?"

"None of your business."

I put Rob's card in the top drawer of my bedside cabinet while I opened the others. The ones from the girls were all jokey as usual. Zoe's was too. But the one from my mum brought tears to my eyes. She wrote that it was good to have her younger daughter *back again*."

"You're not going to get all sentimental on me, are you?" Beth was still seated on my bed. "You're supposed to be happy on your birthday."

"I am happy, and particularly because it's fallen on a Sunday this year. I plan to have a quiet, lazy day while eating chocolate and drinking—"

"Wine?"

"Coke."

"Did I mention that I've asked all the guys to come over."

"No, you didn't. Why would you do that?"

"Because you refused point blank to go out anywhere this weekend, even though I put off Russell especially."

"Which I told you not to do."

"It'll do us good to have one weekend apart."

Russell and Beth had seen each other practically every weekend since they'd first met. One week he came down to London, the next she went up to his place. I'd expected the relationship to last no more than a couple of weeks at the most, but it was still going strong. Last week, they'd gone to the infamous engagement party for Beth's boss,

Leroy, and Deborah. Although Beth had never come out and said it, I was sure she was hoping that event might give Russell ideas, but so far there had been no announcement.

"So much for my quiet, lazy day." I sighed. "What time are they coming over?"

"Midday. I've ordered pizza for us all."

"I haven't even had breakfast yet."

"You'd better get showered and dressed. The pizza can be your breakfast."

When Beth had left my bedroom, I took Rob's card out of the drawer and reread what he'd written.

Happy Birthday, Mo.

Only nine months now until the end of our no dating pact. I'm counting the days, and I'm sure you are too.

Love

Rob

xx

Love? Was that the way he signed all of his greeting cards? And what was with the *xx*? And how dare he assume I was counting the days? Pah. As if. But none of that was important. I was too riled at the audacity of him looking in my personnel file, and when I was back at the office on Monday, I planned to tell him so in no uncertain terms.

All the gang, except Nicky, arrived together.

"Where's the wine?" Jen demanded.

"Coming up." Beth headed for the kitchen. "Mind you, this one refuses to drink anything but Coke."

"Come on, Mo," Carol said. "You have to have a real

drink on your birthday."

"No, thanks. You lot feel free, though."

Beth had just poured everyone except me a glass of wine when there was a knock on the door, and Nicky shouted. "It's only me."

"Come in."

She walked in, carrying a gift-wrapped present.

"What's that?" Beth snapped.

"It's for Mo."

"Have you forgotten our *no birthday gifts* pact?"

A couple of years earlier, the five of us had all agreed that we wouldn't buy each other birthday presents. The agreement was that we would only give one another cards.

"I didn't forget, but I saw this and I knew that Mo would love it." She handed me the present.

"Thanks, but you really shouldn't have." As soon as the gift-wrap was off, and I saw the box, I knew it must have cost a small fortune.

"What do you think?" Nicky said.

"It's lovely." I wrapped the knitted scarf around my neck.

"It matches your hair."

"I thought you'd turned over a new leaf, Nick," Beth said. "And you were going to watch the pennies. What happened to that?"

"Aren't all your credit cards already maxed out?" Jen chipped in.

"It's okay. I've paid them all off. I've paid off my overdraft too."

"Pull the other one," Beth scoffed.

"It's true."

"And how did you manage that?"

"I won the lottery."

We all laughed.

"Yeah, sure," Beth said.

"It's true, honestly. Not the big jackpot. I only won twenty-two grand."

"I'm not sure which I find the hardest to believe," Mand said. "That you won the lottery, or that if you did, you used the money to pay off your debts, instead of going on a spending spree."

"I knew you lot wouldn't believe me." She opened her handbag and took out several sheets of paper. "That's why I brought these." She handed them to Beth who glanced at each one with growing incredulity.

"She's telling the truth." Beth passed the credit card and bank statements to Jen who looked just as shocked.

By the time we'd all seen them, there was no doubt that Nicky had paid off all her debts.

"You're such a jammy sod," Beth said. "I've never won a penny on the lottery."

"That's because you don't do it," I quipped. "I say we make a toast to Nicky."

"To Nicky." Everyone clinked their glasses together.

"How's the new job going, Mo?" Mand asked.

"I'm really enjoying it, but it's my three-month assessment on Tuesday, and I'm bricking it. If they decide not to keep me on, I don't know what I'll do."

"That's not likely to happen, is it?" Jen asked.

"I hope not."

"She's worrying about nothing," Beth said. "The big boss sent her a birthday card."

"Let's see it, Mo," Carol said.

"There's nothing to see. It's just a standard card. His assistant probably sends one to all the staff."

"I bet they aren't all signed *Love Rob,* with two kisses, though." Beth laughed.

"How do you—you read it, didn't you?"

"Of course I read it. While you were in the shower. What did you expect?"

"*Love Rob*?" Nicky grinned. "Is there something you're not telling us, Mo?"

"I'll tell you the same thing I told Beth earlier. Nothing. Is. Going. On. Now, can we please change the subject?"

"What was that app you were working on at the place you used to work, Mo?" Carol said.

"I worked on quite a few while I was at Headrow."

"I mean the one you were doing for yourself. The one that got you fired."

"It was called Study-Ant."

"What did it do?"

"It was designed to let students buddy up with other students to work and revise together."

"That's what I thought. My sister is reading law at Reading university. She mentioned that she was using an app that did something similar to that. I thought about you when she told me. It's a pity you didn't get the chance to finish yours."

"Really? I wouldn't mind checking that out. I don't suppose you remember what it's called, do you?"

"No, sorry, but I can ask Janet if you like?"

"Yeah, please."

She made a call, but it went to voicemail, so Carol promised to let me know when she'd managed to get hold of her sister.

"Hey, Jen," I said. "How are you settling into your new place?"

"It's fantastic. We couldn't be happier, thanks to Mand."

Jen was renting Mand's mother's old house. And, although I wasn't privy to the details, I was pretty sure the rent was considerably below the going market rate.

"How's Pete doing in his new job?" Beth asked.

"He loves it. With a bit of luck, we should be able to start looking for somewhere to buy in another six months. But do you know what the best part is?"

"No in-laws?"

"Got it in one. I can put the dishes in whichever cupboard I like. And no one is following me around, picking up my cups of tea before I've finished with them. It's heaven."

It was almost six o'clock when the gang finally called it a day and went home, but not before we'd had the second takeaway of the day.

"I almost forgot," Beth said, once we were alone. "I bought you a cake, Mo."

"I can't eat another thing. I'm fit to burst."

"You have to have some cake."

"Just a really small slice, then."

While Beth was cutting it, Carol called.

"Mo, I've just heard back from Janet. That app she's been using is called Ztudy."

"How do you spell that?"

"It's study, but with a Z instead of the S."

"Oh, okay, thanks." And people thought the name of my app was weird.

I brought up the app store and searched for it by name.

It took only a matter of seconds to download. I then spent the next thirty minutes playing around with it, and getting progressively angrier and angrier until finally, I could take no more.

I threw my phone across the room, onto the armchair opposite, and screamed, "The thieves!"

"What's wrong?" Beth looked at me as though I'd lost my mind.

"It's the app that Carol's sister has been using."

"What about it?"

"It's mine."

Chapter 25

I'd managed less than an hour's sleep, and that was on the sofa. I'd spent most of the night going through the copycat app's various functions and comparing them to Study-Ant. Although I no longer had access to the code, I still knew my app like the back of my hand.

"Didn't you go to bed?" Beth yawned.

"There would have been no point. I wouldn't have slept."

"Have they ripped you off?"

"No question. They've made a few tweaks, mainly to the display, but otherwise this is my app."

"Who's *they*?"

"They call themselves LockGrid. I've tried searching for them, but I can only find the bare bones of info."

"What are you going to do?"

"I honestly don't know, but there's no way I'm going to take this lying down."

***

"Are you okay, Mo?" Hannah leaned over towards me from her desk.

"I'm fine."

"You look like I do when I've had a heavy night at Jesters."

"I didn't sleep very well."

"You're not worrying about tomorrow's assessment, are you? It's just a formality."

"You can't know that for sure. What if they decide they don't like my work? Or that I'm too quick to express my opinions? Or—"

"You're fretting about nothing. Your work is as good as anyone in the department, better than most. And, yeah, you can be a bit outspoken in meetings, but what you say usually makes sense."

"Only *usually*?"

"I only said that because I don't want you to get big-headed."

"Who carries out the assessments, anyway?"

"It'll be Chelsea and someone from HR."

"In that case, I'm doomed. People who work in HR have always hated me. It was the same at Headrow."

"You're just being ridiculous now."

"I really need a coffee to get me going, but I'm not drinking that slop from the machines. I think I'll take a walk over to Bean Shack. Do you want anything?"

"No, thanks. I've had my coffee infusion for the morning."

I had no qualms about nipping out to the coffee shop. Everyone did it, and besides, I'd banked so many additional hours by working late, that they owed me about a week.

"Look who it isn't." Jed greeted me with his customary smile.

"Hey, Jed. Are you on your own today?"

"Only for the next twenty minutes. Liz is coming in to help."

"Are you shorthanded again?"

"I'm afraid so. My latest recruit, Charlie, suddenly decided to take off and hike around Australia for a year. I don't suppose you'd like your old job back, would you?"

Before I could respond, a voice from behind me said, "Hands off. She already has a job." I turned around to see Rob sitting there. "I'll get the young lady's drink. Would you bring it over, please, Jed?"

"Sure, no problem."

"I have to get back to work," I protested.

"Judging by your eyes, you'll not be doing much work today." Rob grinned. "Come and sit down or I'll tell your boss you've been skiving."

"I'm not skiving." I took the seat opposite him. "I've banked tons of extra hours."

"Relax, I'm only joking. You do look a little rough, though. I assume you were out last night, celebrating your birthday?"

"Then you assume wrong. I stayed in all yesterday and all of last night."

"Why would you stay in on your birthday? If I'd known you had no one to go out with, I would have taken you somewhere."

"You make me sound like Billy-no-mates. I'll have you know I had a party at my place."

"I didn't get the invitation."

"There you are, Mo." Jed put my coffee on the table. "Enjoy."

"Thanks." I waited until he was back behind the counter and then let fly at Rob. "That's because I didn't send you one. I also didn't give you permission to go nosing through my personnel file."

"What?"

"You heard me. Just because you're the CEO doesn't give you the right to access my file."

"It doesn't, you're right. And I didn't."

"So how did you know it was my birthday, then?"

"Is that what this is all about?" He shook his head. "I called your mother and asked her when it was."

"You couldn't have. You don't know her number."

"I figured she might still have a landline, so I checked directory enquiries, and there it was: Mrs S Jackson. I have to say, she seemed very pleased to hear from me, and she even asked when I'd be going to visit her again."

"I hope you told her never."

"I said it would probably be about another nine months or so."

"In your dreams."

"This is the part where you apologise."

"For what?"

"Accusing me of looking through your personnel file."

"Right. Yeah."

"I didn't hear an apology."

"I'm sorry, okay?"

"Did you like my card?"

I shrugged. "I received so many that I can barely remember it."

"I knew it. You loved it. I wasn't sure whether to include two kisses or three."

"Is that what they were supposed to be? I thought you'd just written random letters on the bottom."

"Seriously, though, you do look a bit under the weather. Are you feeling okay?"

"I'm fine. I just didn't get much sleep last night because I had stuff on my mind."

"What kind of stuff?"

"It doesn't matter."

"Tell me. I might be able to help."

"Someone has ripped off my app."

"You mean the one that got you fired from your previous place?"

"Yeah. The sister of one of my friends has been using an app that sounded similar to mine. Out of curiosity, I decided to download it, only to find it was basically my app."

"How can you be so sure? There are numerous examples of similar apps available to download." He took out his phone and brought up the app store. "Look, if I search for study aids, it brings up dozens."

"I'm not stupid. I know that, but I also know there are certain—err—quirks, let's call them, about this app that match mine exactly. They're the sort of details that would never appear just by coincidence."

"Okay, let's say you're right. How did whoever is behind this get hold of your code and repurpose it? You told me that it had been lost when you left your previous employer."

"I thought it was, and I have no idea how they did it. I just know that they did."

"What do you want to do about it?"

"I want to find out who's behind this and tear their heads off, but I don't know where to start. I can't find any information about the company behind Ztudy."

"Hold on while I make a phone call."

"Err, okay?"

"William Maker, please. It's Rob Waites. Yes, I'll hold."

"Are you sure you don't want me to go?" I whispered.

He shook his head and continued to hold.

"Bill, do you have any free time later this morning? Eleven? That'll be fine. I'm going to send a young woman named Maureen Jackson to see you. I'd like you to listen to what she has to say and then do your thing. Okay, great. You won't be able to miss her because she has turquoise hair. Yeah, turquoise. Bye."

"What was that all about?" I said.

"Bill Maker is head of the legal firm that handles all of our stuff. No one knows IP law like he does. I want you to go and tell him everything you've just told me."

"I can't afford to pay a high-flying solicitor."

"You won't have to. With the amount of paid work that we put their way, I'm sure I'll be able to convince him to work on this pro-bono. I have to warn you, though, he's a no-nonsense kind of guy. He'll drill you on every aspect of it, and if he doesn't think you have a case, he'll tell you. Okay?"

"I guess so."

"Good. You'd better drink that coffee so you don't fall asleep while you're talking to him."

***

"Mo, what are you doing?" Beth said.

"I'm under the bed."

"I can see that, but what are you doing under there?"

I reverse-shuffled out. "Looking for all my old notebooks. I put them in a box somewhere, but I can't for the life of me remember where I put it."

"I can."

"You can? Where is it?"

"In the bottom of your wardrobe. I saw it there the other day."

"What were you doing in my wardrobe?"

"Don't you mean: *thank you, Beth*?"

"Are you sure it's there? I could have sworn it was under the bed."

"It's under that other box where you keep all the shoes you never wear, but refuse to throw out."

She was right.

"Brilliant." I pulled open the lid, splitting the parcel tape that had bound it shut.

"What do you want those for anyway?"

"My solicitor reckons our chances of winning are slim without my original code, but that I might just have a chance if I can produce all the notes I kept when designing the app."

"Hang on. Just back up a minute. Since when did you have a solicitor?"

"Since this morning. I was with him for over an hour."

"Second question. How are you going to pay him? Those guys charge a fortune just to say good morning to you."

"It isn't going to cost me a penny."

"How come? You haven't offered him some kind of payment-in-kind, have you?

"No, I haven't. He's going to work on my case pro bono because he gets a ton of paid work from Q-Ventures. Rob contacted him for me."

"Did he now?" She grinned. "So, it's Rob that you've offered a payment-in-kind."

"He did it as a favour. I'm sure he would have done the same thing for any of his employees."

"Yeah, right. That guy is obviously crazy about you, but I can't imagine why."

"Gee, thanks."

"I didn't mean it like that. I meant why would he keep coming back when you treat him like dirt."

"I don't."

"Yes, you do. How long has he been asking you to go out on a date with him now? It must be months."

"It's three months, but the arrangement was that I wouldn't date him until I'd been at Q-Ventures for a year."

"Can you hear yourself? The *arrangement*? Who comes up with something like that?"

"It was my idea."

"I didn't think it was Rob's. What I don't get is why."

"I've explained all of this before. I need to prove myself in the job first."

"That's rubbish. You're a coding superstar."

"Who says so?"

"You do. You're always telling me."

"It's my three-month assessment tomorrow. They might give me my marching orders."

"And I might get a phone call asking me to appear on the front cover of Vogue, but both of those things are extremely unlikely. So, what's the real reason that you continue to put him off?"

Although I was angry at Beth for having a go at me, what she said had more than a kernel of truth in it. We both sat on the bed and before I knew what I was doing, I had opened up to her.

"It's Adam."

"Don't tell me you're still carrying a torch for that loser?"

"No, of course not. I know it's over."

"What, then?"

"I really did think he was the one. That's the only reason I asked him to move in with me. I trusted him one-hundred percent, and it never occurred to me that he might—"

"Cheat on you?"

"I was devastated when I found out."

"I know. I can remember the state you were in. If I'd got my hands on him that day, he'd have been sorry."

"I can't bear the thought of going through that pain again."

"I can understand that, but we're just talking about a date here. It's not like Rob is asking you to move in with him, or to get engaged. Why not just give him a chance and see where it goes? Think of it this way, the alternative is to die a lonely spinster."

"That has a certain appeal."

"No, it doesn't. You like him, so give him a chance."

"Who says I like him?"

"I do. It's absolutely obvious. Don't you?"

"I—err—"

"Mo!"

"Yes, okay, I like him."

"What are you going to do about it?"

"Don't rush me, I'm thinking."

"What is there to think about?"

"Okay. I'll tell him that the arrangement is cancelled forthwith."

"*Forthwith*? You've definitely been spending too long around solicitors."

Chapter 26

"You haven't changed your mind, have you?" Beth said while I was eating dry cornflakes for breakfast because we'd somehow managed to run out of milk *again*.

"About what?"

"Telling Rob that you're scrapping that stupid arrangement and that you'll go on a date with him."

"I can't think about that right now. I've got my assessment this morning, so I might not have a job come lunchtime."

"You'd better tell him, or I will."

"Don't you dare. I'll do it, but not until I've got my assessment out of the way."

"Are we going out to celebrate tonight?"

"Celebrate what?"

"You getting through your assessment with flying colours."

"Now you've really gone and jinxed it."

***

"You're worrying about nothing, Mo," Hannah said.

"I wish everyone would stop telling me that. Anything could happen in the assessment."

"Have you talked to Chelsea?"

"No, I daren't. I'm scared of what she might say. In fact, I'm sure she was avoiding eye-contact with me all of yesterday."

"You really are paranoid, aren't you?"

"Maybe, but that doesn't mean they aren't out to fire me."

I might as well not have been there for those first two hours because I couldn't concentrate on what I was supposed to be working on. I kept having visions of being marched back to my desk by security, cardboard box in hand.

"Mo, they want you up in HR now. Room 413."

"Four *thirteen*? That's not a good omen."

"Good luck. Not that you'll need it."

This was it. The moment of truth. I knocked on the door, and a woman's voice from inside told me to enter. I didn't recognise her, but then I'd met very few people in HR. She introduced herself as Ruth Churchill, and she asked me to take a seat. To her right was Chelsea who looked as serious as I'd ever seen her. That didn't bode well.

"Is it Maureen or Mo?" Ruth said.

"Mo."

"How do you feel your first three months at Q-Ventures have gone?"

"I—err—" What was the point of that question? It didn't matter a fig how I thought it had gone. "I think it's gone well." I glanced over at Chelsea in the hope that she might show some kind of sign that she agreed with my assessment. Just a nod would have done. But I got nothing.

Ruth continued. "In this assessment, we rely very heavily on the feedback we get from your team leader." She gestured to Chelsea. "She's the one who is best placed to judge the quality of your work and how well you've slotted into the organisation."

"Right."

This is the point where she says that I've failed on both counts.

"And I'm very pleased to tell you that the feedback we've received is excellent."

Excellent? Did she just say excellent? I glanced across at Chelsea who was now beaming. Had she been trying to wind me up? If so, she'd certainly succeeded. Not that it mattered now. They thought I was excellent.

"We are very pleased to confirm that your employment status with this company is now confirmed as permanent. That means, amongst other things, that you will be entitled to join the pension and medical schemes."

"Thanks." I was so thrilled that I almost climbed across the desk and hugged them both, but I figured that might not be deemed an acceptable response.

"A couple of other points before you go back to your desk, Mo," Ruth said.

"Okay."

"At Q-Ventures, we believe in rewarding those employees who contribute most to the business. Those who go above and beyond the call of duty. From your assessment, it's obvious that so far you meet those criteria. If you continue to maintain the high standards you've set so far, we will move you up to the next pay-grade in six months' time."

"That's great. Thanks."

"And finally, it's customary for all new employees to attend the Q-Trials as soon as possible after they pass their three-month assessment."

"Right. Err, what is that?"

"It's a team-building weekend. We run them four times a year. They're lots of fun. I'm sure you'll enjoy it."

I wasn't so sure, but I was too thrilled at having been made a permanent employee, with the prospect of a pay rise in only six months, to care about that.

Hannah didn't have to ask how the assessment had gone because it was written all over my face.

"I told you there was nothing to worry about, didn't I?" She grinned. "Will you relax now?"

"Yeah. Sorry if I've been a bit tetchy."

"Don't worry about it. You can buy me a coffee later to make up for it."

"Will do. They mentioned something called Q-Trials. What's that all about?"

"Oh dear." She pulled a sour face.

"What do you mean, *oh dear*?"

"It's about the only time I've thought about leaving the company."

"I don't like the sound of that."

"It's probably not as bad as I remember."

"Tell me."

"Someone high up in the organisation came up with the idea. Someone on the sixth floor, no doubt. It's supposed to build team-spirit, but I'm not convinced."

"Yes, but what is it, exactly?"

"It's run on an old army base somewhere in the middle of nowhere."

"An *army* base?"

"Yeah. It isn't one now. It's been taken over by some commercial organisation, manned by sadists."

"What sort of thing do you do there?"

"Assault courses, zip lines, abseiling, and lots of other muddy, dangerous stuff."

"That sounds awful. Is there some way of getting out of it?"

"Not a chance. The management take this rubbish really seriously. Everyone has to go there once every three years. I've been on two of them now."

"Oh well." I sighed. "They said they're only four times a year, so hopefully it won't be for ages."

"They always put the dates on the company's intranet calendar. Let me have a look." She tapped away on her computer, then sat back in her chair. "Oh dear."

"What?"

"The next one is this weekend."

When Chelsea returned to the office, she confirmed that I would indeed be heading to Q-Trials that Saturday, but even the prospect of a weekend spent climbing walls and getting covered in mud wasn't enough to dampen my spirits. My position at Q-Ventures was now permanent—that's all I cared about.

With the ordeal of the assessment behind me, there was one more thing I needed to do. I was going to tell Rob that the silly no-dating arrangement could be scrapped, and that he could take me on a date if he still wanted to.

It was clear that Beverly, his PA, remembered me from my previous visit because she pushed her chair back from the desk, and looked ready to make a run for it. Behind her, the office was empty, but it was midday, so I figured Rob was probably on his lunchbreak.

"Hi. I was hoping to have a quick word with Rob. Is he at lunch?"

"Mr Waites isn't in at all this week."

"Oh? When will he be back?"

"Next Monday."

"Right, okay, thanks." I almost asked where he was, but I figured that it wasn't any of my business.

On my way back to my desk, I reflected that it was probably for the best that Rob was away this week. He might have suggested we go out at the weekend, but I would be at Q-Trials. I resolved to go and see him first thing the following Monday.

***

"We have to go out and celebrate." Beth was always quick to latch onto any excuse for a night out.

"I'm not going out on a Tuesday."

"You have to celebrate being made permanent."

"I'm going to, with a cup of tea and a bun. I bought us both one on the way home."

"I suppose I'll have to settle for that. Did you go and see Rob?"

"I tried."

"Don't tell me you lost your nerve?"

"No. He isn't in all week, so I'll tell him next Monday."

"You'd better not change your mind between now and then."

"I won't. It wasn't all good news today, though."

"What happened?"

"I discovered I have to go on some kind of team-building thing this weekend."

"That's not so bad. I went on one a few years ago at a luxury spa."

"Something tells me this one will be a different kettle of fish. It's at an ex-army base. According to Hannah, there's an assault course."

"Oh dear." She laughed. "Can I come and take photos?"

"I'm glad you think it's funny. Who comes up with these stupid ideas?"

"It was probably Rob. You said he worked out every day, didn't you? It's just the sort of thing those sporty types would come up with."

"I hadn't thought of that, but you could be right."

"There is one positive about your weekend away, though."

"What's that?"

"Russell and I will have the place to ourselves."

My phone rang; it was my mother.

"You said you'd call to let me know how your assessment went."

"Sorry, it's been manic here. It's good news, they're keeping me on."

"I'm really pleased for you, Mo. You must be thrilled."

"I really am."

"While I've got you, I wanted to remind you about my birthday party, the weekend after next."

"It's in my diary. In big red letters."

"Will you be bringing Rob?"

"I wouldn't think so."

"Are you still playing hard to get with that poor boy? He won't wait forever you know."

"It's complicated."

"Your life always is. I know you rarely listen to anything I have to say, but please take this one piece of advice. If you like him as much as I think you do, don't let him go. If you do, you might regret it for a very long time."

"I—err—"

"There's no need to say anything. Just think about what I said and do the right thing."

"Okay, Mum."

"And well done again on your assessment. I'll ring Zoe and let her know. She'll be thrilled for you too."

Chapter 27

The next morning, Beth was busy tidying the place, ready for Russell's arrival later that day.

"How come you never do that during the week?" I said.

"How come *you* don't?"

"By the time I get home from work, I'm too tired to do housework."

"Ditto. Do you think we should hire a cleaner?"

"I'd be embarrassed to ask someone to clean this little place. What would they think of us?"

"That we're busy professional women?"

"Or lazy slobs. Anyway, I'd better get going or I'll miss the bus."

"I thought you'd be taking the train."

"I wish. The team-building place is somewhere out in the wilds. Some people are making their way there by car, but there's a mini-bus for the rest of us."

"I hope you have fun."

"Somehow, I doubt that."

I was just on my way out when I bumped into Carol, suitcases in hand.

"Morning, Mo." She put them both down.

"Morning. What's—" I left the question hanging there and glanced at the suitcases.

"I'm moving back in with Toby for a while."

"How come?"

"That house share was a big mistake. The place is poky, and the people I was sharing with are obnoxious. Luckily for me, Toby hasn't found himself a flatmate yet, so he said I could stay here until I find somewhere else."

"Why don't you just move in with him permanently?"

"You don't think that me and Toby are an item, do you?"

"I wasn't suggesting that. I just meant that he's looking for a permanent flatmate, so why shouldn't it be you?"

"I'm not sure I could ever get used to the commute. I'm still hoping I'll find something more central."

Toby must have been keeping a lookout for Carol because he opened the door before we reached it.

"Let me take those." He picked up the cases.

"Carol tells me she's moving back in with you again. You're a sly one."

"No." He blustered, blushing in the process. "It's not like—"

"Ignore her, Toby," Carol said. "I've told Mo why I'm moving back here. She's just winding you up."

"Oh right. I'll take these through to your room."

"I'd better get going," I said. "I hope you two are very happy together."

***

It was a three-hour bus journey to the team-building centre, which was in a place that might as well have been called The Backend of Nowhere. The majority of people must have decided to make their own way there because there were only five of us on the mini-bus. Before we set off, everyone introduced themselves. For me and two of the others it was our first team-building event. The other two, Matt and Julie, had been at the company for over three years, so had been on one of these jaunts before.

"Has anyone ever been badly injured?" I said.

"At Q-Trials?" Matt laughed. "I highly doubt it. Hungover, possibly."

"It all sounds a bit dangerous to me. Assault courses, abseiling."

"*Assault courses*?" He looked at me like I'd lost my mind.

"Who told you there was abseiling?" asked Julie.

"Hannah who works—" And that's when the penny dropped. I should have realised that Hannah loved winding people up, and this was just the sort of thing that would have her chuckling away to herself. "I take it I've been fed some duff info."

"Sounds like it," Matt said. "The weather up there is a bit grim, but the exercises themselves are all pretty tame.

"What sort of things will we be doing?"

"Axe throwing."

"*Axe throwing*? I thought you said it was tame."

"It's not like we throw them at one another." He laughed. "There's also knot tying, a scavenger hunt, tug of war, and paintball."

"That doesn't sound too terrible. What are the barracks like?"

"We don't stay in barracks," Julie said. "I think you may have got the wrong end of the stick."

"I assumed because it's an old army camp, that's where we'd be staying."

"The site has been completely renovated. Think Premier Inn or Travelodge."

"We get our own rooms?"

"Yeah, all en-suite."

"This is beginning to sound better and better. What about meals?"

"You have to make those over an open fire," Matt said.

"Oh."

"He's joking. There's a restaurant on site."

Suddenly, I felt a whole lot better about the weekend ahead. Hannah, though, would be in for it when I got back to the office.

***

After settling into my room, which was at least as good as any of the budget-priced hotels I'd stayed in, I took a quick look at the information pack that we'd each been given. In there, was a list of the various activities we'd be undertaking, a map/floorplan of the site and a sheet giving health and safety information. In addition, there were two typewritten sheets, which related specifically to our visit. We'd been divided into two teams: team Q and team V, who would compete against each other over the course of Sunday. On the second sheet were the names of the people in each team. I picked out my name as a member of team V, but then did a double take when I saw the name of the team captain of team Q. It was Rob. I hadn't had a chance to speak to him all week because he'd been out of the office, and it had never occurred to me that he might be taking part in the team-building exercise.

He and I were on opposite teams, but that didn't matter because I was sure that no one was going to treat the competition seriously. If I managed to grab a quiet word with him while we were here, I'd tell him that I was prepared to forget about the one-year no-dating agreement.

I was just about to set off to the restaurant for dinner

when Beth called.

"You're not dead yet, then?" She laughed.

"The activities don't start until tomorrow."

"In that case, you'd better make the most of your last day on this planet."

"I don't think it's going to be that bad. The woman I work with was just trying to scare me to death."

"She succeeded. You looked terrified when you set off this morning. What kind of things will you be doing?"

"Axe throwing, paintball, that kind of stuff."

"*Axe throwing*? That sounds plenty dangerous to me."

"I'll be fine. Guess who's captain of the opposing team?"

"Rob."

"How did you know?"

"Who else was I going to say? I don't know anyone else who works there. Are you in the same barracks?"

"That's the other thing. We each have our own room, and they're not bad. All en-suite."

"Sounds more like a pamper session than team-building. Whose room will you be staying in tonight?"

"Mine of course."

"I thought you might be sharing with Rob."

"I haven't seen him yet, and besides, he probably doesn't even know I'm here."

"You know when I said you were naïve? This is a good example of why. Of course he knows. I'd be amazed if he hadn't arranged the whole thing."

"Not everyone is as devious as you, Beth."

"We'll see. Anyway, I'd better dash, Russell is taking me out for dinner."

"Where?"

"Somewhere expensive."

There were two long tables in the dining room. One of them had been designated for team Q, the other for my team. Our team captain, Wendy Dale, who was a senior manager in the finance department, sat at the head of our table, and asked us to introduce ourselves. While we did that, I had one eye on the other table, where all the team members had taken their seats—all except for the team captain. I was just about to lean back in my chair and ask Julie where Rob was when the man himself came hurrying into the dining room.

"Sorry I'm late, team, I had a puncture on my way up here."

I was hoping to make eye contact with him, but he set about making the introductions on their team, and never once looked over at our table. Moments later, the catering staff appeared and began to dish out the starters. We'd all selected our meals using the terminals in our rooms, so there was no hanging around.

The food was basic, but a decent quality. While we were eating, I kept glancing over at the other table, but I still couldn't catch Rob's eye. He was far too busy talking to the members of his team. For dessert, I'd gone for ice cream, but having seen the sticky toffee pudding, I was beginning to regret my choice. And then, in between spoonfuls of ice cream, I glanced again at the other table and this time, our eyes met. Either he was a brilliant actor, or he was genuinely surprised to see me sitting there because he did a double take.

Then he smiled.

"Did you set this up?" I said, as we walked from the restaurant together.

"Your paranoia knows no limits, does it? I had no idea you'd be here."

"I'll believe you this time."

"That's very magnanimous of you. To tell you the truth, I hate these weekends."

"Why run them, then? You're the boss."

"It was Edward who came up with this idea originally."

"You could have canned them after he left."

"I could have, but they seem to work. And, hard as it is to believe, some people actually enjoy them."

"I doubt that anyone would say anything if you didn't take part in them."

"That's not how I work. If everyone else has to suffer through this once every three years, then so do I."

"I came to see you earlier in the week, but you were out of the office."

"I had a series of meetings with our major investors. All very boring. What did you want to see me about?"

"About—err—"

"Your assessment! Of course. Congratulations, I hear you came through with flying colours. But I suppose you're going to tell me off now for asking HR how you did?"

"No, I—"

"Good. I see we're on opposite teams this weekend."

"Looks like it."

"That's a bit of hard luck for you."

"Because I'm not on the same team as you?" I scoffed.

"No. Because you're on the losing team."

"Says who?"

"Says me. I may not like these weekends, but I like losing even less. So, you see, you're doomed to lose."

"We'll see about that."

"We certainly will. How about I walk you to your room?"

"How about you don't? I'll see you on the battlefield tomorrow."

"I look forward to it."

What arrogance. Until that point, I hadn't been taking the competition seriously, but that had all changed now. I was determined that team V would wipe the floor with Rob and his team.

Chapter 28

Beth's phone call had woken me up at half-past six—a full thirty minutes before I'd intended to get up.

"Big news!" she said.

"It had better be. I was fast asleep."

"I saw Toby go out running just now."

"That's your *big* news? He goes out running most mornings."

"Carol was going running with him."

"That doesn't mean they're an item. Maybe Toby just convinced her she should get more exercise."

"Yes, but what kind of exercise?" Beth laughed. "That's what I'd like to know."

"I really can't see it. Toby's a great guy, but Carol's used to something more—err—upmarket."

"*Upmarket*? I can't believe you just said that, Mo."

"It was a bad choice of words, but you know what I mean. Miles is a pig, but he's a minted pig."

"And I'm supposed to be the unromantic one. Talking of going *upmarket*, have you seen Rob yet?"

"Yeah, I saw him at dinner last night."

"Did you tell him about you know what?"

"I was going to until he proceeded to tell me how his team were going to stick it to mine today."

"What's that got to do with you dating him?"

"Nothing, but first I'm going to bring him down a peg or two."

"You're not going to throw an axe at him, are you?"

"Don't go giving me ideas."

Rob intercepted me on the walk between the living

accommodation and the restaurant.

"I suppose you're going to tell me again that your team is going to wipe the floor with mine?" I said.

"No, that's a given. I was going to say that having you here has brightened up this weekend for me."

"You might not feel the same way by the end of the day when team V has won."

"I really do admire your optimism, Mo, but I'm sorry to tell you that's never going to happen."

Who knew that axes were so heavy? I could barely lift the thing up, let alone throw it. We were allowed three throws each and only one of mine actually hit the target, and even then, it didn't stick in. Fortunately, I wasn't the only one who struggled. Only a total of seven people managed to register a score, three on our team and four on the opposition's. After checking the targets and totting up the scores, the adjudicator ruled that team Q had taken the first event. Much to Rob's obvious delight.

The second task was a kind of scavenger hunt. Both teams were given a different set of clues, which they had to use to collect a number of objects from the surrounding countryside. Our team really knocked this one out of the park. We'd solved all our clues, and found all the objects, while the other team were still struggling with their final two clues. This time it was my turn to lord it over Rob who mumbled something about their set of clues being far more difficult.

The scavenger hunt had taken almost two hours to complete, so we had lunch next. Rob barely touched his food because he was too busy giving a pep talk to all the members of his team. I was ravenous and tucked into the sandwiches and fruit.

Lunch over, the next event was as dull as dishwater. We had to produce a series of different knots based on the instructions we'd been handed. I was hopeless at it, which was hardly surprising because it took me all my time to tie my shoelaces. Fortunately, we had a number of ex-scouts on our side, with the result that we wiped the floor with the other team.

Leading by two events to one, we came to the tug of war. Even from just a quick glance, it was obvious that the other team had a size and weight advantage, but Wendy, our team captain assured us that technique was what really mattered.

For this event, we moved to a field behind the restaurant. There had been heavy rain for several days before our arrival, and the ground was wet and extremely slippery. The adjudicator took his position at the centre-point of the rope, waited until everyone had taken their place, and then gave the signal to begin. Almost immediately, I felt myself being pulled forward, and it looked as though it would be over before it had begun. Wendy, who was positioned at the back, shouted words of encouragement, and for a while we rallied, and were able to hold our ground. But then, Rob bellowed out words of encouragement, designed to drive his team on even more. It was hopeless, we were simply no match for them. Moments later, I plunged face-first into the mud. As I got to my knees, a hand appeared in front of my face. I took hold of it and pulled myself to my feet. I'd assumed my rescuer had been one of my team-mates, but it was Rob.

"Are you okay?" he said.

"I'm fine."

"You have mud on your nose. Let me—"

I slapped his hand away. "I said I'm fine."

"I guess that makes it all square," he said. "So, it's all down to the paintball."

"Bring it on."

The adjudicators allowed both teams a forty-five minute break during which we could clean up, grab a snack and discuss tactics ahead of the fifth and deciding event.

The winning team would be the one who 'eliminated' all the opposing team members. Although I'd never played it before, a couple of people on my team had. Matt, who seemed to have the most experience at the game, gave us instructions on the tactics we should employ. Although I listened, and nodded along, I had only one objective in mind: To 'eliminate' Rob. Taking him out of the game was way more important than whether or not our team prevailed. Which, looking back on it now, I realise wasn't really in the spirit of teambuilding. But I still don't care.

The battle was to take part in an area, just outside the main camp, which was thick with trees and bushes. The boundary of the battle-zone was clearly marked with hazard tape. Anyone straying outside that would be considered to have eliminated themselves. We were told, although we couldn't see it, that somewhere in the centre of the area was an old stone building, which we were allowed to use for cover.

Two adjudicators led the teams to opposite ends of the battle-zone, and on the sound of a horn, the game began. In accordance with Matt's instructions, we split up before heading into the trees. I was surprised at just how excited

I was. Nervous too. I was determined that I wouldn't be the first on our team to be eliminated. I moved from one tree to the next like a ninja, looking this way and that for any sign of the enemy. A few minutes into the game, and I still hadn't seen anyone from the opposing team, or for that matter, from mine. I was beginning to worry that I might somehow have strayed outside the battle-zone, although I hadn't seen the hazard tape.

A horn sounded, and the adjudicator announced over a megaphone that team V had one team member 'eliminated'. Before we started, they'd told us that they would keep us informed of progress until the game was declared over. I was just about to make a move to cover of the next tree when I saw James, a member of team Q. He had obviously seen me too because he was headed my way. I ducked back behind the tree and tried to work out what I was going to do. If I didn't move, I would be an easy target, but if I made a run for it, he might still be able to pick me off. I decided to throw myself to the ground and shoot him while he was still approaching. My thinking was that he would be expecting to have to make his shot at chest height. By the time he realised I was on the ground, it would be too late, and I would be able to get off a shot.

There was no time to second guess myself, so I immediately dropped to the ground, but my plan failed miserably because he had covered the ground much quicker than I'd anticipated. When I looked up, I saw him standing over me, grinning. His gun was pointed straight at my back.

"Sorry, Mo, got to do it."

I closed my eyes and braced myself for the impact of the

paint pellet, but instead I heard a thud. When I looked up, James was staring in disbelief at Matt who had just shot him in the back.

"You're dead, mate," Matt grinned behind his visor. "Come on, Mo, let's get out of here."

I didn't need telling twice; I scrambled to my feet and followed him.

"Team Q - one eliminated."

"Team Q - two eliminated."

"We're winning," Matt said, just before a red blotch appeared on his chest.

I spun around to see Julie who, having despatched Matt, was about to take aim at me. Before she could, I legged it, unsure where I was headed, but desperate to put as much ground as possible between us.

After a while, I couldn't hear any footsteps behind me, so I slowed down. Ahead, there was a small clearing, so I edged my way closer to get a better look. The stone building, or what was left of it—basically four partial walls and no roof—were just a few yards ahead. I was about to make a run for it when I saw movement inside. I couldn't be sure if the occupant was friend or foe, so I stayed put.

Over the next few minutes, the announcements came thick and fast:

"Team V - two eliminated."

"Team V - three eliminated."

"Team Q - three eliminated."

"Team V - four eliminated."

That meant that on my team there was just me and one other team member left alive. Was the person inside the building the other surviving member of my team?

"Team Q – four eliminated."

One of my teammates had just killed one of the opposing team. Whoever that was must be in a different part of the battle-zone, which meant that the person inside the building must be a member of team Q.

"Team Q – five eliminated."

Our team was back in front, no thanks to me, but maybe this was my time to shine. If I could take out the last surviving member of team Q, who was holed up in the stone building, my team would win the event and the overall competition. Putting aside my fear, I was just about to break cover when a figure emerged from the line of trees on the opposite side of the clearing. It was Wendy, our team captain. I tried to catch her attention, but her gaze was fixed on the stone building; she must have figured out there was someone inside. As she edged her way along the wall, I glanced in at the open window, but there was no sign of the figure I'd seen earlier. When Wendy reached the corner of the building, she hesitated, probably listening for sounds coming from inside. She'd no sooner started to move again when another figure appeared behind her; it was Rob. He must have been the one inside the building. I was just about to shout a warning to Wendy when I heard the sickening thud of a pellet hitting her in the middle of the back.

She turned around, dropped her gun, and removed her facemask.

"I thought I had you there, Rob," she said. Even in defeat, she managed to smile.

"Sorry, Wendy." Rob grinned. "But all's fair in love and—"

Before he could get the final word out, the paint pellet

hit him in the back. Stunned, he spun around to face me.

"*War*?" I laughed. "That's victory to team V, I believe."

"Well done, Mo." Wendy brushed past Rob, and came over to give me a pat on the back.

***

That evening, in the restaurant, the two tables had been pushed together, so that the members of both teams could mix with one another. The two team captains were seated side by side, and I was in between Matt and Julie.

After an exhausting day, the meal was enjoyed by all and sundry. Unlike the previous night, alcohol was allowed, but I still stuck with Coke. After everyone had finished eating and the plates had been cleared away, Wendy stood up and clinked her glass with a spoon, to get everyone's attention.

"As captain of team V, it falls to me to propose a toast to the gallant losers." She raised her glass.

The members of our team joined in the toast but changed the words slightly. "Losers, losers."

Rob was next to stand up. "I suppose that means I should propose a toast to the winners." He hesitated. "But I never was a good loser, so I'll just say, cheers everyone."

We all called out *cheers*.

As we made our way out of the restaurant, I made a point of walking out alongside Rob.

"Come to gloat?" he said.

"Yeah."

"Fair enough. I would have done the same. I can't believe I let you outflank me like that."

"I was lucky."

"Luck or not, that shot won the event and the overall competition. Did you enjoy the trials?"

"More than I expected to. Do you think I could have a quiet word with you sometime?"

"Is it quick because I have to shoot off to London. In fact, I'm already running late."

"Hot date?"

"I'm not dating, remember? One of the investors I was meant to see last week had to cancel. The only time he can see me before he goes back to the states is tonight. Sorry."

"That's okay. Maybe we can talk in the office on Tuesday?"

"I'm out all next week too. How about next weekend?"

"I'm away next weekend. It's okay. It really doesn't matter. I'll catch up with you the week after, maybe."

"Are you sure? Was it something important?"

"No. Nothing that can't wait."

Chapter 29

"I can't believe you still haven't told him," Beth said. "It's almost a week since you came back from that teambuilding thingy."

"How could I? He's been out of the office all week. I would have told him today, but I'm going to Mum's in half-an-hour, and I probably won't get back until late tomorrow. I'll try and catch Rob at the office on Monday."

It was Mum's birthday, and for her present, she'd said she wanted her two daughters to spend the night under her roof. I'd readily agreed, and Zoe had arranged for her husband, Jim, to take Ben home after the party had finished, so that she could stay too.

"You're just making excuses." Beth rolled her eyes.

"No, I'm not. You're just in a foul mood because Russ isn't coming down this weekend."

"How many times do I have to tell you? It's *Russell*. And I'm *not* in a foul mood."

"It doesn't sound like it. Have you and he fallen out or something?"

"No. He called late last night to say he couldn't make it. Something to do with his brother."

"What's wrong with him?"

"I don't know. He didn't say. Enough with the Spanish inquisition, already."

"Sorry. I really do have to get going."

"Say happy birthday to your mum from me."

"Will do."

"Any idea what time you'll be back tomorrow?"

"Not really. Mid/late afternoon, I'd guess."

***

"Mum, it's me."

"I hope you aren't phoning to say you're not coming."

"No, of course not. I've just discovered that they're doing maintenance work on the line between here and Leicester, so everything is delayed."

"What time will you get here?"

"I'm not entirely sure. It looks like they've put on a replacement bus service for part of the way."

"The party starts at five because Zoe doesn't want Ben to be out too late."

"Okay. I'll do my best to be there by then."

After the train journey from hell, during which I'd seen parts of England I'd never heard of and hoped never to see again, I finally made it to Leicester. The moral of that story is never travel by rail on a weekend.

Normally, I would have taken the bus or walked from the station to Mum's house, but I was already running late, so I grabbed a taxi from the rank outside the station. The taxi fare was almost as much as I'd paid for the cheap rail ticket.

I arrived at the house at ten past five. The door wasn't locked; it rarely was during the day, so I let myself in.

"Hello! I'm here!"

"About time too," Mum shouted. "We're in the living room."

"Sorry, I'm late, everyone, but the—" I stopped dead in my tracks, as I tried to take in what I was seeing. Mum, Zoe and Ben were seated with their backs to me. Seated opposite them were Jim and *Rob*.

"What are *you* doing here?"

"Don't you mean, happy birthday, Mum?" Zoe shot me a look.

"Sorry. Happy birthday." I gave her a kiss and handed over the present.

"I said no presents," Mum said.

"It's only a box of chocolates, and they've probably melted after how hot it was on that last train."

"Go and sit down." Mum put the box of chocolates on the sideboard behind her. "We've set a place for you next to Rob."

"What are you doing here?" I whispered to him, once I was seated.

"Your mum invited me."

"You could have told me you were coming."

"I thought it would be a nice surprise."

"It's definitely a surprise. Why didn't you give me a lift? You could have saved me from that awful ordeal by rail."

"I've just travelled down from Glasgow, otherwise I would have done."

"Mo, stop interrogating our guest." Mum gave me the same look she used to give me when she caught me raiding the biscuit barrel when I was a kid.

"Sorry."

The party was great fun. Mum insisted we play silly games, ostensibly for Ben's benefit, but which we all enjoyed. The highlight of the evening was when Rob turned out to be the world's worst charades player.

"How did you not get that?" He directed his question to me because he and I had been teamed together.

"Because that looked nothing like a cuckoo."

"I was flapping my arms around like a bird." He gave me a quick action replay.

"I thought you were doing an impression of a windmill. Anyway, you can't talk. You didn't manage to work out I was miming ET."

"I thought you were pointing at something."

"That was what the alien did in the movie."

"Stop squabbling you two," Mum said. "Jim is taking Ben home now, so say your goodbyes."

After Jim and Ben had left, Mum and Zoe went through to the kitchen to wash the pots—Mum didn't believe in dishwashers either. As it was her birthday, I'd offered to do them with Zoe, but Mum had insisted I stay with Rob. My mother—always the matchmaker.

"You said you wanted to talk to me about something," he said when we were alone.

"That's right." I'd rehearsed this conversation in my head a thousand times, but now it was actually time to do it, my mind was a complete blank.

"So?"

"Don't rush me. It's about the arrangement thingamabob."

"*Arrangement*?"

"You know. The one where we aren't allowed to date until I've been working at Q-Ventures for a year."

"I'm not sure I'd call it an *arrangement*, exactly. More a—"

"Can you not be so pedantic, just this once?"

"Okay, sorry. Carry on."

"It was Beth, really. She made me realise that the arrangement was silly."

"I could have told you that ages ago."

I glared at him.

"Sorry, carry on."

"As I was saying, she said I'd already more than proved myself in the job. And she's right. My work colleagues all seem to have accepted me, which is the thing I was most concerned about. Anyway, the bottom line is that I've realised the real reason I've been putting you off is because I'm scared of being hurt again."

"I would never—"

"Shush. Let me finish. Adam really hurt me, even though I tried not to admit it at the time. I'd trusted him completely, so when he cheated on me, it was as if—"

"I would never cheat on you, Mo."

"You can't possibly know that."

"I know how I feel about you. I know I've not looked at another woman since you came up with this *arrangement* of yours."

"What I'm trying to say is that I want to forget about the arrangement, or whatever you want to call it. If you're still interested, I'd like to go on a date with you."

"Oh, I see." He knitted his eyebrows. "I'll have to think about that."

"Of course. I fully—"

He leaned forward and planted a kiss on my lips. It only lasted a matter of seconds, but it left me breathless.

"I've thought about it." He grinned. "And the answer is yes."

"You kissed me."

"Yes, I did. Did you like it?"

"I—err—"

"It probably wasn't one of my best because I'm out of practice. What with not kissing anyone for over three months."

"No, it was good. It was nice."

"Would you like me to do it again?"

"Yes, please."

Before he could, Zoe walked in. "Get a room, you two."

"We were just—"

"It's okay. I only came through to get these." She picked up a couple of plates that had been left on the sideboard. "Carry on."

I didn't need telling twice; this time I leaned forward and kissed him.

"I could do this all night," Rob said. "But I suppose we should arrange this first date of ours. When were you thinking?"

"Err, I don't know. I hadn't thought that far ahead."

"How about Monday night?"

"The day after tomorrow?"

"You don't have anything else planned, do you?"

"No, nothing."

"Monday night it is, then. Eight o'clock?"

"That works for me. Where shall we go?"

"There's only one place we can go." He grinned. "Xquisite of course. If that's okay with you?"

"Yeah, that'd be lovely."

"Right, I'd better be making tracks now. I've got a long drive ahead of me."

"I thought you'd be sleeping on the sofa, like you did last time. I know it isn't comfortable, but—"

"I'd love to, but I have to get back for a meeting first thing tomorrow morning."

"Another one? On a Sunday?"

"I'm afraid so, but I'll be counting the minutes until

Monday night."

Chapter 30

The next morning, Zoe, me and Mum ate breakfast together for the first time since I couldn't remember when.

"This is nice." Mum beamed. "The three of us having breakfast together."

"It makes a pleasant change not to be running around after Ben," Zoe said. "How come Rob didn't stay last night?"

"He had to get back for a meeting."

"I've told you that you should grab that young man before he loses interest." Mum took a sip of tea.

"If you must know, we're going on our first date tomorrow night."

"*First* date?" Zoe sounded incredulous. "I thought you two had been an item for some time now."

"We're just work colleagues."

"Where's he taking you tomorrow?"

"A restaurant called Xquisite."

"Sounds expensive."

"It is."

"Still, he doesn't look short of a bob or two."

The journey back home was only marginally better than the one the previous day, but somehow it didn't seem to bother me. I simply couldn't stop thinking about Rob and that kiss. Kisses. It had been so unexpected.

But what if after all this time, our first date turned out to be a disaster? Our not-a-date had been a success, but there was more pressure on this one because it was the real thing. What if it fell flat, and we discovered we didn't actually like one another? What then? Could we simply go back to being just work colleagues?

***

When I got back to the flat, Beth had a stupid grin on her face.

"Have you been drinking all weekend?" I said.

"I haven't touched a drop." She waved her hand in front of my face, as if that would somehow prove her sobriety.

"Before you ask, yes I did tell Rob."

"Great." She continued to wave her hand close to my face.

"What's wrong with you? You've been banging on for ages for me to tell him the arrangement is scrapped, and now that I have you—what's that on your finger?"

"This little thing? I didn't think you'd notice it."

"You nearly took my eye out with it."

"Sorry. What do you think?"

"It's lovely. It must have cost a fortune. Does this mean—?"

"That I'm engaged? Yeah."

"I thought Russell was stuck in Sheffield this weekend?"

"He only told me that, so he could surprise me. There was a knock at the door yesterday afternoon, and it was him, standing there with a huge bouquet of flowers and this ring. He actually got down on one knee if you can believe it."

"Where is he now?"

"He had to go back early because he's got to go to Cardiff in the morning. Are you happy for me?"

"Err—"

"Mo, you have to be happy for me."

"I am. It's just so quick."

"Compared to you and Rob, you mean? That wouldn't be difficult. And, anyway, I know he's the one. So why wait?"

"You're right. I'm thrilled for you. Come here." I gave her a hug. I genuinely was happy for Beth, even if I did have some reservations.

"Okay, now you can tell me about Rob."

"There's not much to tell. Not compared to your big news."

"What did he say when you told him?"

"He kissed me."

"That's a good start. Did you two get it on at your Mum's?"

"No, we didn't. He had to drive home last night, but we're going on our first date tomorrow night."

"That's more like it. Where's he taking you?"

"Guess."

"Not that chicken wings place again?"

"No, of course not. We're going to Xquisite."

"Nice one. We'd better get our skates on, then."

"To do what?"

"Buy you a new dress."

"I don't need one. I've got the one from our not-a-date."

"You can't wear that on your first official date. He's already seen it. And don't tell me you can't afford it because I've seen your salary slips."

"We don't have time."

"Yes, we do. The shops don't close for another couple of hours. Grab your purse."

***

The next morning, I stopped off at Bean Shack on the way to the office.

"You look like the cat that got the cream," Jed said. "I take it your new job is going well?"

"Fantastic, but that's not all."

"Oh?"

"Rob and I are going on a date tonight."

I'd wanted to tell Jed because I felt like he'd played a small but significant part in Rob and I getting together. Had he not taken a chance and given me the job, I may never have seen Rob again.

"I said from the start that you two were made for one another."

"Not to me, you didn't."

"I told Liz. Where is he taking you?"

"Xquisite."

"I always thought he must be loaded. I'd need to take out another bank loan to afford to eat there."

"Talking of which, is everything okay with the bank?"

"So far. Touch wood. Now, what can I get you to drink?"

"I'm feeling adventurous today, so I'm going to try something different."

"Good for you. What would you like?"

"I'll have a flat white."

"You really have turned into a wild child."

***

Hannah had been on holiday the previous week, so this was the first time I'd seen her since I came back from Q-Trials. She was pretending to be engrossed in something on her computer screen, but her grin gave her away.

"You do know I'll get you back, don't you?" I said.

"Sorry, Mo, I didn't see you there. Get me back for what?"

"You know what. Your little ploy didn't work, anyway. I always knew you were exaggerating."

"Liar. You were bricking it. How did it go?"

"Much better after someone on the mini-bus told me what I could really expect."

"Did you do paintball? That's my favourite."

"Yeah, we did. That was the final event, and our team won."

"Aren't you going to tell her the full story, Mo?" Chelsea had clearly been listening in on our conversation. "Mo shot Rob to win the whole competition for her team."

"Nice one," Hannah said. "You must have enjoyed that."

"Winning the competition? Yeah, I did."

"I meant shooting Rob."

"That was pretty sweet too. While I have your attention, there's something I want to tell you both."

"You're not going to quit, are you?" Chelsea asked.

"I knew it. You've been headhunted, haven't you?" Hannah said. "Is it that company that does the fitness apps? They've been after me all month."

"I haven't been headhunted and I'm not going to quit."

"Phew." Chelsea sat back in her chair. "Thank goodness for that."

"I wouldn't normally be having this conversation with

my work colleagues, but I don't want there to be any bad feelings or misunderstandings when it comes out, which knowing the grapevine in this place, it's forced to."

"What have you done?" Hannah said. "The suspense is killing me."

"I haven't done anything yet, but I'm going out on a date tonight with Rob."

"Is that it?" Chelsea raised her eyebrows.

"I thought it was going to be something really scandalous," Hannah said.

"I just don't want you two or anyone else to think I'm only doing it to get a promotion."

"Don't be stupid," Chelsea said. "You'd still get your promotion even if you went up to his office and poured a glass of water over his head.

"Everyone knows you two have the hots for one another," Hannah said. "No one cares."

"What do you mean, *everyone knows*? Rob and I have barely spoken to one another since I started here."

"Come on, Mo. We'd have to be blind not to see the looks you two give one another."

"It's only a date, anyway. Nothing may come of it."

"Yeah, right." Hannah scoffed.

"So, you guys are okay with it?"

"Of course." Chelsea nodded.

"I am on one condition," Hannah said.

"What's that?"

"I want all the sordid details."

***

"I'm really not sure about this." I was staring at my

reflection in the wardrobe mirror.

"You look great," Beth said. "Do a twirl."

Somewhat self-consciously, I did as she asked, but my reflection didn't look any better when I was facing the mirror again.

"I've never worn a red dress in my life."

"Then you've been missing out."

"Don't you think it clashes with my hair?"

"No way. Red and turquoise are the perfect combo. How come he isn't picking you up, anyway?"

"He offered to, but I said I'd rather make my own way there."

"Because?"

"I thought the walk over there might help me relax."

"You can't possibly *walk* there."

"Why not?"

"Well, for a start, those new heels will cripple you long before you get to the Queensway."

"I hadn't thought about that. I'll take the tube."

"And arrive there smelling of sweaty armpits? I don't think so. You'll get a taxi."

"It'll cost a fortune from here."

"Didn't you tell me last night you'd just got a bonus?"

"Yeah, but—"

"But nothing. Get a taxi ordered."

"Okay. Are you absolutely certain I look okay in this dress?"

"You look amazing. When he sees you in that, he'll probably cancel the meal and take you straight over to his place."

Even though my cab arrived at Xquisite five minutes

early, Rob was already standing outside the door.

"You look terrific," he said, and I could tell by the look in his eyes that he meant it.

"Thanks. Beth said I had to buy something new."

"You and she are really close, aren't you?"

"Yeah, even though she drives me mad a lot of the time."

"Shall we go inside?"

"Sure."

It was like no restaurant I'd ever seen before. There were fountains, a glass wall containing what looked like fossils, and carpet so deep, I was worried I might lose one of my new shoes in it.

"Are you okay?" Rob said. "You're dithering."

I blamed the aircon, but the truth was I was just nervous.

The maître d' showed us to a table inside what I can only describe as a glass oyster shell. Although I could hear voices, I couldn't actually see any of the other diners.

"What do you think of this place?" Rob said.

"It's amazing. I assume you've been here before?"

"A couple of times."

I wanted to ask who he'd been there with, but I bit my tongue. The waiter gave us the food menus and took our drinks order.

"You could have had something stronger," Rob said.

"I like Coke."

"My spies tell me that you got a hero's welcome back at the office last week."

"Yeah. Most people were only interested to hear how I'd shot you."

"I'm never going to live that down. Was your journey

back okay?"

"Bearable, and when I got home, I discovered that Beth was engaged."

"To that toy boy of hers?"

"Yeah, but I reckon I'd better stop calling him that now they're a proper item."

"Are we a *proper item*?" He grinned.

"Of course we aren't. This is only our first date, remember."

"What about that other one? What did you call it?"

"The not-a-date."

"Yeah. Plus, I've seen you with no clothes on in the bathroom."

"I had a towel around me."

"True. Sexy feet, though."

"Thanks, I think."

"And we've kissed."

"We have."

"Several times."

"Three." I smiled.

"You're counting?"

"No, I—err—"

He leaned across the table and gave me a quick peck on the lips. "That's four."

When the waiter appeared, I expected him to be carrying our drinks, but he was empty-handed.

"Sir, madam, I'm so very sorry, but there's been some kind of problem with the power in the kitchen. I'm afraid the restaurant has to close."

"You're kidding?" Rob said.

"I'm afraid not. We will of course give you a voucher

that will entitle you to a free dinner for two at a day and time convenient to you."

Rob looked as though he wanted to climb over the table and strangle the man, so I said, "It's okay. These things happen."

"Thank you for being so understanding, madam. I hope you enjoy the rest of your evening." And with that, he scurried away.

"Well, that's just great," Rob said. "What now?"

"There's only one thing we can do."

"Go back to my place?" His face lit up again.

"In your dreams." I held out my hand. "Come with me."

"Where are you taking me?"

"You'll see."

***

I arrived back at the flat just after eleven o'clock.

"What are you doing back here so early?" Beth said. "Or for that matter, why are you here at all? I thought for sure he'd whisk you back to his place after your posh meal."

"We didn't get our posh meal."

"How come?"

"We got as far as ordering the drinks, but then—"

"He couldn't resist you any longer, dragged you back to his place, and ravished you."

"No. The power failed in the restaurant kitchen, so we had to leave."

"If you didn't go back to his place, where did you go?"

"Guess."

"I've no idea."

"I'll give you a clue. I still can't feel my lips."

"You spent all evening snogging in the park?"

"No, you idiot. We went to Red Hot Wings again."

"Boy, I would have paid good money to see you two, dressed up in your glad rags, eating chicken drumsticks."

"*Wings*. And at least it wasn't just me this time. Rob was dressed to the nines too."

"Priceless. It could only happen to you."

"I'm beginning to think you're right."

"Apart from the whole chicken wings fiasco, how was the date?"

"Fantastic."

"Thank goodness for that. I was worried it might turn out to be an anti-climax after all this time."

"Me too, but it was brilliant. We never stopped talking all evening."

"That doesn't sound like much of a date to me. What about the part where you ripped each other's clothes off?"

"He's really funny. I already knew that, I guess, but he had me laughing all the time."

"Hopefully, not just after you'd ripped his clothes off."

"Beth, I'm trying to be serious."

"Sorry. Carry on."

"He listens too. Really listens and he's genuinely interested in what I have to say. Time just flew by. I couldn't believe it was time to leave."

"Please tell me he at least asked you back to his place."

"No, but he did offer to drive me home."

"And you two finally got it on in the backseat of his car?"

"I refused his offer and took a taxi."

"I'll never understand you. Is that it, then? Is that what

all these months have been building up to? Another romantic night spent in the chicken wings shop?"

"We're going out on another date."

"When?"

"Tonight."

Chapter 31

About one year later.

It was Saturday morning, and Beth, Carol and I were seated at the kitchen table, drinking coffee.

"How long are you going to keep up this charade, Carol?" Beth said.

"I don't know what you're talking about."

"You've been living at Toby's for almost a year now, and yet you still insist it's only temporary."

"It is. Until I find somewhere nearer the centre of town."

"Are you actually still looking at properties?"

"Yes."

"And the last time you went to see a property was?"

"Why all the questions? What does it matter to you?"

"It doesn't. I'm just curious."

"She means nosy," I chipped in.

Beth wasn't done yet. "And what about poor old Toby?"

"What do you mean? I pay him rent."

"I meant the way you're leading him on. The poor guy must be going nuts, seeing you walk around half-naked every day."

"I never do that. Tell her, Mo."

"Hey, leave me out of it."

"We're just flatmates, that's all," Carol insisted.

"You must be aware of the way he looks at you."

"That's all in your head, Beth. You always did have a dirty mind." Carol finished the last of her coffee. "Anyway, I'd better get going. Toby and I are going shopping this morning."

"I rest my case." Beth laughed.

"Why do you insist on winding her up like that?" I said, once Carol had left.

"Because I can, and anyway, most of it's true. She's given up looking for anywhere else, and Toby is crazy about her."

"Has he told you so?"

"He doesn't need to. It's obvious."

"By the way, I saw Jen in town the other day."

"Have they moved into their new place?"

"Yeah, about a week ago. She says they love it."

"Brilliant. I wonder what Mand will do with her mother's house now?"

"According to Jen, she's already put it up for sale."

"You'll never guess who I saw coming out of a charity shop the other day," Beth said.

"Not Dazzer?"

"No, you idiot. It was Nicky."

"I haven't seen or heard from her in ages. I assumed she'd gone back to her old ways and was embarrassed to let us know she was in debt again."

"You couldn't be any more wrong about that. She'd been looking for clothes."

"In a charity shop? Are you sure it wasn't someone who looked like her?"

"She really has turned over a new leaf. After she won that money, she cut up all her credit cards."

"I don't believe it."

"It's true. She showed me her purse. The only card she uses now is her debit card; she never buys anything on credit."

"What about loans?"

"She said she doesn't have any and I believe her. And you know the best part? She was really happy. She said it was time the whole gang had a night out together."

"What did you say?"

"That I'd have to check with Russell."

I laughed. "How times have changed."

Just then, the bedroom door behind me opened, and Russell appeared, wearing shorts and a sports vest. Judging by the sweat on his top, he'd had a rigorous work out.

"Hey, Mo, long time no see."

"Looks like you've had a good session."

"I always do a longer one at the weekend."

"Can I take a look at your gym?"

"Sure."

My old bedroom was unrecognisable. The carpet had been replaced by laminate flooring, all the walls had been painted white, and two large mirrors had been mounted on the far wall. The room was full of all manner of equipment including a treadmill, cross-trainer, weights and a bench, and some other stuff I didn't recognise.

"It's looking really good in here. Does Beth ever use it?"

"Yes, I do," she shouted from the kitchen.

"Only when I twist her arm. She was meant to be working out with me this morning."

"And I was going to until Mo rang to say she was popping over."

"Any excuse," he whispered.

Russell said he was going to take a shower, so I went back into the kitchen.

"He's looking good, isn't he?" Beth said.

"He should be after all the work he puts into that body of his. I take it you two are still going strong?"

"Couldn't be better."

"How has he settled into his new job?"

Four months after Beth and Russell had become engaged, and one month after I'd moved out, Russell had transferred to the same office where Beth worked, and he'd moved in with her. So far, there had been no talk of marriage, but if I knew Beth, it was only a matter of time.

"He loves it, although he still moans about the commute."

"I'd better be going because if I'm late like last year, Mum will kill me."

"Wish your mum a happy birthday from me. I can't believe it's a year since you were up there for her last one."

"Me neither. At least I don't have to go by train this time."

***

Even after living there for six months, I still had to pinch myself every time I climbed into the private lift that went straight to the penthouse where Rob and I lived. And even if I lived there for the rest of my life, I would never get used to the three-sixty degree views across the city.

"I was beginning to think you'd got lost." Rob greeted me wearing only boxer shorts. "I thought I'd have to send out the search party."

I walked over and sank into his arms. "Sorry, but you know what Beth is like when she gets started."

"Have those two named a date yet?"

"Not yet."

"I spoke to Bill Maker while you were out."

"On a Saturday?"

"Apparently he'd been trying to get hold of me for a couple of days, but I wasn't around."

"I've not heard from him in months. I'd assumed there was nothing doing."

"It's not good news."

"I didn't really expect it to be."

"But it's not entirely bad either. Do you want me to tell you now or wait until we get back from your mother's?"

"Tell me now."

"You already knew that your case is weak because you can't produce any of your original code."

"I gave him all my notes, though."

"And that's what allowed him to extract the offer he got from them, such as it is."

"Okay?"

"They're prepared to pay you one percent of profit from the app as a royalty."

"I'm amazed they've agreed to pay anything."

"I wouldn't get too excited because this kind of app relies on advertising for its revenue, which generally means they won't be making very much at all."

"Right."

"There's more. They're prepared to include the following credit on the app splash screen and on all the documentation." Rob picked up a sheet of paper and read, "Ztudy is based on an original idea by Maureen Jackson. What do you think?"

"No way."

"One percent is low. Maybe Bill will be able to get them up a bit."

"I'm not bothered about the royalty. Like you said, that's never going to amount to much, anyway. I'm more concerned about the credit. It has to be Mo Jackson, not Maureen."

He smiled. "Are you sure you want to accept? We could fight for more, but it will probably take months or even years."

"I'm cool with the one percent, provided they get the name right."

"Okay, I'll let Bill know on Monday."

"There's still one thing that bothers me, though. How did they get hold of my code in the first place?"

"Bill hired a private investigator to see if he could find out how that had happened. According to the PI, one of the founders of Ztudy worked at Headrow at the same time as you. His name is Ryan Treadwell. Do you know him?"

"Ryan? That sneaky, little slimeball."

"I take it you do."

"Yeah. In fact, he was the one I asked to try to retrieve my code; he told me it had been erased."

"I think you can guess what really happened to it."

"If I ever see him again, I'll—"

"Forget him. Think of it this way, if things hadn't happened the way they did, you may never have applied for the job at Q, and you and I may never have met."

"Ryan has a lot to answer for." I grinned.

"I know you don't mean that." He gave me a kiss.

"You're right, I don't." I ran my finger down his bare chest. "What time do we need to set off?"

"In ten minutes." He pushed me away gently. "So don't go getting any ideas."

"Half an hour wouldn't make any difference, would it?"

"We're going in ten—no, make that nine minutes. If we're late, it's me your mother will blame. Grab your case while I throw on some clothes."

"Must you?"

"Yes, I must."

"Spoilsport."

"You're being ridiculous," I said when we were halfway to Leicester, on the M1.

"I don't think I am."

"Mum knows we've been living together for six months. I reckon she'll have figured out that we share a bed."

"I know that."

"What's the problem, then?"

"Your old bedroom is right next door to your mother's."

"So? We'll just have to be quiet."

"Oh yeah. Like you're capable of that," he scoffed.

"What does that mean?"

"It means that in the throes of passion, you tend to get—how can I put this? Loud. Very loud."

"I do not."

"Trust me, Mo, you do. Why do you think the people on the floor below us have asked the contractors to quote for additional soundproofing?"

"You're hilarious. I still think you're being stupid. Mum will expect us to sleep in my old room."

"Your sister and Jim aren't sleeping together in her old room, are they?"

"No, but only because they want Ben to go home to his

own bed, so Jim is taking him like he did last year."

"Which is why I should sleep on the sofa."

"Please yourself, but I think you're crazy."

Mum greeted us at the door with a huge smile and a hug and a kiss for both of us.

"Happy birthday, Mum."

"Happy birthday, Shirley."

"Thank you both. You're early. Zoe, Jim and Ben aren't here yet."

"See," I whispered. "I told you we had time."

"Time for what?" Mum never missed a thing.

"Err," Rob spluttered. "Mo said we had time to take the scenic route, but I didn't think we did."

"Take your case upstairs and then we'll all have a nice cup of tea."

Rob grabbed the case and led the way up to my old bedroom.

"What do you think of it?" I pointed to the collage mounted above the bed.

"I like it. Has it done the trick?"

"Yeah, I haven't had any of the bad memories since Mum put it up there. And look." I pointed to a series of framed photos on the dressing table. "She found those too."

"So, you're okay in this room now?"

"Absolutely, which is why you should sleep in here with me tonight."

"We've already discussed this."

"But just look at that bed. Mum has even bought a new mattress. Want to try it?"

"I think I heard your mother calling. Tea must be

ready."

And before I could stop him, he'd disappeared downstairs.

Zoe, Jim and Ben arrived a few minutes later. Rob and Jim had become firm friends, since they'd discovered a shared passion for rugby. Mum laid on a fabulous spread as always, with a special treat of strawberry jelly and ice cream to finish.

Afterwards, we played a number of silly party games, and somehow Rob succeeded in being even worse at charades than he had the previous year.

"How did you not get that one?" I sighed.

"I almost got it right."

"You weren't even close." I scoffed. "Magnificent seven? Give me strength."

"I've never even heard of seven brides for seven brothers. It was before my time."

"Hey, Mo," Zoe said after we'd abandoned the charades game. "Mum reckons you and Rob are running a coffee shop now. Is that right?"

"No, she's got the wrong end of the stick as usual. I told her that Rob has invested some money into Bean Shack, the coffee shop where I worked for a while last year. Jed, who owns it mentioned to me that he wanted to open a second shop, but the banks were still a bit nervous about lending to him. When I told Rob, he offered to buy twenty-five percent of the business. Jed is using that money to fund the opening of the new shop."

"Will you be working in there?"

"No chance. My days as an apprentice barista are well and truly behind me."

It was time for Ben to go home, but when I went through to the hallway to say goodbye, Zoe and my mother had their coats on too. Not only that, but Mum had a small case in her hand.

"What's going on? I know Rob's useless at charades, but there's no need to do a runner."

"I'm going to stay at Zoe's tonight."

"Why?"

After she'd explained what she was up to, they all left.

Rob was in the kitchen, pouring himself a glass of wine.

"Put that down." I took the glass from him, took his hand, and led him towards the stairs.

"Where are we going?"

"You'll see."

"Where are the others? Where's your mum?"

"Shush."

I led the way into my old bedroom and closed the door behind me.

"What's going on, Mo. You're starting to scare me."

"Mum has gone to stay at Zoe's."

"What? Why?"

"She said how pleased she was that I've managed to get over the bad memories connected to this room."

"O–kay?"

"And she said it was high time that I make some new memories in here. With you."

"I don't understand."

I pushed him, so that he fell backwards onto the bed.

"You will."

Also from Adele Abbott:`

Witch Is When It All Began

The day starts out just like any other for private investigator, Jill Gooder. Then, she discovers she's a witch. Mystery, magic and laughs galore.

Whoops! Our New Flatmate Is A Human

Take a shy werewolf, a wizard who fancies himself as a ladies' man, and a vampire dying for her first taste of human blood. Then add a human for good measure.

Murder On Account

Her boss has been murdered. Now she must find his killer. Smart, sassy and kickass tough, private investigator, Kat Royle, is nobody's fool, but does she have what it takes to keep the agency afloat, and find the murderer?

Website: AdeleAbbott.com
Facebook:
facebook.com/ AdeleAbbottAuthor

Printed in Great Britain
by Amazon

85409463R10176